ZODIAC DRAGON BROTHERHOOD

Dragon Ascending

USA TODAY BESTSELLING AUTHOR

GENEVIEVE JACK

Dragon Ascending: Zodiac Dragon Brotherhood book 2

Copyright © Genevieve Jack 2024

Published by Carpe Luna, Ltd. Bloomington, IL 61704

First Edition: August 2024

ISBN: 978-1-962757-14-0

eISBN: 978-1-962757-06-5

v 2.7

About This Book

What Aries wants, Aries takes!

A secret society of dragon killers...
From the beginning, dragons have lived among humans, inspiring creativity, innovation, and sometimes *revolution*. Sent from the stars by the creator, the dragon race thrived until a wealthy medieval nobleman learned their secret. In an effort to protect his riches and position, he formed the Saints Order, a secret society fueled by dark magic and founded on the tenet of eradicating all dragons.

A Zodiac dragon warrior sworn to defend his kind...
Connor is an Aries dragon and member of the Zodiac Brotherhood, a band of twelve warriors charged with defending their race. Thanks to the sacrifice of one brother over fifty years ago, dragons have enjoyed a period of peace under an accord with the Saint's Order. But when a civilian is brutally murdered in front of the

Fontaine Saint-Michel, it's clear that the Order is rising once more.

A mating bond that is one hell of an inconvenience... Desperate to protect his people, avoid war, and force the Saint's Order back to the negotiations table, Connor kidnaps the Order grandmaster's fiancée, washed-up novelist Fiona. But the order isn't interested in peace talks. Worse, Connor's inner dragon has chosen Fiona as his mate.

Prologue

Fontaine Saint-Michel, Paris, France

American photographer Lucy Vale adjusted her camera case on her shoulder, annoyed to find herself alone in front of the Fontaine Saint-Michel. She glanced at her watch. Four in the morning, as instructed. If her client weren't an eccentric billionaire who'd prepaid in cash for this shoot, she'd never have taken this job. But when a man offers you four times your regular rate plus a free trip to Paris for a super-secretive one-hour gig, it's hard to say no.

Still, it annoyed her—the hour, the lateness, the entitlement.

She groaned when she finally spotted him walking toward her under the streetlights, the only thing moving aside from the occasional car zipping along the boulevard. The plaza was oddly silent, although she didn't frequent Paris enough to know if that was common at this hour.

As he strode closer, she recognized him from his picture. *Pictures* actually. And videos. That was the thing about running a global empire, she supposed. He'd spent his share of time under the microscope of journalists everywhere.

But then she glimpsed his outfit. Shook her head. Not what they'd agreed to by a long shot. "Have you brought a change? Your dark clothing will get lost in this light. I'm not a miracle worker."

"I know what you are, Lucy." A jagged blade appeared in his hand, lighting up and casting an other-worldly blue glow between them.

"What do you have there?" Lucy glanced between the sculpture of the archangel Michael vanquishing the devil that formed the pinnacle of the Fontaine and the prop in his hand. So that was it then. This was to be a nerdy fantasy-world thing. "Oh, like the statue! Well, we can try it, but at this hour I can't guarantee I can achieve the results you're looking for."

He reached her, his lips drawing back off his teeth in a chill-inducing smile. A smile that made Lucy's skin tighten and her deepest instincts compel her to run. But it was too late for that.

His gloved hand closed around her throat, cutting off her scream.

"Oh Lucy, I guarantee you will provide exactly the results I'm looking for."

Chapter One

CONNOR

"Jessie, if you burn that sauce, I swear on my father's grave you'll be on tomorrow's menu." My new saucier came highly recommended, but as the owner and head chef of Diabolique gastropub, I have high standards. I run my kitchen like a war room. My staff are my soldiers. Every evening, I wage a battle to serve as many hungry people as possible the most absolutely showstopping meals this kitchen can pump out.

Doesn't hurt that I'm also a dragon and can smell the sauce starting to curdle from six feet away.

Jessie lifts the pan off the burner and stirs vigorously. "Got it, Chef!"

I love nights like this. The bustle. The verve. The spark. Most of the humans working in my kitchen don't realize they're feeding off my dragon energy, growing as culinary artists thanks to a celestial gift the creator sent them thousands of years ago. Dragons like me coexist in secret with humans in order to inspire them, to help evolve their species to its ultimate potential. Diabolique has the reputation of being a proving ground for up-and-coming talent. The magazines and influencers think it's because I'm some great mentor, and I'm no slouch in that department, but it has far more to do with being a dragon. The magic in my skin is working on my staff every day they're here.

In a year, I predict Jessie will be running his own kitchen, and that's all right by me.

The door to the front of house swings open, and a four-foot-eleven-inch fireball of a woman with curly gray hair and a neck tattoo appears in front of me. Carmen is my manager, an Army veteran and grandmother of four whom I keep around because nothing fazes her. Nothing. There could be a shootout on the floor and she'd find a way to calmly usher the customers into the alley to finish their meal *Lady and the Tramp*–style. She's also one of the few humans who knows what I really am.

Tonight her fists are on her hips, her spine rigid enough to add two inches to her height, and her lip is curled the way it does when she's seriously annoyed.

"What happened?" I plate the fish I've been poaching and give her my full attention.

"Table seven wants to speak with the chef."

Everyone stops. For a heartbeat, her words hang in the air. Even the burners on the stoves seem to pause, their flames bending in her direction like they can't believe their ears. The saucier stops whisking. My sous-chef stops dicing. My entire kitchen staff seems to hold their collective breath.

Long ago, I gave up being offended by this reaction. My temper is renowned to the humans in this kitchen. And while none of them but Carmen knows I'm a dragon, they all know I'm an Aries. What you see is what you get and I never back down from a confrontation.

"Table seven." It's the end of the night, but I pride myself on every dish that leaves this kitchen. And I remember every order. "What's wrong with the steak?"

"He says it's overcooked." Carmen tosses her hands as if the notion is preposterous, and it is. There's a reason I hired her despite her advanced age. She isn't afraid of anything, including me, and she doesn't suffer fools.

Tossing my apron onto the counter, I pass her, mumbling that I'll take care of it, and march to table seven. I'm big. Around six foot five and ripped thanks to my dragon genetics plus warrior training regimen. The humans I meet often joke I'd make a good linebacker with my general width, which Carmen says is like two average guys standing side by side. I don't know about that, but I make no effort to diminish my otherworldly attributes as I approach this customer. No. I plan to intimidate this asshole until he's near wetting himself.

The man's gaze locks on to my crossed arms first, then traces up and up and up to meet my eyes. *Yeah, way the hell up here, buddy* my expression conveys. *You ready to tango? Because I was born knowing the steps.* It's then that I notice his date. Interesting. This guy is a four at best, but his girl is a strong eight. Her gaze travels north along my torso in the same way, but her eyes hold more than a little heat when our gazes connect. I flash her a lopsided smile. Her brows lift.

"You asked to see the chef?" I mumble, forcing my attention back toward the man.

"You're the chef?" he asks incredulously.

"Connor Drexler," I say by way of introduction. I don't offer my hand. "What can I do for you?"

He swallows, puffing up his chest. "My steak is overcooked."

I glance at the bright red middle of the piece of meat on his plate. "How rare do you want it?"

"Rare rare. This is clearly medium rare."

I stab a finger toward his meal. "If that beef was any rarer, there would be hoofprints leading to your table."

He crosses his arms and leans back in his chair.

Across from him, his date shifts nervously, her lashes fluttering. "It looks rare to me, Richard."

"No one asked for your opinion," the man barks, like she's a dog he means to redirect.

I picture my hand shooting out, cuffing his ear, and knocking him out of his chair. I know guys like this. He's a little man in a designer suit, a modern Napoleon type, making up for his small stature by throwing money around along with his attitude.

"Oh, I'm very interested in her opinion," I say, returning her smile with a small, lazy one of my own. My voice drops an octave as I add, "on a number of things."

"Hey, asshole, what about my steak? You gonna fix this or what?"

A low growl rumbles in my chest, and my skin grows hot with the desire to turn this fucker inside out. My bones rattle with a growing lust for his blood. They actually rattle as if I'm standing too close to an arriving train.

I'm fantasizing about dismembering this guy and then bending his girlfriend over his bloody remains and giving her what I see she wants when she looks at me with those bedroom eyes.

Thank the creator, Carmen chooses that moment to deliver a swift punch to my kidney as she passes behind me. I do a double take.

"Check the date and time, Chef," she says. "And stop making that noise."

I glance at my watch. Past midnight.

March twenty-first.

My dragon's alignment.

Fuck.

"Are you wearing contacts?" The woman at the table leans forward, catching my eye.

Yeah, I bet she got a show. I need to get out of here before I do something I'll regret.

"Uh, Carmen?" I call her back over from the hostess stand.

"Chef?"

I close my eyes for a beat while I rein in my inner beast, then give her a nod. "Guy wants a rare steak," I mumble. "Can you give him the Bones treatment?"

"It would be my pleasure." She grins wickedly, then grabs his plate and follows me back into the kitchen.

Bones is my German shepherd. Recently he's started getting really picky about his kibble. I've figured out if I put his bowl on the counter, shake it a bit to stir it up, then put it back in front of him, he eats it. It's about the attention, not the food.

Carmen will let the guy's steak sit under the warmer

for fifteen minutes, flip it over, trim it, and rearrange it on a new plate, then bring it back out to him. By that time, I predict table seven will either eat it or bolt.

Meanwhile, I need a breather to make sure my dragon knows who's boss. I cut left and head into my office, bracing myself on the desk and taking a deep, cleansing breath. Every dragon is born under a certain star sign. Mine is Aries. But unlike humans, when a dragon reaches the part of the year aligned with his sign, we undergo changes. It's the only time of year when we're fertile, and so our dragons are at their strongest and most virile during that month. But all that power comes at a price. We run hot, all our emotions razor-sharp and our needs exaggerated to a fine point. Hunger feels like starvation. Anger feels like an explosion. And lust—fuck, we have a special name for it. *Appetency*, mating sickness.

Every year we grow older, our appetites get stronger. For those of us lucky enough to find a mate, our alignment ceases to be a problem. But without our one and only, our need grows and grows until, around the age of a hundred, we literally go up in flames. I'm thirty-eight, and I haven't found a mate yet. Right now my spleen feels like it's sliding down a red-hot cheese grater, and my dragon is telling me that the only thing that will ease the pain is seeing blood or sinking deep into a pretty pink pussy.

Fuck.

I'm still doing the mindful-breathing thing when the phone rings—the old landline. I flip the handset into my palm and bark, "Connor."

"Why aren't you answering your cell?" Seb's voice comes down the line, skating between anger and annoyance. He's my best friend and a dragon warrior like me. A Taurus.

"Because I'm busy running a restaurant. The phone's a distraction. I turn the ringer off while I'm working." I reach for it now, noticing the screen is filled with missed calls from the Zodiac Brotherhood, the group of warrior dragons like me who've taken an oath to defend our kind.

"Right now you need to be distracted. Way distracted. Distract yourself immediately, feel me?"

"What's going on?"

"Check CNN. News coming out of Paris. You're not going to like it, bro."

Deep dread rises like bile as I scroll to the news app on my cell. This is the worst time for something to happen that involves the brotherhood. Our Pisces brother, Solomon, has to step down for personal reasons, and my nephew Mason is taking his place. Only the transition isn't complete because removing Solomon from his position while the wheel of the celestial year was in Pisces would have put us all at risk. We've scheduled an ascension ceremony to take place in one month, at the end of my alignment. The timing gives Solomon plenty of time to train his replacement and gives Mason a year to get up to speed before he's put in a leadership position. Only problem is, the transition to my leadership literally happened tonight at midnight. And for the next four weeks, we'll be down a dragon in the brotherhood. Solomon is gone, but Mason hasn't ascended. And I'm in the throes of adjusting to an influx of power that feels like it might snap me in two.

It's a fucking terrible time to have an incident.

A story labeled BREAKING NEWS: PHOTOGRAPHER LUCY VALE FOUND MURDERED is at the top of my news app. I tap on the included video.

"Horror in Paris," the news anchor announces. "Award-winning photographer Lucy Vale was found dead in front of the Fontaine Saint-Michel in the early-morning hours by a passing tourist, her body brutally mutilated. Police suspect cult activity as sections of her back were flayed and stretched to look like wings. Amateur video shows an inscription, '*Astra inclinant, sed non obligant*,' written in her blood at the crime scene. Experts tell us it's Latin for *the stars incline us, they do not bind us*. French police are seeking any eyewitnesses to this very public murder."

"*Astra inclinant, sed non obligant.*" Every dragon knows that phrase. It's the motto of the Saint's Order, the organization of wealthy humans who are sworn to kill us. They all have it engraved on their rings, a historical slap to dragonkind who come from the stars and are guided by celestial energy. It's basically the Order's way of saying fuck direction from the universe and the connection between all living creatures; we are the gods here and we'll take what we want when we want it.

"Yeah," Seb growls. "If an Order member didn't do this, it's a great fucking copycat."

"Her wings weren't even developed. She wasn't a dragon." My inner beast rages.

"Her dad is half. I met the man once. He couldn't shift, which means Lucy was a dormant."

"Did she even know about her heritage? The Order?"

"I don't know. I don't think so."

"Why the fuck would they do this?"

"I'll tell you why. It's an act of war, that's what it is! Carving up one of our civilians on public soil? It's egregious." The smoky timbre of Seb's dragon rises with his anger. There's a reason the sign for Taurus is a bull. He's as hardheaded as they come. Once he places the blame, no one can convince him otherwise. Honestly, in this case I agree with him.

I brace myself on the desk, everything in me wanting to avenge Lucy's death. *Bite. Shred. Kill,* my dragon growls from inside, wanting control. "Someone's got to pay for this."

Rustling comes down the line, and I picture Seb smoothing the arms of his suit jacket. I know that sound. He's wrangling his dragon into submission. "As much as I'd love to get behind immediate retaliation, you know we can't do anything rash. We'll have our day, but we need to be patient. Follow the process. The sun is in Aries, Connor."

"You think I don't know where the wheel is?" I snap. "For fuck's sake, I almost took off a customer's head today so I could fuck his girlfriend in a pool of his blood. Believe me, I know it's on me." Normally Solomon would gradually transition the reins to me acting as a consultant as the wheel turned from Pisces to Aries, but because the Oracle directed him to step down immediately and focus on training Mason, he's unreachable. I'm going to have to jump into this headfirst.

"Okay, then you know it's your duty to summon the four."

By *the four*, Seb's referring to the next three Zodiac Brothers in the wheel as well as me. It's been a long-standing tradition in the brotherhood. We're at our strongest during our alignment. The brotherhood is composed of one warrior dragon born in each of the twelve sun signs so that we always have one brother with exceptional power to lead. But because that power wanes with the passage of time, the Oracle requires the next three positions in the wheel to be in agreement on any major decisions. That means that while I am technically calling the shots at the moment, Seb as our Taurus, Remus as our Gemini, and Ellison as our Cancer have to agree for me to pull the trigger on any major response. Seb and I are close. Remus is easily swayed. But Ellison?

"Fuck. I know technically I'm supposed to, but you know Ellison will drag his feet. That asshole has never met a risk he's willing to take."

Seb grunts in agreement. "He only gets one vote. As long as we can sway Remus, we're good. But that would be easier if we had additional evidence. Do you think you can reach Donovan?"

Donovan is the reason we have the peace accord to begin with. Fifty years ago, the Libra brother sacrificed himself in exchange for the Order's promise to stop hunting and trapping dragons on land that isn't owned by the Order. Now he serves as the grandmaster's personal good-luck charm, the Order's own dragon prisoner, and the source of the blood used in the spell to make their weapons. He communicates with us rarely and only under great risk to himself.

"I'll try his burner. He was able to get a message through a few weeks ago. He might know what's going on."

"It's a start. We need confirmation that the Order is behind the murder before we retaliate, or we could be throwing the peace accord and everything Donovan has worked for out the window."

"Thank you, Captain Obvious. I'm on it."

"Only trying to help. Believe me, all I want to do is track the killer down and show him what happens to Order members who touch our civilians. I recommend starting at his toes and seeing how many parts we can tear off before he dies."

My dragon twists in my torso, loving that idea. I rub the back of my neck. "Consider yourself called, Seb."

"Where and when?"

"My place. We need to stay on-world or I won't get Donovan's response to my message. Be there tomorrow night. Eight sharp."

"I'll call my pilot and tell him to ready the jet."

I brace myself on the desk, images of Lucy Vale's desecrated body burning in my mind. "Tell me we're going to kill the fucker who did this."

Seb answers with a growl. "Fuck, yeah. I swear it to the creator."

Chapter Two

FIONA

What a day to oversleep! I stride as fast as I can toward the bistro, feeling hungover despite having not touched a drop last night and hoping that my friend Vivian hasn't given up on me. I'm almost twenty-five minutes late for our lunch date. I practice my apology in my head as I turn the corner and navigate toward the patio. Her latest text says she's already chosen a table outside in the sun.

Vivian's smile cuts through the crowd. She raises a massive glass of red wine and waves me over to an annoyingly wobbly table for two. I leave my jacket on as I take the seat across from her. It's sunny but on the cool side. Typical weather for the south of France at the end of March.

"Sorry, Viv. I set my alarm but slept right through it."

"C'est la vie." She waves a perfectly manicured hand through the air, her sleek black hair falling over one shoulder. "You're in the south of France. Kick back, relax."

I breathe a sigh of relief that she's not cross. "Thanks for understanding. Even the French Riviera isn't enough of an excuse for how late I am."

"Honestly, if the worst thing I have to do today is sip wine at this bistro for a half hour waiting for a friend, it will be a good day." She demonstrates the wine sipping, and I'm convinced she wasn't put out by my tardiness.

"That's what I love about you, Viv, always looking on the bright side."

The corner of her mouth lifts. "So... are you sure you're late because the alarm didn't go off? Or did that new billionaire fiancé of yours require your attention this morning?"

I give a theatrical gasp at her probing question and clutch invisible pearls around my neck. "Vivian! I don't kiss and tell."

"What good is it being best friends with a romance author if you can't discuss the steamy parts?" Her eyes fixate on my left hand. "Oh my God, is that the ring?"

I hold the new edition to my left hand out and wiggle my fingers so that the diamond catches the light. She gives a long, low whistle. The thing's an iceberg. "Honestly the largest diamond I've ever seen in my life. The American man at the neighboring table looked twice at it like he thought it might be ice for his flat water."

"It's enormous!"

"Roman had it specially designed."

"Right after he hired a bulldozer to carry it to the jeweler. Fuck, your hand must get tired." Viv snorts.

I bite my lip to keep from following that train of thought. Any woman would be proud to have a ring like this, and I refuse to let on that I'm anything but grateful. But no way would I have ever picked this ring for myself. It catches on everything, and I've cut myself on it twice. As soon as I'm married and enough time has passed, I plan to store it permanently in my jewelry box. I change the subject so I'm not tempted to complain. "Thanks for agreeing to be my maid of honor on such short notice.""

"Your relationship has moved fast! From first date to engagement in a month. I've had car repairs that took longer."

Our server arrives, and I point to the wine I want to order, then to a dish with *canard* in the name because I know it means duck. Vivian fills in for me in fluent French.

"When are you going to learn French, woman?" she asks. "Once you're married to a jet-setter, it would help to speak a second language."

"I'll get right on that."

She plants her elbows on the table and rests her chin on her threaded fingers. "Now, about this morning and why you were late..." She bobs her eyebrows.

I roll my eyes. Vivian and I share a publisher, which is how we met. I've made my career in thrillers, specifically the Alex Rogue series about a retired military police officer who is now a private investigator specializing in crimes committed by fringe religious orders and secret societies. Vivian writes steamy contemporary romance.

I know that look in her eye. She wants all the details.

"Sorry to disappoint you, but Roman did not keep me

in bed this morning." I laugh. "Actually..." I hesitate to tell her this part because she won't approve. "We've decided to sleep in separate bedrooms until the wedding night."

She narrows her eyes as if she can't quite get her head around what I'm saying. "Wait... is this a recent thing, or are you saying you two haven't, um..." She hooks her fingers together.

"Nope," I admit, toying with my crucifix necklace absently. "He's old-fashioned. Wanted to be married first."

"Oh." She frowns. "That's... weird."

I shrug. "Is it? Old money and old-fashioned?" I laugh. "Maybe I'm more open to it having been raised Catholic. His family seems really conservative. I think it goes with the territory."

She takes a long sip of wine. "But, I mean, he's not like a virgin or anything?"

I laugh. "No." And neither am I, but then she knows that. I don't share that Roman's been so busy with work that I haven't even seen him in two days. "Honestly, I just overslept. I'm exhausted. Planning this wedding, the dress, the flowers, the cake, it's taken a lot out of me even with the hired help."

Vivian's face falls. "Do you think it's your fibro?"

"Don't say its name out loud. I don't want to tempt the universe with the wedding tomorrow."

Her eyes fill with pity. I hate that. I can take anything but pity. "I don't want to jinx you, but after what happened before..."

She means the first time I had a full-blown fibro attack, after Marion was killed and my central nervous system seemed to go haywire with my grief. I'd pushed myself too hard and ended up in bed for weeks. I flatten my napkin on the table with my palm. "It's possible. This whirlwind relationship, the travel, the wedding planning, it's all stressful. Not to mention I haven't been able to write in months."

Her eyes widen. "Still?"

"Not a word."

She lowers her voice as if there's an editor spying on us from a neighboring table. "Wasn't your latest Alex Rogue manuscript due, like, months ago?"

I'm relieved when my wine arrives, and I take a fortifying sip before answering. "Try a year. They gave me an extension following the accident, but my writer's block isn't getting better. First I thought it was because I was grieving Marion, but now I just feel like I can't hear Alex anymore. It's like she's chained up inside my head and refusing to have any further adventures. I haven't been able to write anything more creative than a grocery list in a year. I've tried over and over to start *The Milkmaid*. The story is just *gone*."

Her brows sink. "Oh, Fiona. I'm so sorry." She reaches across the table and squeezes my hand. "Grief is a powerful emotion. Losing a sister like you did..." she shakes her head. "It makes sense that it might take up all the room in your head. I'm sure your writing voice will return once you have some peace and quiet in your life, room to heal."

I nod. "After the wedding. I'm sure of it."

"But it does beg the question." She leans back in her chair and studies me.

"What question?"

"Everything's happened so fast with you and Roman. The travel, the gifts, the overwhelming publicity of dating a billionaire. Are you sure about this marriage?"

I almost blow a sip of water across the table. "I better be sure. The wedding's tomorrow."

"But... Please don't take this the wrong way. You and Roman moved *very* quickly." She pins me with a knowing look.

"Four weeks from the time he bumped into me at a bookstore to the night he proposed in a hot-air balloon over Paris. Now here we are, wedding in the south of France. Am I sure I want to marry a handsome billionaire who swept me off my feet and proposed with a diamond ring the size of Plymouth Rock? Yes, Vivian, I am."

My attempt at humor doesn't earn her smile.

"Do you love him, Fiona?"

I glance away, wishing the server would interrupt us. "Why else would I be marrying him?"

She squints at me. Sees through me. Damn it. Vivian knows me too well.

I pinch the bridge of my nose and decide I owe her an honest answer. "Look, I get that the romance writer in you wants a big love story with instant chemistry and explosive feelings. You want Roman to be my Henrik Angel." I purposefully use Alex Rogue's on-again, off-again love interest to drive home the point that this is full-blown magical thinking. "But love like you read about doesn't exist. Roman is a solid option. I'm confident my feelings for him will grow with time."

She gapes at me. "No. No. No. Fiona, that's not why you should marry someone."

"Hmmm." I rub my chin as if I'm seriously contemplating her warning. "Well, it's enough for me." When she huffs in response, I lean toward her. "Let me tell you what I *love* about Roman. He can support me, which I need because my sales are officially in the toilet. I'll have health insurance when my fibro makes it impossible for me to get out of bed, and I'll be able to afford the best doctors, nutritionists, and physical therapists once I'm married to him. Oh, and I'll be able to pay off that property Marion loved so much, literally the last piece of her I have in my life. As it is now, I'm barely keeping my head above water. This engagement is a lifeline."

Now she scowls like she smells something bad. "Oh Fiona... you know what I think?"

I'm afraid to ask. "What?"

"I think that life has handed you a raw deal. I think you're marrying Roman because he asked. I think the trauma of losing your sister has made you feel like you have no control over your life, and so you've fallen into a pattern of reacting rather than directing what happens to you. I think your lack of agency over your own life is the reason you haven't been able to write as Alex Rogue since the accident. Alex had agency. She was a woman who made things happen. I think you're marrying Roman because he's an easy answer to your problems, but maybe you need to find your inner Alex again. You're about to bind your life to this man. This man you hardly know. This man you don't love."

I shift uncomfortably in my chair, my skin feeling too tight beneath her scrutiny. I'm saved when the food arrives. "I'm not one of your characters, Vivian. Stop analyzing my motivations. My reasons for marrying Roman are... complex. Far more complex than because he asked. I love the idea of having a family again. Roman is very close to his father and Donovan."

"Who's Donovan?"

"He's this man who is literally always with his dad, Stefan. Roman says he's just a friend. His father's best friend. Like an uncle, I guess."

Vivian cuts into her steak, suddenly wide-eyed. "As much as I am now painfully curious about the 'very close friendship' of the elder Cifarelli, let's get back to you and Roman. Before I stand behind you at that altar tomorrow, I need to know that you're not making a huge mistake. What else besides financial security makes you believe this marriage will work?"

I expected Viv would have questions. As writers and introverts, we live relatively isolated lives and aren't the type of friends who see each other or even chat every day. Admittedly, I've been sparse with her on the details of my relationship with Roman because I didn't want this type of scrutiny. But considering she flew all the way to France to stand up in our wedding, I owe her an explanation.

So I think about my time with Roman and what drew me to him. "He's hardworking and seems to genuinely care about me. I mean, he came on strong and pursued me like no man ever has before. Oh, and he's read all my books. That's how we met. He recognized me in a bookstore and told me he's a huge Alex Rogue fan. Read the entire series. I know you mean well and you want me to say I'm head over heels for this guy, but honestly, our story is more of a slow burn. You are right about one thing though—Marion's death changed me. Since the accident, I don't have the magic like before, not about anything. Maybe you're right. Maybe I am reacting to what's in front of me. Maybe I'm going along with where the universe drags me. So what. I'm tired Vivian. I can't have the type of feelings you're talking about with Roman because I'm not capable of them right now. Perfect doesn't exist, and I don't have the fight in me to wait for it anymore. This is what I want. It's what's best for me."

With a slow shake of her head, she studies her food, pushing it around her plate with her fork. "It's not what I'd want for myself, but you're an adult and you know what's best for you. You could do worse than marrying a billionaire superfan who seems to adore you," she says sternly. "Tomorrow you'll be married. Once things settle down, your muse will return, you'll finish *The Milkmaid*, and all the magic will be back in your life."

I raise my glass. "From your lips to God's ears."

Chapter Three

CONNOR

Bones senses something's up. The German shepherd has velcroed himself to my side, even following me into the bathroom as I shower off the smell of the restaurant. From the night I found him eating out of the dumpster behind Diabolique and took him in, he's been highly attuned to my dragon's energy. My restlessness is now his restlessness. I'd take him on another walk, but Seb, Remus, and Ellison are due here any minute, plus I don't want to risk missing contact from Donovan. With any luck, he'll respond before the official meeting of the four.

Then again, Donovan will expect the murder in Paris to send shock waves through the brotherhood. If there were any way for him to get a message to me, I suspect he'd already have done it. The Order must be holding their resident dragon in a position where he either can't reach the phone or can't risk contacting us.

Which means I'll have to settle for plan B.

If only I had a plan B.

The doorbell rings, and I hear my Firetender, Zaire, welcome someone inside. The talented artist has served me faithfully since taking his oath three years ago. Our Firetenders get close access to our creative energy, and in return we get an enthusiastic servant. I'm lucky to have him.

"Seb and Remus have arrived," Zaire announces.

Bones leaves my side to go greet the two dragons with an animated tail wag. Remus rubs the dog's head affectionately, and Seb gives him a thump on the side.

"Thanks for coming. Help yourself to a drink at the bar if you need one. We'll start as soon as Ellison arrives."

"Are you sure we can't start without him?" Seb slants a wry grin, his presence filling the room. The Taurus dragon is the picture of casual elegance in a pair of Tom Ford jeans, a relaxed button-up shirt, and a waxed canvas jacket. He clasps my hand and grabs my shoulder firmly in a way I picture him doing with every band he signs as an executive at his record label. Seb is as loyal as they come, but it's true what they say about bulls and china shops. When he thinks he's right about something, he doesn't care how many teacups he has to shatter to prove it.

At his side, Remus, dressed in his faded blue jeans and wild, shoulder-length hair, isn't as sophisticated as Seb but he's easily as intimidating. Equally as large, the tattoos that peek out from the sleeves of his leather jacket cover much of his torso. Remus is quiet but deadly. There's a lot going on upstairs, but he generally keeps it to himself until he can't anymore. And then look out. The tattoo artist may take his time to deliberate, but once he makes up his mind about something, you don't want to get caught between him and his goal.

"Remus. Good to see you again."

"Same." He strips out of his leather jacket and drifts toward the bar at the back of the room.

I need Remus to side with Seb and me about taking direct action on Lucy's murder. Ellison is reliably conservative on issues like this. He'll want to cross every t. But the longer we wait to rustle the grass, the longer the snakes can hide in it, and that means more civilian lives at risk. As he crosses the room, I try to guess where he stands, but his body language doesn't give anything away. Fuck, the Gemini can be hard to read, but then his sign is known for being conflicted. Twins in one body, not always in agreement.

Another knock comes at the door, and Seb and I exchange glances.

"Ellison is here," Zaire announces, escorting him into my living room before bowing and exiting in the direction of the kitchen.

Bones nudges Ellison's leg with his nose, his tail barely wagging. It's a greeting but not an enthusiastic one. *Yeah buddy, I feel the same way.*

Ellison gives the dog a reluctant pat that turns into a push. He doesn't want dog hair on his dress pants. Typical Ellison.

"Thanks for coming," I mumble.

He strides into the room in a tailored and pretentious gray suit, an attaché case in his hand. He's a partner at the law firm of Stuck Up, Backed Up, and Fucked Up, aka Goldberg, Weber, and Strunk. Ellison falls in the backed-up category. The guy's sphincter is constantly clenched. Throw out any idea and Ellison will come up with thirty reasons why you can't do it. It's ironic his sign is Cancer because he is literally a cancer on my proactive Aries ass.

We lock eyes and exchange curt nods. Everything I need to happen today revolves around my ability to lead this team, which means a scuffle with Ellison is off the table.

"If everyone could take a seat, I'll officially call a meeting of the four to discuss retaliation for the murder of civilian Lucy Vale." I remain standing, my back to the floor-to-ceiling windows overlooking the Upper East Side.

"Have you heard back from Donovan?" Seb asks, dropping into one of my leather side chairs and crossing an ankle over his knee.

"Donovan?" Ellison's brows shoot skyward and his mouth bends into a scowl. "Are you sure you want to involve him? Why risk his safety when we haven't even confirmed the Order's involvement?"

Why do you think, shithead? I can feel my blood heat in my veins. "Their involvement is a given. Lucy Vale was murdered in front of a sculpture of an angel slaying a person with wings we all know represents a dragon. The Order's motto was written in blood above her head. What other proof do you need? An attack on a dragon civilian on public soil is a breach of the accord. We need to retaliate before it happens again, show them there are consequences. If we can't get a confirmation from Donovan, we should pick one of them off and hold them until the Order answers for their crimes."

Ellison scoffs. "You do that and we're at war, Connor. We need to contact the Order for an official response first. It's possible one of their members went rogue. We can't jeopardize the peace accord unless the Order officially claims responsibility for the attack."

I take a step toward him, pointing at the ground between us. "Don't you think the message above Lucy's head is enough of an admission?"

"Only one way to find out." Ellison pulls out his cell phone and dials.

"What the fuck are you doing?"

Finger to his lips, he hits Speaker, and we all stare as the device rings once, twice, three times.

"Cifarelli Enterprises, this is Brandy. How may I direct your call?"

"Stefan Cifarelli please."

"May I ask who's calling?"

"This is Ellison Weber from Goldberg, Weber, and Strunk, returning his call on a legal matter."

Like this would ever work.

"One moment please. I'll transfer you."

I squint at Ellison. *Bastard.*

"Stefan Cifarelli's office. This is Pam. How can I help you?"

"Pam, I'm trying to reach Stefan Cifarelli. I'm returning his call on a legal matter."

"I'm sorry. He's not in the office at this time. Can I take a message?"

"Actually, this is a pressing legal matter of urgent importance. Is there a way you could connect us?"

I snort. Have to hand it to the guy, that's sort of brilliant.

"I'm afraid that's impossible. Mr. Cifarelli will be out of the office for a personal family event until the middle of next week. Unfortunately, he's not taking calls, but if I can have your name and number—"

"Odd. I swear he told me to call him immediately."

"Sorry, sir."

"Must be an important event."

"What message would you like to leave for him?"

"Thank you, Pam. I'll just call back next week."

He stabs the End Call button.

"Family event?" Seb mumbles. "What kind of family event has Cifarelli incommunicado for over a week?"

Remus holds up his phone and snorts. "*Page Six* says Roman Cifarelli purchased a custom diamond engagement ring at Harry Winston's recently, and rumor has it he's marrying *New York Times* best-selling author Fiona Morrow."

Seb snaps his fingers. "Doesn't she write those thrillers about a woman who breaks free of a deadly secret society and makes it her life's mission to take every one of them down? The Alex Rogue thrillers?"

"Yeah, that's her."

"Ironic. You think she knows she's marrying into the very threat her main character vows to bring to justice?"

I brush off his question. "Any rumors on *Page Six* about where they're tying the knot?"

Remus taps his screen a few times. "No, but that kid

from Florida who tracks celebrity jets says Roman traveled to the Marseille province in the south of France two days ago."

"No shit. Seems suspicious that the Cifarellis are in France at the same time a dormant dragon is murdered in Paris."

"Coincidental." Ellison scoffs. "Marseille is at least an eleven-hour drive from Paris."

I whip out my phone and do my own calculations. "An hour-and-a-half flight. He's a fucking billionaire. It would be nothing for him to rent a plane or chopper."

"You can't be suggesting that a member of the family did this? If the grandmaster or his son wanted to dissolve the accord, there would be quicker ways to do it than slaying a civilian in public. And why? This accord has worked for them as much as it's worked for us."

"Worked for us? After what they did to my nephew and his mate Reagan?" My voice is raised, something I promised myself I wouldn't do. But after watching the Order hunt Reagan down like an animal and shoot her in the back not even twenty-four hours after forcing her to shift, I know the kind of evil the society is capable of. "I'm saying a member of the family *could* have done this. Might even be using the wedding as an alibi."

"Why? There's no motive." Ellison glares at me like I'm on the witness stand. "For that matter, if it was them, why openly use the Order's motto? It would be far easier to believe this murder was committed by someone who *wanted* us to believe it was them."

"A third party?" Seb scratches the back of his neck. "Someone not on our radar?"

Ellison shrugs. "It's possible."

Searching for a mysterious third party sounds like a great way to waste time. Good thing I'm in charge. "There's one way to know for sure. One of us should go to this wedding and confront Stefan."

"Whoa, whoa, whoa…" Seb holds up a hand. "Calm your fire sign, Aries. That's a good way to end up in a cage. You set foot on Order property, and they have every right to capture you."

I fold my arms. "If they have the wedding in a church, he's fair game."

Seb's mouth forms a firm line. He wants to support me, but I can tell this idea is pushing his boundaries. "For all you know, they could be having the event at the estate of a friend."

"The Château de la Rosalie." Remus grunts, holding up his phone again. "Or so it's rumored."

"Is that an Order property, Ellison?"

Ellison pulls out his laptop and storms the keyboard, mumbling under his breath, "This is such a bad idea." His fingers stop their mad dance, and he shoots me a sideways glance that says *here it is in black and white. You're an idiot.* "Yes, it's registered. It's Order property."

"I want a map of the boundaries. I only need to get close enough to get inside Stefan's head." All dragons have psychic abilities, one of which is the ability to slip into an unguarded mind and read a person's thoughts. Easy enough if they're asleep or distracted. Two minutes in Stefan's dreams and I'll know what he knows about the attack.

A chorus of negativity rings out around me.

"You can't be serious!" Ellison bellows.

Even Seb is shaking his head. "It's too risky. At least clear this with the Oracle first."

Remus, though, studies me as if he's working something out in his head. "I actually think it's a good idea."

Every eye locks on the brother in surprise.

He strokes the two-day stubble on his chin. "Wedding days are pure chaos. They'll be bringing in flowers, food, tables, servers. The family is going to be distracted with a million details, and they'll all be together. With the right balance of stealth and timing, Connor's right, he could slide into Stefan's thoughts and get the truth before anyone knows he's there. And the time to do it is the exact moment we know that every Order member will have their eyes on one spot and one spot only."

I can't help the smile that twitches into existence on my face when I pick up what he's laying down. "During the ceremony."

Chapter Four

FIONA

I'm getting married today. It's supposed to be the happiest day of my life. But as I come awake to the sound of voices outside my room, all I feel is dread. My room. Roman insisted we have separate ones. We've never slept in the same bed. Never shared more than a chaste kiss actually. I told Vivian he was old-fashioned, but that's only part of the story. Although he's always been kind to me, our relationship feels passionless.

I wonder again why he's marrying me. Why would a wealthy, attractive, and powerful man pursue a broke, washed-up novelist with an invisible disability? Our romance has consisted of a whirlwind of fleeting moments and romantic gestures. From the beginning, he pursued me with the intent to marry me. It's inexplicable.

Undeniably, I'm rushing into this. Rushing away from the memory and aftermath of the accident that killed my sister and toward the safety of this man, his wealth, the security he offers. But after my conversation with Vivian yesterday, I'm questioning everything. I shake my head. What Roman has to offer will be enough for me.

It has to be.

The door opens, and one of the servants rushes in. "*Levez-vous, Madame*," she sings, buzzing around the room to open the drapes and flood the dim space with natural light. "It's almost noon. The hair and makeup team is already here. I am Esther. I will help you into your dress when the time comes." She stops and turns a beaming smile on me. "What can I have them bring you for breakfast?"

"Just coffee," I mumble, rubbing my eyes.

The woman taps her phone and orders coffee, croissants, and fruit in French. I crack my neck. A croissant in the south of France before walking down the aisle to marry Roman certainly won't hurt anything.

I stumble toward the bathroom and take a quick shower, then wrap myself in a deliciously plush cotton robe just as a half dozen men and women swarm into my room. Coffee is thrust into my hands, and I'm encouraged to sit in a chair so that an impeccably groomed man with a comb can go to work on my tangled tresses.

Esther speeds by and clicks on the television to the local news station. "Something for you to watch while you're stuck there."

"English subtitles please," I request.

She presses a few buttons, and the English translations scroll across the bottom of the screen. "Looks like more drama for the royals," she says with a laugh to no one in particular. The Prince of Wales's face splashes across the screen.

I sip my coffee and take a bite of a croissant that melts in my mouth like it's made of butter-flavored air. Mmmm. A redheaded woman brushes crumbs off my chin and starts blotting base there with a makeup sponge. I drop the rest of the croissant back on the plate.

Esther pulls my dress out of a massive, zippered bag with the help of two other workers, and they start fluffing and steaming the fabric. It seems like far too much lace. Too much overall volume. It's the dress version of the Blob. I tell myself it's just my simple childhood roots rearing their head. Admittedly, I know nothing about fashion. My sister and I were raised in a Catholic orphanage until we were fifteen and then bounced from foster home to foster home. I thought Versace was a brand of car until I was twenty-three.

I deferred to the fancy designer Roman commissioned, and I'm sure I won't regret it. At least I think I'm sure.

The next time I glance at the TV, there's a segment playing about a murder in Paris. My writer's curiosity kicks into gear. The video pans to a body in front of the Fontaine Saint-Michel.

"What's this about?" I sit up straighter, causing the man behind me to tug me back into place by the hair.

"Have you not heard of this, Ms. Morrow? Famous photographer from *Etats-Unis,* um, New York, murdered night before last. Lucy Vale." Esther shakes her head. "Butchered her body. My husband suspects satanists."

"Satanists!" My brows shoot skyward.

"Because of the blood."

"Was she drained of her blood?" I'm not sure why my mind goes there except that it seems very satanic.

"No, not that." Esther waves a manicured hand like she's try to find the words. "The murderer wrote an inscription above her head in her blood." She points at the screen where *Astra inclinant, sed non obligant* stains the concrete. "The flesh of her back was flayed to look like wings, right under that statue of the angel killing the devil."

"Religious extremists," my hairdresser hisses with disgust. "Terrifying."

"How something like this could happen." Esther tsks and shakes her head. "Such a public place and no one saw it?"

"*Astra inclinant, sed non obligant* is a famous Latin quote. It means something like the stars guide us, they don't bind us. Certainly sounds cultish. Maybe she was involved in one. Someone might have wanted her dead to keep her quiet." I stare at the screen, my imagination running wild with stories of how and why Lucy was murdered. "Maybe she knew something she shouldn't. Someone should check her camera."

I reach for my coffee and take another swig.

"We must start on your nails, madam," a pretty, doe-eyed man to my right says.

I switch the coffee to my other hand, still focused on the screen, when the door swings in suddenly and Roman is there, staring down his nose at me. He looks regal in his tux, like Italian nobility. A modern Medici.

The redhead doing my makeup does a double take. Her lashes flutter.

"Excuse the interruption." He casts me a tight smile. "The license is here. All we need is your signature, and then the American officiant will legalize everything immediately following the ceremony." He places a form on the table in front of me and holds out a pen.

He's already signed it.

Roman explained this to me before. We can't legally be married in France since we aren't citizens, so we're having a simultaneous remote ceremony to make this one legal. "Oh, uh, they're painting my nails. I'll sign it when they're dry."

He frowns. "This is important. They will fix any damage to your manicure." He clears his throat.

The nail tech stops painting and releases my hand. Everyone stops. Esther is still holding the steamer, but it's nowhere near the dress. The man behind me stops working on my hair. Just like that, everyone is staring at the license and holding absolutely still.

What. The. Fuck.

I carefully raise the pen between my half-painted fingers. Roman smiles and gives me a little nod of encouragement. It's intimidating as hell. I slide a teasing smile his way, pen hovering over the signature line. "Haven't you ever heard that it's bad luck for the groom to see the bride before the wedding?"

The corners of his mouth bend higher, but his dark eyes don't twinkle with the smile. "Then it's a good thing neither one of us believes in luck."

"Right." On our first date, Roman admitted that he

liked my Alex Rogue character because she didn't believe in luck or magic. Like Hercule Poirot, the character is governed by logic and deduction. I guess Roman believes I share that personality trait with Alex, but the truth is, she's entirely fictional. As childish as it may be, I do think that luck and magic exist in this world, and I find myself sad that I'm marrying a man who doesn't. "Are you nervous at all about today?"

He glances down at the license and sighs as if annoyed I haven't signed it yet. "Of course not."

I wait for him to ask me if I'm nervous, but he doesn't. Just glances between me and the license while the room grows uncomfortably quiet again. Although he doesn't actually say anything, the message is clear in the set of his shoulders, the way he hovers over me, the weight of expectation hanging in the air. Immediate compliance is expected. I get the distinct impression I'm the first person to make him wait for anything.

Why am I hesitating? Christ, I'm about to walk down the aisle and exchange rings with this man in front of a garden full of guests. Why should the legal documentation of what's about to occur feel oppressive?

"Fiona?" He takes a step closer. "Is there a problem?"

I glance up at him. *Yes, of course there's a problem. I'm having an existential crisis around our upcoming nuptials.* "No." I chuckle. "I must need another coffee."

I scroll a sloppy signature on the line and hand the form back to him.

He gives me a small nod of acknowledgment, then kisses me on the forehead. "There. Easy enough." He winks. "Meet you at the altar."

He starts to leave, but then I remember something I've been meaning to ask him. "Has your father arrived? I thought maybe I could ask him to walk me down the aisle considering..." Considering I'm an orphan whose only family recently died in a terrible accident.

His expression softens. "What a wonderful idea. Unfortunately, his flight is delayed. I'm not sure he'll make it by the start of the ceremony."

"Oh! Maybe we should push back the wedding. You can't get married without your family here." Our small guest list is mostly his friends and relations, but I can't imagine he'd want to move forward without his only living parent.

His smile falters, his jaw tensing. "I'm afraid that won't be possible. The officiant is on a tight schedule. Besides, my father has been married twice. He knows how this works." He gives a dark laugh.

Roman slips out the door, and it's like the entire staff breathes a sigh of relief. Everyone starts talking again.

Esther turns to me. "You must be a very strong woman to have landed such a man."

I chuckle as the man beside me starts painting my nails again. "Yeah... Strong."

Two hours later, I find myself standing in the outdoor gardens at the end of an aisle the staff has created between rows of white chairs. I cling to the handle of my bouquet to distract myself from the itch that runs the length of my body. I itch like a kid with chicken pox. My dress is some kind of scratchy couture, sewn together by the devil himself to torment my flesh like nothing else I've ever worn.

It's a beautiful, sunny day with miles of blue sky. Blush-colored roses, freesia, and calla lilies cascade from pedestals at the end of each row of chairs, and more blooms line the altar. It's too early for this garden to be in bloom, but you'd never know it from the topiaries and large planters surrounding me. I can't even fathom how much it must have cost to ship all of these in and set them up here.

I wiggle, wondering if the heaviness in my stomach is nerves or dread. Maybe it's a little of both. Every bride gets cold feet I suppose. Giving in, I scratch my neck. It doesn't help. Out of habit, I feel for my crucifix, then remember that Esther removed it from my neck because it showed through the dress.

Swallowed in a monstrosity of lace and wearing shoes that pinch my feet, I try my best to stay in the moment, but my painfully tight bun is making my head pound. As beautiful as the flowers are, the scent is cloying, almost suffocating, and I breathe through my mouth to keep from getting sick. Or maybe it's not the flowers or the hair or the dress. My stomach sinks again, a growing knot in my gut telling me this is wrong.

Vivian chooses that moment to appear beside me in a gorgeous lilac mermaid dress. Her eyes widen when she sees my face. She knows. She knows she was right yesterday. I am standing at the head of the aisle on what should be the happiest day of my life, thinking about running. Thinking about calling the whole damn thing off.

"Fiona?" she whispers. "Take a deep breath."

I swallow hard. "I'm fine," I say automatically.

"You don't have to do this," she whispers.

Roman takes his place beside the officiant. If I asked Vivian to, she'd get me out of here. I know she would. But then what?

How unfair would it be to leave Roman now? All the media outlets, every news station, would report how the billionaire groom was left at the altar. He doesn't deserve that. From the moment we met in that bookstore, he's done nothing but treat me with respect. I might not love him, but I definitely don't want to hurt him.

"I'm fine," I say through my teeth. "Just nervous."

That seems to appease her. She nods and squares up to face the aisle.

I force my regrets and apprehension down, down, down until I can hardly hear the whisper of warning my gut is sending me. A string quartet nestled under a canopy of feathery greens begins to play a classic piece, Handel if I remember correctly from my meeting with the coordinator. Vivian strikes a plastic smile and walks to her spot, stepping up onto the dais across from Roman. The music changes, and it's my turn.

Time seems to slow. Step. Step. Step. One foot in front of the other, I walk myself down the aisle. Until finally I reach my place facing Roman. Vivian fluffs my train, then takes the bouquet from my trembling hands.

The officiant starts talking about love and family, lives joined. My mind wanders. I am really doing this.

What would Marion say if she were still alive? Silently I say a prayer. *God, if you're listening and I'm not supposed to do this, if I'm not meant to be with Roman, stop this wedding from happening. Send an earthquake or a storm. Anything. Send me a sign.*

I pray it over and over again, my joints starting to ache from the anxiety welling within me.

I can't look directly at Roman, not when I'm thinking these thoughts. I pick a floral arrangement over his shoulder to focus on. Looking at him without looking at him. That's when I see something move along the side entrance to the garden, the aisle Roman took to the altar. I'm drawn to it, happy for the distraction. There's an irregularity in the pattern of the flowers. An animal? I can't make it out. I draw a deep breath through my nose. Whose cologne is that? It smells like salt air, cucumber, and mint. Soothing and clean. The thing shifts again. There's nothing there, but there is. I can't explain it. And I can't tear my eyes away from it. I stare at the non-thing. Really stare.

And it *blinks*. It blinks!

Jesus fucking Christ, there is an alien predator at the end of the aisle, and its eyes are trained on me!

Chapter Five

CONNOR

Looking back, I should have had a contingency plan, but I've never been much of a wait-and-see kind of guy. I'm a man of action. Coming here on my own to read Stefan's mind made sense. I never suspected a scenario where the man wouldn't attend his own son's wedding. He's conspicuously absent. Something is definitely off, and I don't like it.

Once I've registered that my target is missing, I turn around to leave. It's the obvious next step. Every moment on this property increases my risk of being detected and captured by the Order. The four will want to know about Stefan's absence. We all need to go back to the drawing board and come up with a new plan.

Only, the second I notice the woman at the altar, I can't move. Oh hell do I notice her. My dragon slams into the wall of my skin like a tiger leaping for its prey. I burn, my mouth goes dry, and my wings twitch with the desire to take her. Everything has changed. My world, my priorities, everything that I am and will ever be is different now.

Because of *her*.

The woman standing on the dais is the most perfect specimen of a female I've ever laid eyes on. And she's staring straight at me. Even wrapped in all that French lace with her gorgeous auburn hair bound in a bun that looks painfully tight, I see something wild in her amber eyes, something flinty, as if the right word could spark a fire in her that would send this entire event up in flames. My dragon twists and chuffs, a vivid image of the dress burning off her filling my mind. Nothing but creamy flesh and palpable tension would be left between us.

This is Roman's fiancée?

No. No. No. I refuse to believe it. It's a travesty. She *can't* be with him. What must he have on her to force her to dress in this costume and jump through gold hoops for these people? I close my eyes and get control of myself. I'm not here to be distracted by a woman, especially not one who's chosen to marry my nemesis. For Creator's sake, I have no business even looking in her direction.

My dragon disagrees. His desire to claim her is a drum whose beat grows louder in my ears. *Thump. Thump. Thump.* I fist my hands. Breathe deep. Close my eyes so I can't see her. Count to ten. I take a step back, then another. I can do this.

And then I hear her in my head. I'm not trying to hear her. I haven't made any effort to enter her mind. But I feel her inside me and I realize she's projecting a mental plea, a panicked plea, so intensely she might as well be screaming it. *If you're out there and I'm not supposed to do this, if I'm not meant to be with Roman, stop this wedding from happening. Send an earthquake or a storm. Anything! Send me a sign.*

She's praying to her god, not to me, but she wouldn't be thinking those words if she didn't want the earthquake, if she didn't want to stop this wedding from happening. She's having second thoughts. And this, this is why I can't leave. The beast within me has a carnal, primal need to answer her call, to save her from this travesty of a ceremony.

She's begging for a storm. I am the storm.

Fiona. I breathe deep as I mentally repeat her name. I know it from Remus's research. Fiona Morrow. Fiona. My dragon sings her name inside my head.

For all intents and purposes, I'm invisible, camouflaged in the shadowy recesses of the garden, but her amber eyes look directly at me. I swear she can see me.

The Saint's Order only initiates men. There are women who know about the Order—wives, girlfriends—but they don't wear the rings. The rings possess the magic necessary to detect cloaked dragons, but even with one, the order members have to be actively using the rings to see us. Fiona has no ring and shouldn't be able to see me, but her eyes widen slightly and there's recognition in them. She sees me. She *sees* me. The deepest part of my soul. And I see her.

Mine, my dragon growls. *Claim her. Claim her.*

My dragon is me, and I am my dragon. We are two halves of the same soul. But my dragon half is far more impulsive. Far more driven by instinct. At that moment, the moment my dragon decides this woman is mine, the entire world constricts to three irrefutable facts. One, I want this woman more than I've ever wanted anyone in my life. Two, the mere idea that I allow her to marry the piece of shit standing across from her is unacceptable and worth dying to stop. And three, the pain and discomfort ratcheting up inside me is mating sickness, and she is my only hope of relief.

She's my only hope because she is, undeniably and unmistakably, my mate.

I am so fucked.

"Fiona? Fiona?" Roman is trying to get my mate's attention, but her eyes are on me. It's time for her to say her part, her vows. That won't be happening.

I hold out my hand to her. I'm cloaked, invisible, but I call to her with my mind, my soul. Lips parting, she takes a half step toward me, the pointed toe of her shoe extending over the edge of the dais before Roman grabs her arm and says her name again.

A growl rumbles in my chest. I can't let him touch her. He can't have her. It can't happen. Heads turn, one by one, to look in my direction, each face more confused than the last.

I charge up the aisle. No one can see me, but the Order members sense me. They jump to their feet, knocking over the white folding chairs and pushing each other out of the way. Their rings glow to life, morph into neon-blue swords and crossbows.

She's in my arms now, wide-eyed and breathless. Once she touches me, she can see me, and her eyes lock on my face as I launch into the air with her cradled against my chest. Her arms shoot around my neck, clinging to me as we soar higher, and I fucking love it.

A blue bolt skims past us. A bit of lace falls from Fiona's side, and I glance back to see Roman holding a crossbow. *Fuck!* It's one thing for him to shoot at me, but how dare he risk hitting Fiona! He aims again, but then the dark-haired woman who'd been holding my mate's bouquet knocks the crossbow aside and the shot goes wide.

I pull the key I wear around my neck from my shirt. The talisman holds ancient dragon magic, allowing us to fold space. I close my fist around it and fly toward the sun, muttering the spell we all learn as children. I pass through the portal that forms just as another bolt narrowly misses us, and I dive and roll into the light. The next second I'm hurtling through the sky above a remote stretch of forest. Fiona's clinging to me, her body rigid. She's clearly terrified. Fuck, I've stolen this woman off the altar and carried her through a portal in time and space. I need to take her somewhere safe where we can talk, and thank the creator, I own just the place.

I land in the woods outside my secluded hunting lodge and set her down, taking my time to make sure she's steady on her feet. Who am I kidding? My arms around her are as much to indulge my need to touch her as to help her balance. Her skin is soft and warm. Fuck, I want to taste her. I want to bury myself in her.

"You're safe," I assure her, my hand gliding up to cup

the back of her neck. My wings are out, and I wrap them around us for warmth. It's cold here. At least for her. I bring my lips close to hers. "I have you."

She blinks twice, taking me in as if she can't quite believe I'm not a hallucination. Then she opens her mouth and screams.

Chapter Six

FIONA

I can't remember the last time I screamed like this. Maybe the night Marion and I snuck out to the local carnival at thirteen and walked through the Haunted Funhouse, but even that pales in comparison. I scream and scream and scream until my lungs burn.

The creature who abducted me has to be six foot five and is built like a Nordic god. Maybe he is a god. All I know is he looks unsettlingly like my character Henrik Angel and was invisible at the wedding. Is he an alien? An angel?

It would be impossible to mistake the creature for human despite his straight nose and pillowy lips or the scar that breaks through his right eyebrow. My abductor has wings. Great, taloned, deadly, working wings that flew us here, wherever here is. His wings though aren't the feathery sort. More like a demon's wings. And we are definitely not still in the south of France. I prayed to God to send me a sign if I was doing the wrong thing marrying Roman. Is it possible that this angel or demon is the answer to my prayers?

Whatever he is, he's stunning. Breathtaking. Inhumanly beautiful. Shit, with his dark blond hair sweeping his shoulders and ocean-blue eyes, he looks like he walked right off a Viking war ship. And his body is a masterpiece of long, lean muscle. Golden-skinned, chiseled male perfection. All my deepest instincts urge me to press my lips to the mouth that is so close to mine. Only my logical mind keeps me from acting on that impulse.

He's not human.

He abducted me.

He looks like my character but has wings like a demon.

And so I keep on screaming.

"Relax. I'm not going to hurt you," he says firmly. His bright, direct eye contact steals my breath.

My scream cuts off, and I struggle to drag air into my lungs. Did I just feel his words inside my head? He said them. I heard them. But I also *felt* them like a soft rustle of leaves blowing through my skull. My eyes widen even further. By now they must be large enough to influence the tides.

"Take a deep breath. I'll explain everything," he says. The salt air, cucumber, and mint scent I'd smelled before wafts into me again. I inhale deeply, realizing it's his cologne I smelled at the wedding. The scent seems to travel straight to my core and sends another confusing flush of heat down low in me. My nostrils flare, trying to get a better whiff. I have the insane desire to bury my face in his chest.

Fuck! Angel, demon, or alien, his presence is intense.

I stumble backward, my nervous system still fighting the insane reality around me. He catches me when I start to fall, lifting me easily. My feet bicycle in the air like something out of a *Flintstones* cartoon.

"Relax, Fiona. I promise you, everything will be fine if you just listen to me." His words blow through my mind again, soothing but not soft. Directive. Dominant. That deep, primal urge within me wants me to obey.

I stop running. Slowly he sets me down. "Wh-what the fuck are you?" Tears flow from the corners of my eyes. I've never been the type of woman to cry easily, but I'm terrified.

He releases my shoulders and raises one enormous hand to my face. Fuck, he's big. I recoil, afraid, but he only wipes away my tears with his thumb.

"Are you an angel?" My gaze traces over his wings.

He gives a low chuckle. "No."

I raise my hands between us. "Demon?"

"No!" He takes my hands between his own. "I'm a dragon."

"A dragon?" I wasn't expecting that, and the answer leaves me completely confused.

"Whatever Roman's told you about us, it's not true." His voice is low, deep, and commanding.

I study him for a moment and then remember Roman shooting at us with some sort of blue weapon. I have no idea what this winged man means by being a dragon, but I'm beginning to think he's far more worldly than any angel or demon. My eyes narrow.

"You... you abducted me!"

He holds up his hands. "Easy. Let's just talk about this."

"You kidnapped me on my wedding day."

His blue eyes narrow and his jaw hardens, lips forming a cocky grin. "You didn't want to marry that guy."

I scoff and shake my head. "What the fuck are you talking about?"

He frowns slightly as if considering something. "You were staring at me, begging me with your eyes to keep you from making the biggest mistake of your life."

For a moment I'm stunned silent. No way am I going to admit to this *dragon* that I was second-guessing my marriage. "Begging you? I never said a word to you."

His smile is back. Slow. Wolfish. "But you admit you were thinking it."

Something clicks inside me, like my body has thrown a switch from fear to anger. Fire pumps through my veins as if I'm a stick of dynamite whose wick has burned down to nothing. "Motherfucking, arrogant freak! You cannot be suggesting I am somehow to blame for my own abduction!" I poke a finger into his chest, my face feeling flushed as fury courses through me, overpowering any remaining fear or instinct for self-preservation. "I don't care what you thought you saw in my eyes. You're *wrong*. Take me back. Take me back NOW."

He narrows his eyes and pulls me closer, his delicious warmth surrounding me. "Sorry, sweetheart, you're *mine*."

"Yours?" I huff, struggling against him. I break free of his hold and stand on my own, facing him, the cold slamming into me once more. I don't care how warm he is or how beautiful. This is bullshit. "I most certainly am not yours!"

Something in his face changes, almost like I've slapped him, and all the warmth and humor drains from his eyes. "You are until I get what I want," he says through his teeth.

"What do you want?" I bellow. The wind picks up and I shiver, folding my arms over the useless lace dress.

"The Order to answer for the murder of Lucy Vale."

I draw back, more confused than ever. "The Order? Who the hell is the Order?"

"Like you don't know."

I stare at him blankly. "Lucy Vale? That's the woman who was murdered in Paris. The one with the Latin inscription over her head, written in her blood."

"That's right. You didn't think we'd let the Order get away with murdering one of our kind without answering for it, did you?"

I swallow. "Your kind? Like... *dragons*." I play back the conversation in my head. Nothing makes sense. Why does this man think Roman wants to kill him or his family? I shake my head. "Roman isn't part of any Order. And he certainly isn't a murderer."

The wind blows again, tiny flakes of snow swirling

down from above in its gusts. Where the hell are we? I hug myself harder against the cold, against the realization that my life just got turned on its head.

"Come inside. You need to get warm." He grabs my upper arm and turns us toward a house I would have called luxurious in any other context. All rich wood and stone with a wraparound porch and a pair of rockers out front. It looks like it belongs in a vacation catalog for Montana or Wyoming.

"Where are we? How did you...? How did we get here so fast...? You didn't just fly me here did you?" I shiver hard but somehow feel hot. My joints ache. My head throbs.

He frowns, then speaks slowly, as if he's talking to a preschooler. "I'm a dragon. I'm the thing your fiancé is trying to kill. And I find it hard to believe that the woman marrying the son of the grandmaster of the Order doesn't know anything about it or us."

"Jesus fucking Christ!" I scratch at the lace of my dress, suddenly feeling like the itch has turned to pain. "I told you, I don't know anything about any order. But I do remember Roman shot at you today, and no wonder! You're a fucking monster."

That seems to piss him off. A growl rumbles through his chest. "I'm not a monster. I'm your ... mate."

"What?" I can't really hear him over the wind, but it almost sounded like he said mate. *Mate*? What does he mean by mate? Is it like in the Australian sense? Like he thinks I'm his friend? My head swims and I hold it between my palms, suddenly nauseated. "What do you really want? Is it money? I'm sure he'll pay." My voice shakes. My head throbs. I feel clammy despite the cold, and my skin is on fire. I know this feeling. *Shit. Shit. Shit.*

"I don't want money," he mumbles, his brow creasing.

God, his eyes are boring into me. It's like he can see into my soul. My cheeks heat. Maybe he can. Fuck, I can't believe this is happening. My heart pounds against my folded arms. I'm trembling, and the telltale tingling in my fingers and toes tells me that my intuition is right. The stress has triggered a full fibro flare. This is bad. Very, very bad. I need to lie down. I sway on my feet.

"Hey, are you okay?" His hands are on me again, and I'm not strong enough to push them away. "You don't look so good." Cucumber and mint. It's incredibly soothing. He's warm, and suddenly I'm so, so tired.

"How the hell do you think I am?" My eyes roll back and I slump in his arms.

"Whoa!" He catches me before I hit the ground. Before I can protest, I'm in his arms again and he's walking me toward the house. My cheek rests against his biceps, although I can't be sure if it's flesh under his Henley or steel. The man is a wall. A very big, very hard wall. I close my eyes against a wave of dizziness.

"What's going on, Fiona?"

"How do you know my name?" My voice sounds small. I'm so tired.

"A story about your engagement."

"You know my name, but I don't know yours. What to call you," I babble. The world around me starts to spin, and I close my eyes. It feels like I'm drunk.

He repositions me to unlock and shoulder open the

door. All I register about the inside of the house is that it smells clean and the dark eases my pounding head. He carries me into a bedroom and lays me down like I'm made of glass. The bodice of my gown digs into my back and I inhale sharply against the pain.

"My name is Connor. Tell me what's happening."

"Need to rest," I mumble. "Hurts."

"What hurts?"

"Everything." I close my eyes and hold absolutely still.

"You can't sleep in that." I hear him opening drawers.

In the back of my mind, I have a fleeting instinct to run. Fight. Do something to try to save myself from Connor, whoever he really is. He's distracted. I might get away, find help. But I can't keep my eyes open. Every joint in my body aches to the point I'm afraid to move, and a slash of pain down my back feels like an open sore. I know it's just my nerves. My body is attacking itself. I might as well have been hit by a truck for the pain and fatigue I'm experiencing. I can't move. I can't form words. I can't keep my eyes open.

"I'm getting you out of that dress." I feel Connor grab hold of the fabric, and I make the weakest attempt to stop him. "Relax. If I see anything I haven't seen before, I'll let you choose from the prize table."

I don't know what he thinks he's going to do. It took two women ten minutes to get me into this monstrosity. The next thing I hear is fabric tearing and the dress is off me in seconds. Holy fucking shit. He tore it off me like it was made of paper!

"That dress was fifty thousand dollars," I mumble.

"It belongs in fifty thousand pieces," he mumbles back.

A tiny voice at the back of my head cheers at the thought that even if Roman rescues me, I never have to wear the itchy mountain of lace again. My corset blissfully loosens, and then it's gone. All at once, I'm bared from the waist up to the monster who abducted me.

There's a long pause, and I pop open one eye to see him studying my breasts and the deep, puckered scar that cuts from my right collarbone to just left of my navel. It healed a long time ago, but the discolored strip of flesh is still shocking. Not as shocking as learning a seat belt can do that to you in a violent accident, but shocking nonetheless.

Channeling all my disdain for the ugly injury into my gaze, I glare at him and say, "I'll take the oversized stuffed animal."

"Huh?" His face goes blank.

"You said if you saw anything you hadn't seen before, I could pick from the prize table. I'll take the oversized stuffed animal."

His lips twitch, and then he laughs in a way that warms my insides as thoroughly as if I were resting near a fire. "I'll see what I can do," he says softly. "What happened to you?"

"None of your fucking business."

He snorts. Sitting me up, he pulls a sweatshirt over my head that's big enough for me to wear as a dress. I'm lifted and then tucked under a blanket. Then he starts pulling the pins from my hair. I'm relieved when it's finally free. I hurt everywhere, but at least my skin no longer itches from the lace and my head no longer aches from the torturous bun.

"Sleep, Fiona. I'll watch over you."

Watch over me. My kidnapper. I'd laugh if I thought it wouldn't hurt. Instead, I close my eyes and pray for sleep.

Chapter Seven

CONNOR

Something's wrong. Fiona's sick. Really sick. I can sense her pain down the spiderweb of a connection the mating bond has woven between us. But it's pain without a clear source. This isn't emotional or psychological. She's in physical pain.

I bring her something to drink and then leave her to rest when it appears she's fallen into a deep sleep. Then I call Morwyn. The Virgo is the best doctor I know, dragon or human. I tell him it's an emergency and insist he has to come himself. Taking him away from his clinic, demanding he come here, it doesn't go over well, but I don't care. I'm Aries. For the next month, I'm calling the shots.

And I can't stand to see her like this.

The surge of my protective instincts has me running a hand down my face. Fiona is an unexpected complication. I went to France to confront Stefan, not to find a mate. Now that I've wrestled my dragon into submission, I realize the mess I'm in.

There's absolutely no way I can mate the fiancée of the grandmaster's son. Nonnegotiable.

If Roman takes Fiona's abduction to the press, avoiding human detection is going to be a pain in the ass. Under the rare chance that the Order is not behind Lucy Vale's murder, my actions today could be viewed as breaking the accord. I might have started a war instead of helping avoid one.

In sum, I've royally fucked up, all because I allowed my dragon and my dick to take control of my brain.

I pause my self-loathing when Morwyn arrives. After a quick explanation, I show him to her room. He agrees to assess her, but only if I wait in the hall. Patient privacy. I pace outside the door, trying not to think about him touching her. I hate the idea of Morwyn alone with her, of him looking at her skin, at her scar. I catch myself growling and make a beeline into the kitchen to distract myself, but I only end up pacing a different floor.

Way too much time passes before the door opens again. My dragon is on the verge of throwing a full-out hissy fit at the delay. Morwyn must notice, because he darts a cautious look in my direction, his black bag clutched in his hands between us as he meets me in the foyer.

"So? What's wrong with her?" I grumble. Fucker better start talking.

He gestures for us to move to the table outside the

kitchen. Good idea. Fiona needs her rest, and I'm liable to raise my voice.

"Explain again why Roman Cifarelli's fiancée is in your hunting cabin?" he asks.

I blow a breath out my nose. "I'm holding her to force Stefan to meet with me about Lucy Vale's murder."

Morwyn's eyes narrow. "Why didn't you take Roman? Or better yet, corner Stefan?"

"Stefan wasn't there."

"Stefan didn't attend his own son's wedding?"

"He was conspicuously absent. Mark my words. Something weird is going on here. I took the girl because she was the easier target. I acted alone."

He nods, his jaw tightening. "No shit you acted alone. You acted impulsively. Ellison tells me the four cleared you to read Stefan's mind, not abduct his future daughter-in-law. So what happened, Connor?"

As a Virgo, Morwyn is a living lie detector. He knows I've handed him a partial truth, but I don't have the patience for his games right now. "Never mind. What's done is done. Tell me what's wrong with her."

"Have you ever heard of fibromyalgia?"

"Heard of it? Yeah, I guess. Why, does she have it?"

"Yeah. She's had it for over a year now. She knows what to expect."

"And what's that?"

"Days, weeks, sometimes months of pain, weakness, and fatigue. She says her last one lasted a couple of weeks. She couldn't get out of bed for days."

"Fuck. Can't you give her something for it?"

"I've given her pain meds, but only rest and relaxation will help her recover. I don't need to tell you that her being held hostage here is not what she needs to feel better. You should take her home. She'd heal faster in her own place."

I cross my arms. "I can't exactly return her. Seb hasn't even had a chance to deliver my ransom message to Stefan yet."

"Then I think she should come to the clinic with me. We can take better care of her until you work this out."

My blood runs icy at the thought of her going anywhere without me, and my dragon gives a possessive growl. "She's *mine*."

Morwyn frowns, eyes narrowing as his head rolls back on his neck. "Oh shit, Connor. You didn't... She's not..."

I clear my throat and hold up a hand. "She's my responsibility. End of story. The clinic is too risky. The Order will have eyes everywhere. She stays here."

No way is Morwyn buying that explanation. He sees it. My dragon is putting off mating vibes like pheromones. The set of his shoulders changes, and Morwyn's finger pokes hard into my sternum. "Look, fucker, I get it. It's your alignment, and your dragon is calling the shots. But that woman in there is seriously ill. If you're keeping her here, you better take care of her. And I mean *all* of her daily needs, asshole. I'll be stopping in every so often to see how she's doing. If you so much as think about using her to ease your mating sickness—"

"Fuck you. I wouldn't do that. She's sick."

"Right. We all know how in control we all are during our alignments." He quirks an eyebrow.

"Hey! I'm as chill as I need to be. She's safe with me."

He studies me for a long moment and then nods. "I believe *you* believe that, Connor. But do you truly understand how fragile she is?"

"Of course I do." My words snap out more aggressively than I want them too.

He sighs. "Just keep your little dragon to yourself. Fiona needs food, rest, and for you to do what you can to manage her stress."

"Got it covered."

He stands his ground, his hand brushing back the tail of his lab coat to come to rest on his hip. "You're sure I can't convince you to let me take her to the clinic? There's no shame in admitting you need help given the circumstances. During my alignment, I often call in another dragon to—"

I slash my hand through the air between us. "I'll. Take. Care. Of. Her. End of discussion."

He scowls. "Fine, *brother*." Reaching into his bag, he pulls out a bottle of pills. "No more than one every twelve hours. Make sure she eats, drinks, and bathes. She'll need help to the bathroom. Once she's feeling better, work up to daily walks. Help her sleep if you have to. Your nearness should hasten her recovery."

"Nearness. Yeah," I say absently, examining the pills. I've never had to take care of anyone before other than Bones, and Zaire helps with most of that. My first instinct is to call my Firetender for help with Fiona too. But no, I want to care for her myself. Mates do that for each other. "I'll take care of her," I promise again, as much for my own benefit as for Morwyn's.

"Fine." Morwyn makes a noise deep in his throat, as if he's resolved on the matter but still doesn't think it's the best idea. He turns and strides toward the door. "Get to the Oracle, Connor, so she can talk some sense into your Aries ass."

Chapter Eight

FIONA

My abductor is in the room again. Connor. He said his name was Connor. He offers me a white oval pill. I recognize it as a drug I've taken before to help with pain when I've had a flare. He helps me sit up and pops it into my mouth, then raises a glass to my lips. Something herbal but fruity washes over my tongue. Lavender lemonade maybe. For a second I consider he might be drugging me, then realize if he wanted me dead, I'd already be in the ground, and my own body is doing a good enough job keeping me sedated. I drink the entire glass, yelping when his supportive hand hits a sore spot on my back. He lowers me onto the bed with a curse and mumbled apology.

Exhausted, I fall asleep as soon as my head hits the pillow.

The next time I open my eyes, there's food. He tries to sit me up to feed me, but I can hardly keep my eyes open.

Everything hurts. He helps me take another pill and feeds me some fresh bread. Where did he get fresh bread? I swallow and then fall asleep again.

The next time I open my eyes, there's a giant stuffed dragon next to my head. Despite myself, I laugh. This must be my prize from the prize table. I grab it and hug it to me. I should be trying to escape. I should try to contact Roman. I should...

My eyes open again. He's carrying me to the bathroom. Sitting me on the toilet. I do what I have to do. He carries me back to bed and gives me another pain pill.

He's taking good care of me. I guess I'm useless to him dead. I hope Vivian isn't worried about me. Vivian. Roman. Everyone must be looking for me.

When I open my eyes again, Connor is stretched out next to me in bed. He's fully dressed, on the outside of the covers, facing me. I watch him sleep for an embarrassingly long time. No one should watch their abductor like that. He truly does look like a Viking. Like Thor. A Nordic god. I'm unnerved by his resemblance to Henrik Angel, quite literally a man plucked from my imagination. He had wings before, but they're gone now. Did I really see wings or was that a fever dream? I have the unmistakable urge to run my hand along the skin of his arm.

He opens his eyes.

I close mine.

My cheeks heat, and I can almost forget that gnawing pain consumes every joint in my body, that I can barely move, that I'm a prisoner here, held by a creature so beautiful I can hardly look straight at him because it's like staring into the sun. I sleep again.

I wake again to light streaming through the window into the small room. The pain is less today, and I'm not sure if it's because of the pills my captor has been giving me or if my fibro flare is running its course. For the first time, he's not in the room. I glance down at the stuffed dragon in my arms and then throw it to the other side of the bed. How long have I been out? The pills on the bedside table say every twelve hours. I try to think back. How many times did he help me swallow them? The bottle says ten pills. I pour the remainder out in my hand. Five left. I've been out almost three days. Jesus. Has Roman tried to get me back? Is Vivian freaking out?

I tip the pills back into the bottle and set them on the nightstand.

For the first time, I'm awake enough to take in my surroundings. This is a cute room. Rich woods and dark-blue-and-green-plaid linens. A leather recliner in the corner has a navy-colored pillow with a Labrador on it. The drapes are a matching navy. If I didn't know better, I'd think I was in a five-star hotel rather than my captor's cabin.

My captor. Connor. What the fuck is he? I remember wings. We flew fast. Far. Not human. Dragon. Something about an order. That murder in Paris. People who want him dead.

I sigh and glance in the direction of the en suite bathroom. It's right there but feels so far away. I try to push up into a sitting position, but my head spins. Stripes of pain erupt down my back like I've been clawed open. I flop back down on the bed with a whimper.

The door opens and the Viking walks in. Damn it. Why does he have to look like that? And see me like this? So vulnerable. So weak. I bet he's loving that his prisoner can't put up a fight.

He swallows, and I have to admit he doesn't look like he's loving this. He looks concerned. Really fucking concerned, like he's afraid I might be dying. "I heard you moan. Are you okay?"

Am I okay? Am I the fuck okay? Oh shit, here it comes. I'm angry, and something about this guy just makes me want to erupt. "No, motherfucker, I am not okay. My entire body hurts like I'm on fire, I haven't eaten since the bread and cheese you fed me like, I don't know how long ago, I think my painkiller stopped working, and I'm stuck here with you in the frozen tundra of God knows where, rather than in my own bed with my new husband in the south of France. Why on earth would you think I'd be okay? You empty-headed, lizard-brained, Viking-sized piece of shit!" I clap a hand over my mouth to stop the verbal diarrhea pouring out of me.

Oh. My. God. Have all my instincts for self-preservation gone out the window? What the fuck was I thinking talking to this thing, this creature, like that? I'd never speak to Roman like that. I'd never speak to anyone like that. But something about Connor just seems to bring it out in me.

He peers at me through narrowed eyes for a moment. And then, as if he's as surprised as I am and thoroughly amused by my behavior, he starts to laugh. He winks at me like I'm a kitten scratching at him uselessly with my tiny claws. "Glad you're feeling better, Fi."

"Who said you could call me Fi?"

"No one. I do what I want."

"Obviously, or I wouldn't be here, would I?"

There's a beat where I think he's going to say something, and then he's scooping me into his arms.

"Where are you taking me?"

"Bathroom."

"How did you know I needed to use the bathroom?" A chill runs through me at the idea that he can somehow tell.

He sets me on my feet in front of the toilet. "It's been twelve hours since I last carried you in here. Call it a lucky guess."

I wait. "Aren't you going to leave?" I nod toward the door.

"You need help?" He gestures toward my lower half.

"No!" I say emphatically. All I'm wearing is Connor's huge sweatshirt and my underwear, and I do not want him pulling down my underwear. Then I realize we've been here before and he's already helped me with it. My cheeks heat again.

"Right. I'll be on the other side of the door if you need me," he mumbles.

I wait until he delivers on his promise before slowly drawing up the sweatshirt and using the toilet. It takes me four times longer than it should. When I'm finished, I manage to pull myself together and wash my hands, catching my reflection in the mirror above the sink. Shit, I'm a mess. My hair is sticking out at odd angles, stiff in places from leftover hairspray but falling or sticking out in others. Mascara trails under my eyes to my chin, and a sheet mark is etched from my temple through my left eyebrow from sleeping on my side.

I feel a wave of embarrassment and then check myself. Why does it matter how I look? I'm his hostage. He should have to see me like this the entire time. He should know exactly what he's done to me. Then again, I know I'll feel better if I get cleaned up.

I dig in a drawer and find a hairbrush, the feel of it running through my shoulder-length tresses positively heavenly. I use the hand soap to wash my face. It's painful and slow, but I do it. When I'm done, I still have dark circles under my eyes. I don't look pretty by any means. But I feel more like myself. Now if I only had a—

"There's an extra toothbrush in the drawer," he says through the door.

I bristle. How did he know I was thinking about my teeth?

"I heard the water running. Thought you might want to clean up."

Oh. Of course.

Slowly I open the opposite drawer from where I found the hairbrush and find a toothbrush still in its box and a small tube of toothpaste. I brush my teeth quickly but thoroughly. When I'm finished, I open the door to find the Viking standing right outside.

"You're welcome," he says gruffly.

"If you expect me to thank you for the simplest accommodations when you are the entire reason I need them, you've got another thing coming!"

"Another think coming."

"What?" I sneer.

"The expression is another *think* coming. Not another thing. Aren't you an author?"

"Oh, fuck off."

The corner of his mouth twitches, and I get the help-less-kitten feeling again before he sweeps me into his arms like I weigh nothing and carries me back to the bed, propping me up on a bunch of stacked pillows. He grabs the stuffed dragon from the other side of the mattress and tucks him into my side.

"How's that?" he asks, adjusting me.

I give him the finger.

With a huff, he plants his hands on his hips. I'm getting under his skin, and the thought gives me an unexpected thrill. I want to punish him for what he's done to me, and I find that although my body is in pure fibro hell, my mind is unusually clear. But there's something more. Deep down, I sense he's safe. He won't hurt me. Maybe he can't. Taking out my pain and frustration on him is as easy as breathing and surprisingly distracts me from the pain.

"I'm going to make us something to eat. Do you have any allergies or foods you just can't stand?" he asks.

"What, no bread and water? No gruel? What kind of prison is this?"

"Fucking pain in the ass," he murmurs under his breath. He heads for the door. "Fine, you'll get what you get."

"Wait!"

He glances back at me.

"When am I getting out of here? Did you get what you wanted from Roman?"

He frowns, his gaze drifting away again. "I'm working on it."

"He didn't kill that woman. You've made a mistake."

He slips out the door, and this time he leaves it open.

I should get up. The door is open. If nothing else, I should scope out the place. See what I'm up against. Make a plan to escape. But the thought of moving makes my body ache. I hug the stuffed dragon to my chest, resting my chin on its plush head. He's obnoxiously cute, rose gold with movable legs and a sweet face. I decide when I leave here, I'm taking him with me. I close my eyes. Tomorrow. I'll worry about escaping tomorrow.

The sound of pans and utensils clanking together somewhere in the house wakes me sometime later, and then the scent of bacon wafts into my room. My stomach grumbles. Can the Viking cook? I smell cinnamon. I adjust myself on the pillows. My mouth is watering.

He appears in the door with a bed tray and places it over my lap. The sight of what he's made for me almost makes me cry. A Dutch apple pancake, lightly sprinkled with powdered sugar and cinnamon, piping hot and steaming in a mini cast-iron skillet. Four slices of perfectly crisp bacon crisscross a side plate, neighbored by coffee with a tiny silver pitcher of cream. Juice that looks like he squeezed the oranges himself finishes off the meal.

I adjust myself higher on the pillows and wince. My stomach is growling, but lifting my arms to feed myself is going to be a chore. Lo and behold, the Viking grabs the extra pillow and shoves it behind me, then starts cutting up my pancake. My face heats. Is there anything more humiliating than having a man who looks like him feed me like a child?

I push the unwelcome feeling aside. Why do I care? He's a criminal. My kidnapper. Why do I have to keep reminding myself of that?

"Open," he commands.

I'm too hungry to put up a fight. I open my mouth, and he shovels in a bite. "Oh my fucking God," I blabber as I chew the literally best food I've ever tasted in my life. "Did you just *make* this?"

His answering grin makes me ashamed to have forgotten my disgruntled-prisoner routine. Fuck, I'm weak. My body needs food. I open my mouth and let him feed me another bite.

"I'm a professional chef. The least I can do is make sure you eat well while you're here."

"A chef? Wait, wait, wait." I rub my head, trying to sort out what I remember about the day he took me. "You had wings."

"I do."

"And we traveled…. You flew with me in your arms. You're not human."

He shakes his head and feeds me another bite. "Nope. Not human. The wings are real—I just keep them tucked away when I'm not using them. It's easier that way."

"You called yourself a dragon." I search his face. This isn't a joke. It isn't an elaborate con.

"Are we going to replay our entire conversation?" He studies me, one of his eyebrows lifting. "You really don't know anything about the Saint's Order or dragons, do you? You were marrying Roman Cifarelli, the son of the grandmaster himself, but had no idea who he really is?"

I shrug. "Honestly, I think you've got the wrong guy. Roman is too busy running his companies to be involved in a secret society. You are definitely wrong about him being in any way involved with killing Lucy Vale. He was in the south of France when she was murdered."

"He was with you? Physically with you at four a.m.—the time she was murdered?" he asks through his teeth like the very thought disgusts him.

I want to tell him yes, but again, I find I can't lie to him. "Uh, well, no. Actually, he was working. I hadn't seen him in two days."

He scoffs and cuts another bite of pancake. "I don't have the wrong guy."

Why couldn't I just say I was with him? Now he's convinced Roman's involved. "Or maybe you're just some whacko, genetic freak who's trying to shake him down for a payday."

A growl reverberates through the room, through me, and it's like when you hear a bird sing and realize the loudest sound is coming from the tiniest bird body. The growl resonates, much bigger than a man of his size should be able to produce while perched at the end of my bed. Louder than a lion's roar. It's a growl that speaks to that same primordial thing in me that responded to him before. I may not have ever heard of dragons, but I know in that moment that he's dangerous. I gulp and realize I've unconsciously pressed myself into the pillows, putting room between us.

He holds out another bite of pancake. "I'm not going to hurt you. But this is not about money. I have plenty of money. More than I could ever spend."

I eat the bite. "So, like, *dragons* are just living among us? You're a chef. Are there dragon doctors? Lawyers? Teachers?"

He redirects his attention to my pancake. "Yup. And now you're in on the secret. How's it feel to know that battle-ax of an eighth-grade teacher you had in middle school might have actually been a dragon?"

I slowly reach for a slice of bacon, picturing the nun who taught me algebra. "Actually, that would explain some things.

"Cream or sugar?" he asks, pointing at the coffee.

"Just cream."

He pours in the perfect amount, which is weird because I prefer just a splash and normally people over-pour. I bring it to my lips and take a long sip. He helps me place the mug back on my tray. "So if it's not money you're after, what do you want from Roman exactly?"

"Not him actually. Stefan. The grandmaster. I want Stefan to meet with me to discuss Lucy's murder. She was one of us, a dragon hybrid."

"A what?"

"A hybrid. Her father was a dragon. Mother was a human. She was murdered in a public place in violation of our peace accord. I want him to either claim responsibility for it or help us find the person responsible."

My eyes narrow even further. "What makes you so sure this order is even responsible? I heard that the police in Paris are blaming satanists based on the inscription."

"The inscription, written in blood above her head, was *Astra inclinant, sed non obligant*."

"The stars guide us, they do not bind us."

"You're familiar with it?" It's his turn to narrow his eyes.

"I'm a writer. It's a famous quote."

"And inscribed on your fiancé's ring."

I give him a confused look.

"Big platinum number with a Saint George Cross on the face?"

I feel my face grow cold. I know the ring he means, although I don't remember any inscription. Roman told me it was a class ring for a British boarding school. "It's a common quote," I mutter.

"It's the motto of the Saint's Order, a secret society sworn to kill dragons."

"Kill you?" I laugh. "Who would try to kill you? You're the size of a house."

The corner of his mouth twitches as if that amuses him. "You watched Roman shoot at us with a crossbow. Those weren't toy bolts."

I open my mouth but can think of no response to that. Instead, I fill it with another piece of bacon. "So you are suggesting to me that Roman is a member of a secret society."

"He's the son of the grandmaster. A VIP of the Order."

I snort and shake my head. "There has to be another explanation."

Connor huffs. "That was a statement, not a question. How well do you even know this guy?"

My shoulders hunch defensively. "Well enough to marry him."

"But not well enough to know he is part of a secret society formed to kill or enslave dragonkind."

I take another swig of coffee. "You have to be mistaken. Secret societies are my specialty. I think I would have noticed—"

"Right," Connor drawls. "Because you write those, uh..."

"Alex Rogue thrillers. About a character who solves murders committed by cults and secret societies." I take another sip. "Well, I used to. Not writing much lately, obviously, what with the engagement and wedding. I've been busy. And now this." I slide my hand through the air, indicating my general circumstances, then thumb the stupidly large engagement ring on my finger.

His entire demeanor changes, his smile fading and his presence becoming like a darkening storm gathering above me. I set the coffee down and lean deeper into the pillows. I don't feel like I'm in danger with him, but something I've said has definitely pissed him off.

"How long have you known Roman?" His timbre is low and commanding again.

Do I admit that it's only been a month? That our relationship was never physical? For some reason, I don't want to talk to this... dragon about Roman. It's none of his business anyway. I shouldn't be cooperating. "I need to rest."

"Never mind." Lightness is back in his eyes, as if the storm has passed. "None of my business."

I hold up a hand when he tries to feed me another

bite. "If I eat any more, I'll burst." I feel wasteful. There's enough left for two more people.

He cuts another bite and feeds himself, using the same fork he used to feed me. I guess he's not worried about germs. Another bite and his eyes flick up to mine. Slowly, meticulously, he finishes everything left on the tray, licking the remaining syrup off the tines of the fork with the flat of his tongue.

Everything south of my bottom rib clenches, and my brain gives me a very vivid fantasy of that tongue between my legs.

Ugh, why did he have to be my kidnapper? Even racked with pain, my body knows that being with this man would be a religious experience. I squeeze my eyes shut against the rogue thought. I'm engaged to Roman. I'm sure Roman will be perfectly acceptable in bed. I try to picture it. I can't.

Connor flashes me an insouciant grin and lifts the tray from my lap. "Rest. I'll wake you when it's time to take your next pill."

Chapter Nine

CONNOR

I manage to hold it together long enough to gently close Fiona's door. My. Mate. Did. Not. Sleep. With. My. Enemy. Praise the creator! When I asked her about him, I didn't feel a shred of emotion for him down our bond. But that image she sent me when I licked her fork.... She is not unaffected. I didn't broach the subject of her being my mate again, but that will come with time. Deep down, she already knows she's mine. I have to trust in that.

As I see it, I have a few things going for me. She doesn't know I can read her thoughts when she projects them down our bond. Plus I'm sure I've convinced her that Roman isn't the man she thought he was. Fuck, Roman convinced her of that himself when he shot at her. Stupid fucker. All I have to do now is get her to accept me as her mate. I snort. I've never had trouble seducing women in the past. Once she's healthy, I'll have her on her back in no time.

My smile eases wider as I set the tray down in the kitchen, then break into a touchdown dance, thrusting my fists into the air.

"I take it things are going well." Seb's dark laugh comes from the family room. It's an overcast day and the room is dim. I didn't see him there, waiting in the shadows.

I lower my arms and clear my throat, playing it cool. Pretending he didn't just see me do a happy dance in my kitchen. "Seb," I say in an artificially low voice. "I was just, uh..." I can't think of any reasonable excuse, so I point in the general direction of the sink and trail off.

"Never mind." He rises from a leather chair and strides toward me. Once he steps into the light, his face betrays his true emotions. Dark circles stain the skin under his eyes and his expression is bracketed by lines of deep strain.

"What's wrong? What's happened?"

"What's wrong? While you've been holed up here with the fiancée of the Order's second-in-command, I've been putting out all the fires you've caused."

"Fires? What fires?"

"Everyone's pissed. Ellison is having a total meltdown over what this means for the accord, and Remus hasn't said a word since he found out you took that woman. Every time I try to talk to him, he just growls and that vein in his neck throbs like he's going to blow. Be thankful he's not here because I think he's saving up all his words for you."

"Fuck them." I lift my chin in his direction. "We all agreed I should go. They can't get mad now that it didn't work out the way they expected."

Seb gives a frustrated grimace and runs his hand through his hair. "We gave you the okay to go to the wedding and read Stefan's mind. You abducted the bride of the grandmaster's son from the altar in front of witnesses."

"Don't be so dramatic. Stefan wasn't there. I adapted the plan. It's called thinking on my feet."

"It's called potentially starting a war."

Now I'm pissed. I point at the floor between us and try to keep my voice down to keep from waking Fiona. "*They* started the war the night they killed Lucy."

"You shouldn't have taken a hostage, Connor. That's not how the brotherhood works."

"The wheel is in Aries, my friend. It's my prerogative."

Seb gets in my face. "Go fuck yourself. You're the brotherhood's leader for a month, not our king. I have half a mind to return her to Roman myself."

Pure fire blazes in my blood, and I cross to the window to distract Seb from seeing it on my face. I'm sure my eyes are glowing green, reflecting the dragon within. It's all I can do to stay in control. I take a deep, calming breath before I speak again. "Look, what's done is done," I say. "This is going to work. Stefan will be forced to meet with us to address the Lucy situation. Did you get the message to him that we have her and if he wants her back, he needs to meet with us?"

Seb rolls his eyes. "Couldn't."

"Huh?"

"It seems Stefan isn't just missing from his son's wedding—his secretary hasn't been able to reach him in days and says he wasn't planning on coming back to work for another week or so. Also, no one seems a bit concerned about it. Roman is running the company in his place and presumably the Order too. We've left a message with him as well, but he's not returning his secretary's calls or ours either, and when we hired a human messenger to deliver the ultimatum to him at the Château de la Rosalie, there was no response to that either. The messenger confirmed Roman got it. Roman is deliberately not responding to us. Oh, and no one knows Fiona's been abducted either. There's no word of it on social or in the papers. As far as the world is concerned, all the party guests are still celebrating at the château. Of course all the party guests were Order members. It follows that if Roman wanted to keep this quiet it would stay quiet. He hasn't even reported it to the police."

"Because he knows what this is all about. He knows it's in retaliation for Lucy and he doesn't want to involve humans."

"He isn't returning our calls. And we haven't been able to reach Donovan either. Something is very, very wrong about all this."

"Do you think they went into hiding?"

"I don't know. I can't begin to guess what's going on. None of us could have foreseen this turn of events because none of us thought we were *kidnapping a woman* three days ago."

I smooth my eyebrow with the pad of my thumb,

wondering how much I should reveal to Seb about why I actually took Fiona. One look at the fire in his eyes and I decide to keep it to myself. "Uh, right. What's done is done. I did what I thought was right."

"You acted impulsively and broke the rules."

I shrug, turning back to him and spreading my hands. "What would you suggest I do? She's here and she's sick. I can't just return her where I found her."

"Sick? What kind of sick?"

"Apparently she has fibromyalgia and all the stress brought on a flare. She can hardly move."

"Fuck."

"Morwyn was here and checked her out. I'm keeping her comfortable. He says being near me will help her recover faster, but I'm not going to move her until she's better."

Seb plants his hands on his hips and shakes his head slowly. "You really screwed the pooch this time."

"I get it, okay? My dragon may have been running a little hot, and we acted without thinking first. I'll go see the Oracle. I'll do whatever she recommends."

A harsh laugh bursts from Seb's throat. "If only it were that easy, my friend."

"Huh?"

"Ellison already went to see the Oracle because Ellison follows through and follows the rules."

"Yeah, yeah. Ellison is the greatest." I grunt. "What did the Oracle say?"

"She said, and I quote, 'Tell Connor that he's made his choice and now he must live with the consequences.'"

"What the hell does that mean?"

"Your guess is as good as ours."

Damn, being in trouble with the rest of the four is nothing compared to being in trouble with the Oracle. "Maybe I should go see her myself. Apologize. Ask her advice."

Seb's humorless grin grows wider. "You can't."

"Why not?"

"She's in seclusion."

"Seclusion?" I've never heard of the Oracle being inaccessible. She's always in her sanctuary, reading the stars. She exists to see the future and guide our species.

"According to her acolytes, it's a time to be cut off from the world and devote herself to prayer and connection with the creator."

"How long does that go on?"

The way Seb licks his bottom lip, I know I'm not going to like the answer. "Anywhere from a week to a year, according to her acolytes."

"Fuck."

"Yeah, fuck." Seb frowns.

"Well, she'll have to come out of seclusion for Mason's ascension to the brotherhood."

"That's three and a half weeks away."

I scratch the stubble on my jaw. The part of my soul that is my dragon stirs, his voice low and coarse as he whispers in my head, *This is good. It means more time with Fiona. Time we can use to win her over. To convince her to be ours. Claim her as our mate.*

"Thanks for letting me know," I say dismissively.

He brushes invisible lint from the arm of his sport

coat. "No problem. I, unlike some, take my responsibilities as a member of the four seriously."

The barb raises my hackles, but I don't take the bait. "What exactly do you expect me to do here?"

"It's not for me to decide," Seb says incredulously. "What are *you* going to do? As you keep reminding us, you're calling the shots."

Inside, I can feel my dragon smile wickedly. *Yes, we are.* "I'm going to stay here and guard Fiona while helping her recover. Roman is a smart boy, and resourceful. If he wants his fiancée back, he'll answer our calls or have his daddy come out of hiding to do so. The plan is, we stay the course and protect our own."

Seb bows. "I'll let the others know. It should be fun watching Ellison's head explode."

Chapter Ten

CONNOR

If I learned even one thing from Seb's visit, it's that I have exactly three and a half weeks to make Fiona fall in love with me. That's the length of my alignment and how long I'm in charge, the ultimate authority given that the Oracle is in seclusion. Once Seb takes the reins, nothing can stop him from removing her and sending her back to that bastard, or just moving her home. Nothing but a mating bond. No dragon would ever keep a mated pair apart. The sanctity of a completed mating bond has never been questioned, even with a human. Fiona might not know it yet, but our relationship is metaphysically predetermined. If she allows me in, it will click into place.

I text Zaire a list of things I think Fiona will need now that she's recovering. I want him and Bones here too, to make it feel more like a home. She needs to feel safe. I want her to be comfortable.

So comfortable she never wants to leave.

Which means the last resistance I had to this bond has been snuffed out. I don't care if my nemesis put a ring on her finger. She was never truly his. The moment she saw through my camouflage at the wedding and I heard her voice in my head, heard her practically begging me to take her, I knew this bond was meant to be. She's mine now.

I'm almost done with my text to Zaire when there's a knock on the door. Morwyn for his promised checkup. As always, his brown hair is as wild as Einstein's and his tall, ropy body is dressed in blue scrubs and a lab coat.

He folds his wings away as he enters the foyer, the membranous appendages passing smoothly through his lab coat thanks to our dragon magic. "How's she doing?"

"Better." I give him a recap, and he disappears into her room.

Seconds turn to minutes, and I pace outside her door again. I can't stop myself. Fucking Morwyn. Why does he have to be alone with her? Probably touching her. Talking to her. Alone. A growl percolates in my throat, and it takes everything I have to keep my dragon at bay.

Something tight within me loosens when he finally emerges from the room.

"Well?" I bark.

He shoots me a stern look, eyes narrowing. "She's much improved."

I release a relieved breath. "So I should continue with the meds and stay near her so that she heals faster?"

Morwyn frowns. "She should only take the pain meds if she needs them. And as for staying close to her, that depends. What do you plan to do about your attachment? You do know if you keep a hostage forever, it defeats the purpose."

"What the fuck are you talking about?"

"I heard your growl, Connor. Your dragon is unusually protective of this woman. Unusually possessive." He squints at me as if he knows, as if he can see the bond between us.

"Yeah, well, fuck off. I'm taking good care of her. That's all you need to worry about, Doc."

"Hmmm." He removes the stethoscope from his neck and slides it into his black bag. "Try to get her out of bed tomorrow. By then your dragon energy should have her feeling remarkably better."

"Good." I accompany him to the door, planning to lock it behind him.

"She's still frail, Connor," he warns. "Keep a leash on your dragon. I mean it. She's human. You could kill her."

"I'd never hurt her."

"And your dragon?"

"My dragon is completely under control."

He reaches out and wipes sweat from my temple. *Fuck.*

"Clearly."

Our eyes lock, and the intelligent, knowing gleam in his makes me want to slug him. Instead, I forcibly open the front door.

He spreads his wings and pulls his key out from under his shirt. "I'll take that as my cue to exit." He shoots into the air and is gone.

Fiona sleeps most of the day, waking only briefly to

eat, drink, and take her pill. But she's making it to the bathroom on her own. She's getting better. I've never locked her door, but that evening, I make sure to leave it open again so that she knows it's unlocked. Still, she doesn't leave her room.

The next morning after breakfast, I decide it's time to follow Morwyn's suggestion. "Get up. We're going for a walk."

Her eyes widen a little. "I'm not sure I can."

"If you can walk to the bathroom, you can walk outside. Doctor says fresh air will be good for you."

She curls her lip. "Doctors don't know everything. Besides, I have no clothes."

I toss a set Zaire keeps here on the bed. They'll be large on her, but they'll work. He's a slender man. "I'll meet you in the foyer in ten minutes."

Fifteen minutes later, after three tugs on the bond between us, she joins me in the foyer. I wonder if she feels it the way I do, the connection between us. Or maybe to her it just feels like anxiety. I look her over. The shoes are big, but they'll work for a short walk. Zaire will be here tomorrow with clothes for her.

I pull a coat from the hall closet and wrap it around her, then tug a hat over her shiny auburn hair. I notice the engagement ring on her hand just before I cover it with a mitten. Better that thing stays hidden. I want to drop it into the nearest volcano. "Where are we that I need to get so bundled up this late in March?"

"Someplace cold," I say, intentionally vague.

"I hate the cold."

I flash a wolfish smile. "Stay close to me. I'll keep you warm."

"Give me a break," she mumbles.

I step closer to her and wrap a hand around the side of her head. Our eyes lock and she leans toward me, her lips parting. I don't even think she knows she's doing it. "My core temperature is 105 degrees," I say, my voice all grit. "I run hot, baby. Your own personal furnace."

She seems to catch herself and knocks my hand away. "Let's get on with it."

I open the door and lead her out into the early-spring sunshine. We start walking toward the path that leads into the woods. Wyoming is stunning this time of year, and the air feels crisp and clean in my lungs, the scent of pine trees frosted in light snowfall a lingering perfume in the air.

"You're not wearing a coat," she says, seeming to notice my T-shirt for the first time.

"No." I watch her out of the corner of my eye.

"Don't you ever get cold?"

I slant a cockeyed grin in her direction. "Never."

"Never?"

"I run hot, remember?" I waggle an eyebrow at her.

She scowls.

"Dragons are impervious to extreme temperatures. I sometimes feel the heat or the cold, but it doesn't bother me. I can't burn in fire or freeze to death."

"Oh." She stares at me like she might ask me something more but doesn't.

"How did you meet Roman?" My voice is abnormally low. I hate saying the bastard's name, but I tell myself I need to know how close she is to the Saint's Order. Deep down though, my curiosity serves another purpose. If I can figure out what made her fall in love with him, maybe I can make her fall in love with me.

"At a bookstore. Why? Are you looking for tips to pick up women?"

I snort. "No. I'm trying to figure out how a woman like you ends up with a guy like him, then ends up almost marrying him without knowing a thing about him."

She shoves her hands into her pockets. "Just lucky I guess."

I growl.

"Do you have to make that noise? You sound like a bear."

I laugh. "You should be thanking me. Might keep away the real bears."

"There are bears here?" Her gaze sweeps over the woods.

"Occasionally." I fan a wing out to surround her shoulders. "I promise I'll protect you."

"I'll never get used to that," she mutters with a glance toward my wing. "How does that work, anyway, I mean with your T-shirt?"

"The magic in our wings rearranges the molecules in the cloth. Basically, our clothing parts to accommodate them."

She stares at my wing for a beat and down our bond I sense her urge to reach out and touch it, but she quickly turns her attention back to the trail and doesn't.

I frown and tuck the wing away. "So you met Roman

at a bookstore. And then what? Love at first sight?" I can't keep the irritation from my voice.

She looks annoyed as she glances again in my direction. "Why are you so interested?"

I sigh. "I'm just having a hard time believing you know nothing about the Saint's Order. I'm trying to put it together, that's all. It would help me to understand... things."

She scoffs. "You want to know if I'm lying about this because if I am, you can't trust me."

I give a single nod.

"Fine. I met Roman in a bookstore. He was buying my newest release. He'd already read all twenty-two of my other books and recognized me right away from my picture on the back cover. After some small talk, he asked me for coffee. We discussed Alex Rogue for hours, and then he asked me if I liked Italian food and if I'd like to go to dinner. I agreed, and he flew me on his private jet to Italy. Over the next three weeks, he filled my apartment with flowers and we went out once or twice a week. Out as in all over the world—London, Munich, Sydney. And then a little over a week ago, he asked me to marry him. We planned everything in six days." She stops walking and stares absently into the woods. "It's amazing what money can do."

"Is that why you married him? The money?"

Her hand snaps out and slaps me across the cheek. It stings a little, but she shakes it like it hurt her a lot more. She even had the foresight to remove her mitten before she did it. I chuckle at the fire I see in her eyes. She's got pluck, and she's right, that comment was out of line, even if I sense down the bond that there's a grain of truth to it. "Uh, sorry," I mumble. "Seems like a strange reason to marry someone. Just because they read your books and took you to dinner a few times."

She frowns, still rubbing her hand. "You'd be surprised how few people in my life have actually read all my books. Even my late sister hadn't." She slips her mitten back on. "I want to go back. I'm tired."

I sweep under her knees and swing her into my arms. She yelps in surprise, but I ignore it and carry her toward the house.

"I didn't ask you to carry me!" she insists.

"No. That's just a bonus. We are full-service here at Dragon Lodge. Bathroom trips. Meals. Walks in the woods. We do it all for you."

Her eyes meet mine, and I swear the corner of her lip twitches, but the hint of a smile vanishes as soon as it appears. She wriggles out of my arms the moment we reach the door and stomps back toward her room, slamming the door.

I let her go, but I dig out my e-reader and download her series.

Chapter Eleven

FIONA

I'm officially a bad person. I'm one of those women you read about in online gossip magazines, rife with problems so deep and complex there is no other explanation than a chronic habit of bad decision-making. By some ironic act of fate, I am lusting after my kidnapper.

I crawl back into bed, more tired than I should be from such a short walk, my mind reeling. The electricity that flowed through my body when Connor carried me back to the house still hums in my veins, and images of his eyes, his lips, his wings flash across my mind.

Do I have a wing fetish or something? Is that a thing?

None of this makes sense. He kidnapped me! From my wedding! I should be planning my escape and cowering in fear every time he enters the room, not having feelings of sexual attraction. But that's exactly what I'm feeling. Every time I look at him, it's like I'm on a swing at the top of the arc and my stomach is doing that dropping thing just before I swing in the opposite direction. My entire body wants to smile in his presence. Some kind of dragon mind trick? It has to be.

None of this makes sense. From the moment I first saw him at my would-be wedding, my entire world has been out of control. And today, if I'm being honest with myself, his accusation came far too close to the truth. Money did play a part in my almost marrying Roman. The fact that a stranger can see it is almost too much to bear.

I hold up my left hand and look at the gaudy iceberg that serves as my engagement ring. Roman shot at me. Shot at me with a goddamned crossbow. A medieval weapon. I remember the bolt brushing my side as it cut through the lace of my dress. And if that's not the weirdest part, Connor, the man with wings who abducted me from that shit show, looks disturbingly like one of my characters. Now here I am in a lodge in the middle of nowhere, eating gourmet meals and being cared for by a man who is also apparently a dragon.

None of this makes sense. I wish I could talk to Vivian.

For a few minutes, I toss and turn, scissoring my legs under the covers. When I turn on my side and slide my hands under my head, the rock digs into my cheek. I roll onto my back again and slide the ring from my hand, placing it on the nightstand. I stretch my fingers and immediately feel better. Then I curl around the stuffed dragon and finally feel at ease. *Ahhh.*

CONNOR

For the rest of the day, I give Fiona her space, sensing she's struggling with everything that's occurred. It's traumatic, I'm sure. If it's true that she barely knew Roman, she's learning she almost married a killer while also experiencing the draw of the mating bond, which has to be confusing to her human body. I want her to heal, and pushing her too fast or constantly pressing her for information isn't what she needs right now. So I keep her well-fed but otherwise stay out of her hair.

It gives me time to start her books. No one would argue she's a talented author, but I wonder if Roman's interest in her is how close her work comes to reality. Alex Rogue destroys secret societies just like his. Or are her stories a ploy to cover up her part in that reality? I have to know for sure before I get any closer to her.

When night falls, I let myself into her room and take a seat on the recliner in the corner, where I have a clear view of her and the bed, my e-reader in my hands.

"Are you going to sit there all night and watch me sleep?" she asks, her voice a little breathless.

"Yes." Fuck. That came out more dragon than man. I shift in the chair. Being in the same room as her does things to me. "I'm going to continue reading this book." I hold up my device. "Alex is just about to infiltrate the seedy underbelly of elite academia."

"You're reading *Skull and Bones*?" She huffs in surprise.

"It's book one." I shrug.

"Why?" Her eyes pop. "Really, you shouldn't..."

Odd. Down our bond, I get the sense she truly does not want me to read her books. There's a hint of embarrassment. "Just want to get to know you better." When that seems to make her even more uncomfortable, I add, "I do this with all my prisoners. Helps me to understand who I'm dealing with."

She looks away from me, toward the ceiling. "Fine."

"Are you hungry? You didn't eat much dinner."

"No. Just tired."

"Thirsty?"

"No." She sounds annoyed again.

I lean back, put the footrest up. "More reason for me to stay in here. In case you need help again or get hungry later." I open the cover on my e-reader and start to read.

She sighs. "Suit yourself." She closes her eyes, but she's restless. She's feeling it too, this magnetic attraction the creator built into all mates. She doesn't understand it, and fighting it is keeping her awake. I send a curl of dragon energy her way, wrapping it around her mind and encouraging her to relax, to let go.

Minutes pass, and her breath evens out. I feel her slip into sleep.

Up until now, I've only read the thoughts she's projected into my head, made louder by the bond between us. But I need to make sure our connection isn't making me blind to a trick by the Saint's Order. She wasn't forthcoming on our walk today, and I need to be damned sure she's telling the truth about her knowledge and involvement with Roman and the Order.

Dreamwalking isn't something dragons do casually. Jumping inside someone's head is risky. You never know what you might find in a place where there are no phys-ical restraints or social mores. I don't relish stumbling upon my mate dreaming about Roman, for example, but I'm aware it's possible. One could also argue that it's a violation. No doubt there are ethical lines I'm crossing. But I dismiss any qualms immediately. I'm warranted because she's technically the enemy since she was marrying into the Order.

Plus she's our mate, my dragon adds. *Must learn what brings her pleasure. Must prime her mind to our affections.* He coils and chuffs inside me, causing my wings to twitch and the tips of my talons to sprout from my second knuckle. Sweat breaks out on my brow again, and my stomach pitches. Mating sickness. It's getting worse with her nearness. I close my eyes and will myself under control.

The truth is, I could accomplish everything I need to without dreamwalking, but it would take too long. I'm a man of action. This is the fastest road to where we're going—*everywhere* we're going—and I'm taking it. To her it will all feel like a dream anyway. I've got nothing to lose and no one to stop me.

I dive into her head.

Blackness, that's always the way it begins, then everything goes hazy like I'm walking through a cloud. Once the clouds part, I find myself in a swanky cocktail lounge, the mirrored wall behind the bar reflecting shiny bottles of top-shelf liquor. Interesting. This is not what I expected to find in Fiona's dreams.

A slim woman in a strappy red dress sits at the bar, her back to me. This figure is at the center of the dream.

That's how I know it's her. Fiona's hair in real life is a dark auburn, a deep brown that holds a hint of red when it catches the light. In her dreams, her hair is the color of honey. Almost blond. Dream Fiona is also taller than in real life, slimmer, the muscles of her back and shoulders toned as though she's been practicing ballet since childhood.

It's not surprising that Dream Fiona doesn't look like Fiona in real life. Most humans hold a version of themselves in their dreams that doesn't match reality. In dreams, their self-image is constructed, carefully curated, and sometimes pieced together from celebrity parts they especially admire. It's normal. Only, it's hard for me to swallow because in Fiona's case, reality is so much better than this. I glance down at myself, in my jeans and flannel, and decide I don't fit the surroundings. I mentally construct a new outfit. A dark tuxedo jacket over a black shirt and slacks. Formal but on the casual side. Something James Bond would wear to the casino. That's what this scene reminds me of, something out of James Bond.

I swagger up to the bar just as the bartender slides a lemon-drop martini in front of her, stating her drink order as if he could possibly have confused her with someone else. She's the only one in here. I take a seat on the stool beside her, but when I get a better view of her profile, I almost cringe. The woman in the red dress is undeniably beautiful, but her face is not Fiona's.

This is highly unusual. People don't normally center someone else in their dreams. I glance around the bar again, perplexed.

What exactly is going on here?

All the features of Red Dress's face are hard, cold, angular. Her green eyes are positively icy as she brings her martini to her lips. I catch her looking at me without turning her head.

"Buy you a drink?" She pivots on her stool, turning the full force of a straight white smile in my direction. Stunning. Of course she is. She isn't real.

"Isn't that my line?" I say, playing along. "When a man approaches a beautiful woman at a bar, he's usually the one to offer."

"But I already have a drink," she says, soft as a kitten's breath. "How will it look if you aren't also drinking?" Her jaw clenches, and she straightens on her stool. "Order. A. Drink."

I raise a finger and order a scotch, neat. The bartender pours it with a flourish.

Only when he's gone does she speak again. "Have you brought the package?"

"The package?"

She rubs her temple with two perfectly manicured fingers. "Jesus, Henrik, I don't have time for these games. Did you get it or not?"

Henrik. It takes me a minute to connect the dots. Henrik Angel. He's a character in the Alex Rogue series, a potential love interest. Which means I'm talking to... "You're Alex Rogue, the private investigator who cracks cult murders." *Fuuuuck.* This is Fiona's character. I'm in one of her fucking stories.

"Shhh." She looks over her shoulder. "What the hell are you doing? Do you want to blow our cover? Now do you have the photos from the Milk Cult initiation or not?"

"I'm sorry. I don't."

She turns away and takes a sip of her martini. "This is never going to work. Whoever this pretty face is, it isn't Henrik. This guy's dumb as a box of rocks. Don't expect me to hop into bed with him if he doesn't have a clue about investigating."

"Who are you talking to?" I look over my shoulder, but there's no one there. We're the only ones in this joint.

"Give me time. I'll try something else," a small, familiar voice says from somewhere on the other side of Alex. Somewhere near the floor.

"We're out of time," Alex snaps. "We've been out of time for six months now. You need to get me out of this fucking bar so that I can do what I do best or you can kiss everything you've ever loved goodbye."

"I'm trying!" the small voice cries. So slight. So weak.

I stand from my stool and try to move around Alex, but her hand shoots out and lands in the center of my chest, her red nails splayed like claws. She leans over to whisper in my ear through pillowy red lips. "Trust me, fella, you don't want to bother with her. Stay here and have a drink with me. I'm much more exciting." One icy-green eye winks.

Brushing her hand away, I round her stool and see Fiona on the floor, crammed in a nook of the bar near Alex's left stiletto. All the air leaves my lungs like I've been punched in the stomach. Fiona is beat up. No, she looks like she's been in an accident. The skin under her amber eyes is black and blue, her lip is split, and her pink

T-shirt is soaked in blood from her right collarbone to her left hip, exactly where I saw her scar before. Minor cuts pepper her exposed skin, but it's the sight of her fingers that will live in my nightmares. Most of her nails are gone, and bone pokes through the tips. Blood pools in her palms as she holds them out to me.

"I can't free her. I've tried everything." Fiona's wild eyes lock on mine, tears streaming from their corners.

A heavy chain is manacled to Alex's slender ankle, binding the character to the bar. It looks like Fiona has been trying to pry the metal cuff off with her bare fingers at the expense of her nails and skin! Fuck, she's been killing herself to free Alex Rogue. Is this what writer's block looks like?

Creator help me, I've never seen anyone like this inside their head. Dreams reveal a person's self-concept. Usually people are more attractive in their dreams than they are in reality. Fiona is a wreck. Her hair and eyes are dull. Her skin pale. Her cheeks gaunt. She's wasting away. Beat up. Destroyed.

"I don't know what to do," she weeps, more to herself than to me. "It won't budge."

Fortunately, I can help. A dragon's most formidable weapons are psychic in nature. We can break minds in the same way we inspire them. If I can get inside someone's head, I can manipulate their dreams, lay chains or break them. This is something I can fix.

I squat down in front of her and place my hands on her shoulders because it seems like the only place that won't hurt. "It's going to be okay, Fiona. I'm good with locks."

"You are?" Her eyes brighten.

"Yeah." I turn my hand over and manifest a key, then rub my thumb over the manacle on Alex's ankle. A lock appears in the metal. "There we go."

She gasps. "That wasn't there before."

"It was always there, I'm just helping you see it. But you have to do it, Fiona. I can show you the lock, and give you the key, but you have to turn it. Do you think you can do that?"

Without hesitation, she swipes the key from my palm, leaving a streak of blood on my skin. I watch her fumble with it until it slides into the lock with a click. Using both hands, she turns the key, struggling to maintain her grip as it's slippery with her blood. The process looks painful, but when that manacle pops off and clatters to the floor, she laughs even as happy tears stream down her cheeks.

Alex hops off her barstool. "Fucking hell, you did it!" She grabs the sides of Fiona's face and plants a kiss on her nose. "We are going to solve this case and save those girls."

Fiona nods, and then Alex grabs her purse off the bar and heads for the exit.

My eyes don't leave Fiona. I scoop her off the floor. She doesn't even attempt to stop me, just snuggles in against my chest and breathes deep. "You smell so good. Like cucumber and mint and sometimes like the sea."

"Yeah? You smell good to me too. So good." I run my nose through her hair. "Like lilacs and new grass. You smell like spring."

"How are you still here?" Her voice sounds tired, like

she could drift off at any moment. "Alex is more fun. You should go with her. The fans would love that, her finally falling for you."

"I don't care about Alex. Everything I need is right here in my arms."

"That can't be right." She meets my eyes, and it feels like I'm staring straight into her soul. "Do you know who I am? I'm a writer who can't write. An orphan. No family and barely a handful of friends." She glances down at herself, at the blood and scars. "I'm damaged. Ruined. I've lost everything." She sighs deeply. "I'm nothing anymore but a pile of broken parts."

I adjust her in my arms, the lump in my throat expanding into a fist, and bring my forehead to hers. "You're wrong about that. You're everything to me, Fiona. Everything. Everything I prayed for. Everything I've waited for." I press a kiss to her lips and taste blood. Our eyes lock.

She blinks and blinks again.

"You're everything to me, Fiona," I repeat. "And you're *mine.*"

"Yours," she whispers dreamily.

The clouds move in, and a heartbeat later I'm back in the chair, thrown out of her head. She must be waking up. I have my answer. Fiona doesn't belong to the Order. If she did, there would be something in her head about it, some fear of me or desire to hurt me. All I found in her head was a woman who needed me and melted in my arms like she belonged there

Through slitted eyes, I see her turn on her side and stare directly at me, her arms squeezing that giant stuffed dragon to her chest. Great. Now I'm jealous of a stuffed animal. I do my best to pretend to be asleep. After some time, she sighs and rolls over to her other side. It takes a lot to shake a dragon, but my breath trembles when I release it.

Chapter Twelve

FIONA

You're everything to me, Fiona. And you're mine.

I wake hearing Connor's voice in my head and turn on my side to find him asleep on the chair in the corner. Holy shit, what a dream. This flare and the stress of the past week must be muddling my thinking. It's too soon for me to be experiencing Stockholm syndrome, so why is my brain producing stories of my captor helping me. Of him holding me. Of him wanting me.

Stupid fucking brain.

For longer than I should, I watch him sleep, and a rush of longing comes over me. Longing for what we had in my dream. His arms. His words. His kiss. I touch my lips.

Flipping over, I turn away from him and give myself a stern talking-to. *Fiona, you're not making any sense right now. Think about something else. Think about your goddamned fiancé!*

That pulls my thoughts up short. I stare at the engagement ring on my nightstand. Roman's ring was exactly as Connor described it. Does it share the Latin inscription left at the site of Lucy Vale's murder? And he shot at me. Oh my God, I can't even believe I'm considering this, but it's more than possible... it almost feels likely... that Roman is what Connor says he is, a member of a secret society called the Saint's Order, a society that could be responsible for Lucy Vale's murder. But if it's true, how did I miss the signs?

I wanted to believe Roman was everything I needed him to be. Now I have to face the truth.

Believing what my captor tells me about Roman though doesn't make Connor someone I can trust. He isn't human. He's a dragon, whatever that means. A man with wings. Aside from that, I don't know anything about the circumstances that brought us to this point. I don't know the nature of the war between the dragons and the Order, who's right or who's wrong, or what motivations might be at play. Furthermore, I don't immediately care. All I care about is getting free of this place and going home. I can tell both men to go to hell once I get there.

And you can finally write my story.

My entire body lights up at the sound of Alex's voice. She appears in my imagination, grabbing her purse off the bar, the drive with the photos from her Milk Cult informant safely inside. She's speaking to me again! Finally.

I need to get back to the motel and pop this into my laptop before I can take the next steps. Write it, Fiona! she orders in her MP voice.

I feel her words like a slap across my face and roll onto my back again, my eyes flipping open with a wave of energy I haven't felt in days.

I know what happens next. I'm ready to write again.

The ceiling here is made of knotty wood. One of the knots looks like a face. A face that's laughing at me. I'm a prisoner in a cabin in the middle of... who knows where. It's—I glance at the clock—five a.m. I have nothing to write with. No laptop. No pen or paper. For the first time in over a year, my writer's block is gone, and I'm in the only situation in the world where I can't do anything about it.

Clunk. I hear the footrest on the recliner fold down and quickly shut my eyes again, pretending I'm asleep. I don't think I can face Connor after that dream. Just the cucumber-and-mint scent of him causes something low in my belly to flutter. Footsteps cross the room, and then the door opens and closes again. He's gone.

Opening my eyes, I try to sit up in bed, expecting my body to hurt as it has the past few days, expecting to have to pay for yesterday's walk and all the emotional currency I've spent since I've been here. Among people with disorders like mine, there's a metaphor called spoon theory to describe our limited energy resources. I only have so many spoons in a day, and simple things like eating or self-care use up many of them. Bottom line is, I should be short on spoons after everything that's happened. But I don't hurt. I feel better. A lot better. Cautiously, I draw my legs up and over the side of the bed. So much better. I've never recovered from a flare this quickly and thoroughly, even after days of bed rest. What the hell?

I only hope it's not a fluke.

I hobble to the bathroom, noticing my balance is better and I can stand up straighter than before. I can't resist the lure of the shower. My hair is still caked with hairspray, and I know the heat will further loosen up my body after my being in bed for so long. A groan of pleasure escapes me as I step into the spray and pull the curtain closed, pleasantly surprised to see some high-end shampoo, conditioner, and body wash in the shower rack. I help myself, lathering my hair with an impossible level of energy. I don't just feel better; I feel good!

I'm in the middle of rinsing my hair when I hear the door open. My breath catches and I freeze. Images of the Viking drawing back the curtain and stepping into the spray fill my head, and things low within me clench hungrily at the idea. I touch my lips again, thinking about the dream. The dream but I'm healthy. The dream but we kiss and then—

He clears his throat. "Just leaving some fresh clothes for you on the counter." His voice sounds strained.

"Uh, thanks." I run a hand over my breast, my wet skin smooth as silk beneath my palm. My nipples have formed hard peaks at the sound of his voice. What the fuck? It's like the tone is caressing me from the inside, the perfect vibration to pluck something needy strung tight within me. I lean the back of my head against the shower wall and trace where I feel the vibration, along the space between my breasts, down my stomach, under my navel, to where it ends between my legs. God, that voice. That smell. Rivulets of pleasure tracing down my skin become sensual torture.

"Oh, and I've left something else for you on the, uh... bed." His voice comes again, this time lower, grittier, more breathless.

"Okay." I concentrate on controlling my own breath, the ache between my legs growing more intense. I rub circles across my clit to ease the throb.

"If you see another man in the cottage today, it's just my employee, Zaire. He's going to be joining us for a while."

"All right," I choke out as if every word coming from his lips isn't stoking a fire deep within me. Electricity zaps through my veins at the thought that nothing but a shower curtain stands between me and the man from my dreams. I arch my back, closing my eyes and absorbing the sensation his voice releases in me. The wetness between my legs is from more than just the shower. I picture his hand where my hand is, his tongue.

I hear the door open like he's leaving. "Fiona..." His rough, growly voice travels up my spine, along my throat.

"Yeah?" I try not to sound breathless, but it's all I can do not to get myself off right here, right now.

"I'm trying my best to keep my hands to myself out of deference to you and your situation, but I can smell your arousal, and if you keep teasing me, I'm going to bury myself in you so deep you'll forget we were ever two separate people."

I yank my hand from between my legs. "I don't know what the hell you're talking about!"

His low laugh rumbles from the room and the door closes behind him.

Could he actually smell my arousal? Shit, I guess he is a dragon. My cheeks blaze with embarrassment even as my nether regions throb with unmet need.

I finish showering, angry and sexually frustrated, and pull back the curtain to reach for a towel. A stack of clothes and toiletries waits for me near the sink. I check the labels. My size. The pair of wide-leg jeans is buttery soft and stretchy and goes perfectly with the lightweight long-sleeved gray sweater he's left me. He even bought me underwear and a matching bra. A man like him, especially one who's shown some attraction to me, might have picked something for his pleasure. Black lace, flimsy, with wires. Maybe a thong. But this is sporty, simple, and comfortable. There's also some makeup, hair-care items, and the complete skin-care line of an expensive brand I only sometimes splurge on because the cream alone is three hundred dollars.

I take a deep breath. *He abducted you, Fiona. He's a criminal and possibly insane. An alien creature. Stop crushing on him!* With a huff, I decide then and there to end this nonsense of fantasizing about the dragon. Yes, he's hot and the first man to make me feel anything below the waist since the accident, but he's a criminal, a kidnapper, a wedding ruiner.

Leisurely, I make use of all the items and emerge from the bathroom feeling like a new person, resolved to do what I have to do to get out of here.

Which brings up an even bigger question. It's been five days since I was taken. Why hasn't Roman moved heaven and earth to get me back? Does he even know I was ill? Unless he has and Connor hasn't told me for some reason.

Connor, my kidnapper, whom I'm picturing in my dreams and when I touch myself in the shower. God, this is fucked up.

I leave the bathroom and pull up short when I see an Apple Store bag on the bed. I rush across the room to rifle through it. What. The. Hell? It contains a new MacBook Air and a selection of notebooks, pens, highlighters, and sticky tabs in various colors. I pull the laptop box out and carry it to the desk by the window, ripping it open. My hands shake as I plug it in and go through the steps to get it up and running. The Wi-Fi is called DragonsLair5G, but of course I don't have the password. But I don't need it. The unit is already set up for me, fully charged and preloaded with word-processing software. I'll be starting from scratch on *Milkmaid* anyway. Nothing I've written so far was worth saving.

I sit down at the desk and open a blank Word file.

Alex appears in my head in her military police uniform. She salutes me. *Let's go, Ms. Morrow. The Milk Cult isn't going to stop itself.*

My fingers hit the keyboard and fly.

Chapter after chapter flows out of me. It's like a river of words has been dammed up in my brain for twelve months and finally, finally that dam has burst. The story behind *Milkmaid* is crystal clear to me now. After the thirteen-year-old daughter of a fellow investigator from her stint as an MP goes missing, Alex traces a chemical in the girl's best friend's blood back to a rave where other girls were similarly drugged. Alex poses as a drug seeker at the same party the following weekend and witnesses a man spray something on a young woman's arm. The drug makes the woman extremely compliant, and Alex has no trouble getting her out of there and to the lab of close friend and former lover Henrik Angel. Henrik's people isolate the substance on her arm, and after some highly illegal research, identify it as a military bioweapon called M1LK, an abbreviation for the chemical compounds used in the formula. Nicknamed Milk, the chalky white chemical produces an instant high. With its other attributes, it's a nearly perfect date-rape drug. Armed with that knowledge, Alex returns to the rave and follows the man she saw using the drug. She links him to a secret society called the Milk Cult.

When my hands start to cramp, I take a break and check my word count. It's one p.m. I've written eleven thousand words. I jump from the chair and dance around the room. It's the most I've ever written in four hours. Hell, the most I've ever written in a day. My stomach growls and my mouth is dry as a stone, but Alex is back, baby. Alex. Is. Back.

I stop spinning when I notice the door is open. Has it been open the entire time? No, I don't think so. Someone's been in here. Shit, I must have been too engrossed in the story to notice.

My stomach growls again, and I go in search of food. And if I'm being honest with myself, I wouldn't mind seeing Connor either. I should loathe him. I should fear him. But I find him strangely compelling and undeniably interesting, plus I should say thank you for the laptop.

I do a cursory check of the hallway and then walk toward the back of the house where I spot a sunroom with a wall of windows. My eyes catch on Connor in the backyard. Oh hell do they catch. In the light of a crisp spring day, he's shirtless, his jeans riding low on his hips, with pine trees and snowcapped mountains framing him like some sort of majestic work of art. He's chopping wood. I watch him set up another log, raise the axe over his shoulder and bring it down in a perfect arc, splitting the piece in a single blow. I sigh, noticing that tendrils of steam are curling off his skin. He's sweating. My eye moves to the snow on the trees. It can't be more than forty degrees out there, and he's sweating.

"You must be Fiona."

I jump and twirl around to find a middle-aged Indian man with a short beard standing behind me.

He smiles. "I'm sorry to startle you. Would you like something to eat? I came into your room to offer earlier, but Connor told me not to disturb you if you were writing."

"Oh yes." I'm starving. So that's why my door was open.

His gaze assesses me quickly. "I'm relieved to see everything fits. Connor was very specific, but one never knows with women's clothing."

"You bought this for me? And the other things?" The man looks familiar, but I can't quite place who he reminds me of.

He laughs. "No. Connor ordered them. I simply picked them up on my way here. I'm Zaire. I work for Connor."

He extends his hand and we shake. When he smiles, I realize why he looks familiar. "Zaire. You are *the* Zaire. The reclusive artist Zaire. My friend Vivian owns one of your paintings—*Rhapsody in Red*. Absolutely gorgeous."

A blush stains his cheeks, and he has to look away. "You flatter me. I remember that painting. It was a joy to complete."

"But that painting..." *Cost her thousands of dollars*, I finish in my head. "Why are you working for Connor when you're *you*?"

He draws a deep breath and blows it out slowly. "Ahhh, it's my privilege to serve him, but um, I believe it would be better if you spoke to him directly about our arrangement." He gestures toward the hall. "He'll be in soon. Please. Join me in the kitchen. I'll fix you something."

With one more glance over my shoulder at the wood-chopping porn happening beyond the windows, I follow Zaire into the kitchen where he seats me at a charming nook. He starts pulling things out of the warmer and setting them on the table. It's more food than a family of four could eat. My stomach growls again, and I don't refuse when he serves me a plate that looks like something from a magazine.

"Duck breast with pomegranate sauce, red potatoes, green beans," he announces. "Connor took a chance that you like duck, but he left something else—"

"I love it!" The bite I place on my tongue is a medley of perfectly seasoned duck meat with hints of a sweet pomegranate sauce that complements the flavor flawlessly. It's so good I moan.

Zaire laughs. "It is his specialty. He'll be glad to hear you like it."

I can't help but make more yummy sounds as I take another bite and then sip the coffee Zaire slid in front of me. "This is not what I was expecting when I learned I was being held hostage."

The man's eyebrows shoot skyward. "He's holding you hostage?"

Before I can answer him, the door opens and I do a double take as a German shepherd the size of a small horse charges toward me.

Chapter Thirteen

CONNOR

Bones lopes into the cottage and goes straight for Fiona. I know the feeling. I've been chopping wood for the past several hours to try to cool my fever for her, and the moment I lay eyes on her, she's all I can see. All I want to see.

All my blood rushes to my dick.

It doesn't help that the clothes I bought for her are five hundred times more her style than that abomination Roman called a wedding dress or my sweatshirt. She looks relaxed and comfortable, her silky hair in shiny waves around her shoulders. The color is back in her cheeks too. She almost looks happy. *Please, Creator, let her be happy.*

"You found lunch," I rumble, unable to keep the dragon out of my voice.

I watch her scratch Bones behind the ears and kiss him on top of his head. First jealous of a stuffed animal and now of my own dog. My inner dragon whimpers at the thought of those fingers touching me in that way. In any way.

"Yeah. Zaire helped me." She looks up from the dog, and our eyes lock. My heart does an interpretive dance inside my chest. Very undragonlike. I'm in so much trouble.

"Good. I'm glad you've made each other's acquaintance." I give Zaire a knowing look, and he excuses himself from the room.

She waits until he's gone to ask, "Why is one of the most famous artists in the world doing your dishes?"

I laugh. "Because he wants to be."

Her brows pinch together. "No, seriously."

"Seriously," I say. "Zaire is here because he produces his best work when he's feeding off my dragon energy. Living with me opens his mind and allows him to be his creative best, and in exchange, he serves as my Firetender."

"Firetender?"

"Like a live-in butler," I explain. "It's a sacred position to my kind."

Her mouth drops open. When she doesn't say anything, I pour myself a cup of coffee from the carafe on the table, although what I'd really like is a whiskey given that I sense the tension ratcheting up between us.

"So you're like a muse or something?" she blurts. Her expression is a mixed bag of wonder and confusion.

I sip the coffee, staring at her over my cup. I trace the graceful line of her neck with my stare, wondering what her skin would taste like if I kissed her there. *Take her*, my dragon urges. I shove him down deeper within me. "I'm a dragon. It's the nature of dragons. We were sent here by the creator to inspire humans, to help you evolve. Perhaps you've already felt my influence in that department. Have you made use of the laptop?"

She pushes a bean around her plate with her fork. "Yes. Thank you for that. And yes, it's terribly strange, but I guess I can't deny it. I have felt inspired today."

Thank fuck. I hit her with my most charming smile. "Then you understand why Zaire stays."

"Right." She takes another bite. "But if you *are* some kind of muse—"

"Dragon," I say, correcting her again.

"If you are a dragon, why would the Order want to kill you?"

I lean my elbows on the table, bringing my face just a little closer to hers. "The Saint's Order is an organization of the richest, most powerful men in the world. Men who benefit from the status quo. It's not that they want us all dead. They want the ones of us who might inspire their competition dead. The rest of us they'd like to imprison and use to advance their own causes."

"The Saint's Order is about *stopping* innovation?" she asks incredulously.

I raise my cup. "Innovation, change, progress... Anything that does not benefit them directly. They see us as a danger to them."

She seems to take that in. "And this is why you're enemies?"

I look her in the eye. "There's nothing a rich man fears more than a poor man with good ideas."

"How long has this been going on?"

"Dragons were sent from the stars by the creator over ten thousand years ago."

Her fingers graze her throat. "That's a long time to stay hidden from humans."

I chuckle. "We weren't always hidden. In the middle ages, an aristocrat who became known as Saint George slew a dragon in retaliation for the beast inspiring the princess George was courting to pursue her own dreams, dreams that did not include marrying George. Dreams that involved a place for women in a patriarchal society. Saint George founded the Saint's Order, to stop the folly dragons induced by inspiring the common man and woman to greater things. Only after the formation of the Order were dragons forced to live in secrecy and our history with your species demoted to mythology."

She sips her coffee. "I know the story of Saint George. I've heard it differently though, that the princess was being sacrificed to the dragon and that Saint George slew the dragon to save her."

I snort. "Human history is written by rich human men, Fiona, and rarely tells the whole story."

"Hmm. Every story has two sides though, and I'm only hearing yours when it comes to the Order. Maybe you're not telling me everything either. Maybe there are things about dragons you haven't revealed. Things that make the Saint's Order necessary."

I bristle. "It would take me years to teach you everything I know about being a dragon, but I can tell you without a doubt that the Saint's Order isn't necessary. No more necessary than child labor or human sacrifice." I say it through my teeth, feeling my hackles rise at the mere thought.

"Was kidnapping me necessary?" Her expression darkens, the happiness I saw only moments ago lost.

"I told you. All I wanted was to preserve the peace between us and the Order. If Stefan would just meet with me—"

"You'd send me home?" Her amber gaze flips up to mine and arrows through me. "That's what you said, yet here I am after five days. Why am I still here, Connor?"

My dragon rises. *Because you are mine and I will never let you go,* he urges me to say. I shove him down and mop sweat from my brow with a napkin. "Stefan hasn't responded to our ultimatum."

"What?"

I don't like the hurt I feel along our bond, but it can't be helped. I face the hurt and I tell her the truth. "He's ignoring our calls."

"But that doesn't make sense!" She raises her voice, agitating Bones. He rushes to her, doing a tap dance and nudging her legs, but she ignores him. "I shouldn't be here long. If Stefan won't respond to you, then ask Roman. You say he's second-in-command. I'm sure he'll give you anything you want to have me back."

My jaw clenches to the point of pain. "No, actually. We've already reached out to him. He hasn't responded. Also, he's told no one you're missing. As far as the world is concerned, you're honeymooning in the south of France."

Her face twitches as if she can't decide whether to laugh or cry. "You're lying. What about Vivian? My friend

Vivian Hargrave saw you take me. She'd tell. They could never keep her quiet."

I think back to the day I took her. "Your bridesmaid? The one with the black hair who shoved Roman?"

"Yes, that's her."

"I'm not sure what happened to Vivian. I'll try to find out for you."

For a moment she says nothing, just stares down at the remains of the meal on her plate, frowning. "You bought me the laptop." She traces the handle of the coffee mug with her fingers, her brow furrowing. "You must have ordered it right after I got here."

"Yeah."

She huffs. Takes another deep breath and huffs again. "Why would you bother with the laptop if you believed Roman would do as you ask?" There's an edge to her voice, one that wasn't there a minute ago.

"I thought you'd want to write."

"Why would you assume I'd be here long enough to use it? If you're telling the truth and Roman knows what he needs to do to get me back, then why assume I'd have time to use the laptop?"

Uh-oh. I see why she's angry now. She thinks I'm lying about contacting Roman. "I didn't. When I bought it for you, I didn't care if you used it for an hour or a day, I just wanted you to have it. If he does as we ask, you'll be free to go. You can take the laptop with you."

Fists clenching, she stands, pushing back her chair and glaring at me with all the fury that could possibly fit in her slender frame. "Take me home. Take me home now. If Roman hasn't responded yet, he'll never give you what you want. I'm useless to you."

I grunt and shake my head. "Not a chance, sweetheart. I'm not buying it for a second. No man gives up a woman like you without a fight. He's bluffing. Releasing you is exactly what he wants. You're mine until he caves." *You're mine for always.*

"A woman like me? I hate to break it to you, but I'm far less famous than I used to be. I'm no prize."

I allow my gaze to rake over her, settle on her mouth, her breasts, her waist. I picture the scene she sent me when she was in the shower and let my dragon's heat fill my expression. "I don't give a fuck about your fame, and he didn't either. He knows what he had in you. He wouldn't be a man if he didn't."

"So that's it, huh? No wonder you and Roman are at war. He's refined and sophisticated. He's not a brute who goes around abducting innocent women to get what he wants. I have a life, you know. I have friends... work." She grinds her teeth.

"Your friends will understand, and I bought you everything you need to do your work," I force out.

The tension between us has reached a fever pitch. At some point we've both rounded the table—I don't even recall moving, but here we are. My hand is wrapped around the back of her neck, and we're face-to-face, her mouth dangerously close to mine. I can feel her breath on my lips.

"Let me go."

"No."

"The only reason you bought me the laptop is to

make yourself feel less guilty." She lifts her chin an inch. "I should have known it was all about you. Kidnap a woman on her wedding day and hold her prisoner! All you are is a fucking criminal. A fucking criminal who knows how to beat an egg."

Her insult snaps like a whip. We're nose to nose, grimace to grimace, her chest rising and falling rapidly in a way I find incredibly distracting. Her eyes dart to my mouth, and the pull between us steals my breath.

The urge to kiss her, to claim her, makes my skin burn. She draws back with a soft grunt, leans forward again. Draws back. Our breaths come in pants as we inhale each other's air, both of us fighting this thing between us for different reasons.

With a hard shake of her head, she surges out of my grip and past me, pushing me away as she runs for her bedroom and slams the door. I could easily catch her, but I don't.

I bring my forehead to my fist, the mating sickness sending spikes of pain and need through me again. "Come on, Bones."

I head outside again to cool off.

Chapter Fourteen

FIONA

He knows what he had in you. He wouldn't be a man if he didn't.

I stand in the middle of the bedroom, replaying the dizzying interaction in my head. The way Connor looked at me sent a rush of need through my veins I've never felt before. The pull to move closer to him was like a tightening corset, like God was pulling the strings, squeezing us together, squeezing us into the shape the universe wanted. My God, I almost kissed him, and if I *had* kissed him, I'm not sure I could have controlled what would have happened next.

Is he lying to me about Roman? He must be. There's no way Roman wouldn't do whatever it took to get me back. I was practically snatched right out of his arms. He did shoot at us, but he might be a good shot. If Vivian hadn't pushed him out of the way, would he have hit Connor and not me? It is weird though that he's told no one I'm missing. *If* he's told no one I'm missing. I have no way of telling if that's true or not. No internet access. No television.

You need to use this time to tell my story, Alex demands, thrusting herself into the center of my head. She's dressed in a maid's uniform. She wants to pose as a maid in the Milk Cult's headquarters to investigate what they're doing with the drugged girls.

If I have no choice but to be here, I might as well use the time productively.

Do I have a choice to be here? Should I have tried to run today? Tried to escape? No. I'm not strong enough. Not yet. It's my first full day out of bed.

I sit down at the desk, turn on the computer, and start writing again.

❧

HOURS LATER, THERE'S A KNOCK ON THE DOOR. I'M DEEP INTO chapter ten. Alex has crawled out the window and onto a ledge to avoid detection and is listening to the Milk Cult leader talk about selling the girls. If Alex doesn't find where the cult is hiding the girls soon, she won't be able to save them or her friend's daughter in time.

The knock comes again. "Ms. Morrow?"

"Come in, Zaire," I yell.

Zaire gives a shallow bow when I look his way. "Connor invites you to join him in the dining room for dinner."

"Do I have a choice?"

He looks confused. "Of course you have a choice. I can bring you a tray if you so wish."

For the second time, I sense that Zaire doesn't know the full story behind why I'm here. I wonder how long that will last and how I can use it to my advantage.

"Would you like for me to bring you a tray, Ms. Morrow?"

The tantalizing scent of Italian reaches my nose, and my mouth starts to water. "No, I'll be right there. I just need to freshen up." I point to the bathroom.

"Certainly." He turns to leave.

"Oh, Zaire, you wouldn't happen to have the Wi-Fi password, would you? I want to research a few things for my novel."

He smiles brightly. "Of course! It's RAMSWAY455. All caps."

"RAMSWAY455," I repeat back to him. "Thank you."

"You're welcome. I'll tell Connor you will be joining him shortly."

I wait until he leaves the room to type in the password and almost give myself away by screaming when it works. I click on the search bar and search my own name. A bunch of gossip articles come up about my wedding to Roman, all focused predominantly on Roman. Some older articles are about my books. There's absolutely nothing about me being abducted.

Ice fills my veins. Connor is telling the truth. Roman hasn't reported it. I do a quick search on Vivian Hargrave. Nothing but publicity for her new release. The last post she made on any of her social media sites is about her getting on the plane to attend my wedding.

Which begs the question: Where is she now?

I fire off a message to her cell phone, then close the laptop, more confused than ever, and hurry from the room before I draw suspicion. I find Connor in the formal dining room off the foyer. He's waiting with a glass of red wine in front of an empty plate.

He didn't lie to me. Pure intuition, if I can trust such a thing, tells me he hasn't lied about anything.

He stands when I walk into the room. He's changed out of his flannel and into a dark button-down shirt, sleeves rolled to his elbows, revealing two immaculately corded forearms. With his hair pulled up into a bun, he's too attractive to be real. Maybe I fell asleep at the keyboard and am dreaming this, dreaming of Henrik Angel come to life. My tongue feels thick.

"Thanks for coming," he says. "I'm sorry I raised my voice before. I'm sure this has all been overwhelming for you."

It's a sincere apology, although I get the sense apologies don't come easy for him. He shifts awkwardly.

"Thank you for that." I stretch my fingers, sore from typing.

His gaze locks on the bare finger of my left hand. "You're not wearing your engagement ring."

"I took it off days ago."

"I thought it was so you could sleep."

I lick my lips. "I'm not sleeping now."

I watch his throat bob on a swallow.

"I hope you can understand how hard it is for me to believe things have unfolded the way they have. Even if everything you've told me is true." There. That's safe enough to admit.

After a moment, he points to the chair across the table from him where a place has been set. The long table. This thing probably seats twelve. I stroll to the opposite end and sit.

"I feel like I'm in another zip code," I say, enunciating my words so he can hear me all the way down there.

Even from across the table, I see him swallow. "It's for the best."

"Why?"

The way he looks at me makes something low within me clench. "Because when you're near me, I have trouble keeping my hands to myself," he says in a low, dark voice.

My stomach whooshes like a trapdoor has sprung beneath my chair. I cross my legs against an instant ache. Maybe the table isn't long enough after all.

I'm relieved when Zaire chooses that moment to enter the room and slide a caprese salad in front of each of us, then disappears.

"He doesn't eat with you?"

"Sometimes he does. These days he's usually too involved with his work to take the time."

"He paints here?" I look toward the hall as if I can see the art studio through the wall.

"He paints everywhere. His life is painting."

"And serving you."

A muscle in his jaw twitches. "Don't knock it until you've tried it," he drawls.

"Someone thinks highly of themselves."

"He chooses to be here. He likes it with me."

"Like I choose to be here? Which is to say, no choice at all." Anger sparks inside me and offers some relief to the hot, burning need that's building low within me.

He heaves a sigh and stabs his salad.

"I'm sorry." I give my head a hard shake. "I didn't come out here to fight. I don't know what comes over me, but every time we're in the same room, I feel like I want to fight or..." *Oh shit. Shut the fuck up, Fiona.*

"Fight or fuck," he finishes for me with a deep laugh. "Would it help you to know I feel the same way?"

My cheeks heat. "Maybe."

"When's your birthday?"

"December first."

He presses two fingers into his ridiculously full lips.

"What's so funny?"

"You're a Sagittarius. A fire sign. As am I, an Aries. We bring out each other's fire."

"So we're destined to fight? Even if you hadn't kidnapped me and I didn't hate you?"

He flinches, his smirk morphing into a pained scowl. "You don't hate me, Fiona," he says with absolute certainty. "You just don't understand how to interpret the feelings I evoke in you."

Fuck. I hate that he's right. I should hate him. I don't. I take a bite of my salad and chew slowly to distract myself from his comment. "Both fire signs, huh? I guess that means if we were together, we'd burn out quickly. Like a shooting star."

"No," he says in a voice so smooth it feels like a caress. "An Aries and a Sagittarius never stop burning for each other. And they're never bored. Both of our signs love a challenge."

I snort. "I've had enough challenge for one lifetime. I think I could take some boredom."

He frowns, biting his lip like he's trying to find the right words. "I'm reading your series. It's been a while since you had a new release."

"Over a year."

"What happened? Did something change?"

I put another bite in my mouth. Too serious. Too personal. I don't like to talk about it. Time to turn the tables. I point my fork at him. "So you're a chef who's a dragon who kidnaps women on the side. How does one work their way into that job? Is there some kind of program or internship? Do you practice throwing CPR dummies in wedding dresses over your shoulder?"

His eyes flash with inner fire. "I was born the son of a dragon warrior and chosen to serve as the Aries member of the Zodiac Brotherhood. I'm a defender of my race. The cooking, well that comes naturally, although I did attend the Culinary Institute."

"Seems like a strange choice for a warrior. Shouldn't you do something tough like be a soldier or deal in weapons or something?"

He snorts. "Being an executive chef in a top restaurant in Manhattan is harder than it looks, and typically, dragon warriors don't need weapons. We have claws and teeth."

I ignore the claws and teeth remark. He can stroke his ego on his own time. "Zodiac Brotherhood. I'm picturing you all logging in every morning to read your horoscope before going about your dragon day." I fake an exaggerated gasp. "That's what it was, wasn't it? *Horoscope Daily* said Aries should steal a bride last Saturday, and you took it to heart."

He drops his fork. "We're called zodiac dragons because we were sent by the creator from the stars to advance humanity. The brotherhood consists of one dragon for each sun sign because that's when we're at our strongest. The sun is in Aries now, so I lead the brotherhood. As for your other question..."

He rises from his chair and walks toward me. Stalks me really. He approaches with the predatory grace of a panther, never breaking eye contact.

"What are you doing?" The utensil in my hand clatters to the table.

His hands land on the arms of my chair, and he lifts and turns me until I'm facing him. He's hovering over me, caging me in. This close, his size is intimidating and I gulp, my eyes widening.

"This question of why I took you seems to be coming up again and again, Fiona. I think we should set it to rest right here. Right now."

I tip my head. "It wasn't the horoscope?" I know I'm pushing him. Needling him. It's stupid. He's the size of a truck and in my face. But I can't stop myself. Maybe there is something to his fire-on-fire theory. "Oh right, you stole me to get my fiancé's father to talk to you because you can't use a phone like a normal person. Looks like that didn't work out so well."

His face is close enough to feel the heat of his skin. His cheeks are flushed with it and it radiates, warming my entire body. As big as he is though, I'm not afraid until his eyes change. His pupils shift from round like a human's to slitted like a cat's, the blue bleeding to green and growing wider, deeper in color, until they glow from within. My heart stutters as I realize I'm looking directly at the dragon inside the man. There's no other explanation.

When he speaks again, his tone is ashes and cinders. "You want to know the truth, Fiona? I didn't plan on taking you that day. I went to your wedding to take a peek inside Stefan's head to investigate what he knew about Lucy Vale. But when I saw you, when I heard you call to me, begging for an escape, I took you. I wanted you and I took you. I answered your call."

Ice forms in my veins. "My call? What call? I never called to you."

"I believe your exact words were 'If you're out there and I'm not supposed to do this, if I'm not meant to be with Roman, stop this wedding from happening. Send an earthquake or a storm.'"

Oh my God, oh my God, oh my God. Those were my thoughts. Those were my words. "Are you... Can dragons read minds?"

"Normally, no. Not like that. But you were projecting. You were in distress. I could hear you because you wanted me to hear you."

Goosebumps march up my arms. It feels like my entire body is lit up from within, on the edge of something strange and wonderful and equally terrifying.

"I could hear you, Fiona, because we have a bond. I am your *mate*. And you are *mine*."

His words do something to me. I feel them enter me and branch like lightning in a summer sky. I can't take my eyes off his lips. My breath is ragged in my lungs, and my heart skips, stuttering at the pure overwhelm that's happening in my nervous system. If our two fire signs bring out the fire in each other and make us want to fight or fuck, without a doubt neither of us is interested in fighting right now. A heavy weight in my core turns over, a growing tension between us that needs to be relieved.

Some small part of me knows I should fight this. I should stop and think about what I'm doing, the repercussions. But with his scent in my nose and his heat on my skin and his claiming words in my ears, I can't think of anything but him. I can't think of anything but the undeniable fact that there is a fire between us that must be fed.

I grab the sides of his head, dig my nails into his hair, and pull his face to mine.

Chapter Fifteen

CONNOR

Fiona's mouth is heaven, and I pillage it like mine is an army straight from hell. I give her lips, teeth, and tongue in a bruising, savage kiss that holds all the pent-up, carnal need I've been holding back the past five days. This kiss is shooting stars, spinning galaxies, exploding suns. It's everything. The alpha and the omega. The beginning and the end.

I have her out of the chair and pressed against the wall before I can question it. And maybe that's for the best. Questioning might mean discipline, control. All I want is her. Now. When my dragon took control and told Fiona she was my mate, I thought for sure I'd gone too far. It's too much, too fast. But now? I'm happy to give my inner dragon full rein just as long as Fiona keeps kissing me, keeps touching me.

"Mmmm." Her deep, throaty moan spurs me on, and

I dive deeper into her mouth, exploring her taste, the way our tongues battle for dominance.

I grind against her, my dick throbbing to be inside her, to claim her properly. But her pleasure comes first, always. No self-respecting dragon would have it any other way. I work my hand under her shirt and flatten my palm against her abs, then stroke up to fondle her breast, teasing her nipple through the black cotton bra I chose for her. The thought that she's wearing the clothes I picked out for her, that she's physically wrapped in my affection, is a fucking turn-on.

She repositions herself to straddle my leg, riding it, rubbing herself against my thigh. It's so hot I think we might both go up in flames. It's been a long time for me. A long fucking time.

"Please," she whispers into my mouth.

"I've got you." I slide my hand down, under the elastic waistband of her pants until the tips of my fingers brush over her clit. My dragon's rumbling purr sparks in excitement at the feeling of her sex. She gasps when she hears it, and I ravage her mouth again, my fingers gently teasing her slit.

"That sound you're making, I can feel it inside me." She blinks slowly, lost in the experience.

"You're the only one besides me who can hear it or feel it."

Her eyes pop open, her brows sinking even as she shakes her head. "Anyone can hear that. It's so loud Zaire must hear it across the house."

I slow my fingers between her legs. She needs to

know this. She needs to understand the connection we share. "You are the only one. Plug your ears."

She obeys, her face open. Her smile grows. "It's even louder."

I increase the pressure, circling her clit with my thumb, teasing her opening. "That's because you're hearing it down the bond, from the inside. You're not hearing it in the traditional sense. You're experiencing it. You hear my trill the same way I heard your call. I'm projecting it to you. It's the most natural thing in the world between mates of my kind."

"Oh," she says breathlessly as I sink one finger inside her. She tips her head back and closes her eyes, sinking down to ride my hand. "But I'm not your kind. I'm human."

I give her another finger, massaging her inner wall while I thumb her clit. "Our species are compatible." And then I lose myself. I push her shirt up to her neck, tear through the cup of her bra, and suck her nipple into my mouth.

"Oh God." She writhes in my arms.

It's like I've crashed through some invisible boundary. Her fingers find my belt and frantically unbuckle it, then make short work of my zipper. Our kiss grows deeper, more frantic, as her hand wraps around my cock, and she curses into my mouth. Curses about the size of me.

I insert another finger in her tight, hot sheath. "I'm going to spread you wide. I'm going to show you what it means to mate a dragon."

She's close, but her eyes are closed, her head tipped back, lips parted. That won't do.

"Look at me, Fiona. Say my name when you come."

She moans but doesn't obey me.

I take her by the jaw, make her face me. "Look at me."

She opens her eyes, and I see the pleasure in them, the fire, the passion. But there's something missing. Something off.

"Say my name," I growl.

I've stopped my fingers, but with a final thrust of her hips against them, she throws herself over the edge, her inner walls clenching around my fingers.

She doesn't say a word.

"Say my name," I demand again. I rest my elbow on the wall above her head as her hand starts to move, stroking me, hard and fast. Fuck, watching her come has me wound tight and I'm close, closer now that she's enthusiastically pumping my cock through my fly. My balls tighten.

Her other hand grabs *my* jaw and squeezes. "Say my name," she demands through her teeth.

"*Fiona*," I grit out because I can't deny her anything she asks. I come and come and come until her bared belly is covered in me. We're both panting and raw, our foreheads braced against each other, using the wall to hold ourselves up.

"Why wouldn't you say it?" I ask, feeling exposed. I grab a napkin off the table and clean us up.

"Will you answer a question for me?"

"Of course."

"This entire time, have you been able to hear my thoughts?"

"Some of them, the ones you were projecting."

She nods. "You told me you could see it on my face. When you took me. You didn't say you could read my mind."

"I can't read your mind. Not exactly. It's different—"

"You've been manipulating me, using my thoughts to seduce me. You saw what I was thinking that day in the shower, didn't you?"

"Yes."

She still holds me roughly by the face, her eyes hard and cold as she says, "You know why I didn't say your name? Because I don't know you, not really. And this house of cards between us is built on a lie. I can't give myself to you because a person can't give away what they don't have. I'm your prisoner. Nothing more."

She pushes past me, calling to Zaire that she'll take her meal in her room.

"Fuuuck." I tuck my shirt back in and zip my fly just as Zaire enters, still looking in the direction she fled. "Would you like me to do as she asks? Or encourage her to return to the table?"

"Did you give her the password?"

"Yes. She asked me for it, as you predicted."

"Excellent. Yeah, bring her dinner to her room. Bring her anything she wants."

"As you wish." He nods.

He takes off toward the kitchen. I lean my back against the wall, closing my eyes and breathing in the lingering scent of my mate.

Chapter Sixteen

FIONA

Only once I'm safely in my room do I realize how hard I'm trembling. My nerves are shot. Everything in me wanted to say his name. I wanted to tell him I was his and he was mine and that we could live in this lodge in the middle of nowhere forever. Lord knows after the orgasm he gave me with his fingers alone, we'd likely spend the first ten years of forever breaking in our bed.

But it's been a long time since I was an idealist. I'm thirty-two. I've had my share of lovers and boyfriends. Connor kidnapped me, and while some of his explanation has proven to be true— Roman isn't the man I thought he was— he definitely has been manipulating me. I've been at his mercy here, eating his food, wearing his clothes. And all that time, he's been reading my thoughts.

I think about the feel of his purr down our bond. How

far does it go? Can he put thoughts into my head? Has he put thoughts into my head?

There's a knock on the door. I wipe under my eyes and let Zaire in. He sets a tray brimming with Italian food next to my laptop and leaves with one of his trademark bows. I follow him to the door, close and lock it, then test the knob. I'm surprised to find that the lock works. Of course, Connor probably has the key. Still, the lock provides me with some level of privacy.

I stare at the food, then look around the room.

What I know for sure is that I can't trust Connor with my heart until I know the truth. I open my laptop and log into my iMessage account. No response from Vivian. My heart gives a painful squeeze. I message Roman's personal cell phone.

Me: *I'm being held in a large cabin someplace cold by someone who calls himself a dragon. All I can see out my window is woods and mountains. It looks like north central US, but I don't know for sure. I don't know how long I'll have access to this account.*

I hit Send and look over my shoulder at my closed door. A few minutes pass and then...

Roman: *Has he hurt you?*

Me: *No. Just confused and afraid. Why am I still here? Why haven't you found a way to get me back?*

I stare at the three dots in the chat bubble, holding my breath. I'm not ashamed of the ring of desperation in those words.

Roman: *I don't negotiate with terrorists.*

Me: *Even when those terrorists have your fiancée?* A sick feeling comes over me.

Roman: *All in time.*

What the hell is that supposed to mean?

Me: *Is it true? About the Saint's Order? Do you and your father lead a secret society?* I hit Send before I can talk myself out of the question.

Roman: *I'd have shared all this with you once we were wed.*

Oh my God. It's true.

Me: *Is that why you haven't reported me missing to the police? Because you don't want them to find out about the Order?*

A full minute passes.

Roman: *The police cannot be involved. Stay brave. All will be righted in time.*

"Oh my God," I whisper at the screen. When Connor explained about the Order, my intuition told me he was telling the truth, but reading confirmation from Roman, knowing it's all true, is something else. It hits me in the stomach. I feel alone. Desperately alone. Like the entire world I thought I knew is false and I can't trust anyone. Then I remember that there is one person who might understand like no other.

Me: *What happened to Vivian? She's not answering my messages.*

Roman: *She's with me. We're keeping her safe until we have you back.*

Keeping her safe? By not allowing her to answer her messages? By not allowing her access to her socials or the press?

Me: *Let me message her. I need to speak to Vivian.*

He never responds. I open a new chat window and

try Vivian again. There's no answer. I email her and get an out-of-office message. If Vivian is being denied access to any form of communication with the outside world, which she is if she hasn't reported me missing, she isn't being kept safe—she's being held prisoner. He's definitely holding her against her will, most likely to keep her quiet.

"What the hell?" I whisper. Who are the bad guys in this scenario? Are there any good guys?

I close my laptop, bury my face in my hands, and weep. My brain feels like a pumpkin that's been kicked down the street. Eventually though, all my tears turn to fire. A star is imploding inside me, hot and bright and angry.

This is all very much like the secret societies I write about.

The implications are chilling. Why was Roman interested in me if he couldn't even share the truth about who he was? And on the flip side, why is Connor? He says I'm his mate, and I witnessed a very real metaphysical bond between us. But isn't it a little convenient for him given his war with Roman? Am I some kind of prize for whoever wins this test of wills?

Alex pops into my head, dressed entirely in black like she's ready for a mission. *Stop being a baby, Fiona!* she yells. *Quit obsessing about the men in your life and do what you do best. Write my story!*

I open my laptop, click on the word-processing app's icon, and dive back into *The Milkmaid*.

❦

I can count on one hand how many times I've stayed up all night writing over the years. My creative energy usually gives out after a few hours. But tonight it's like Alex is talking as fast as she can, narrating what's happening to her as she learns the cult is trafficking women and forms a plan to free them. By morning, I lean back in my chair, crack my knuckles, and realize I've written an additional twenty thousand words. I'm more than halfway through *Milkmaid*, and the only thing stopping me from continuing is that my body is giving out. My fingers are cramping and achy, and I can't keep my eyes open.

Rubbing the back of my neck, I climb from the chair and roll into bed in the wee hours of the morning. I'm asleep as soon as my eyes close.

The dream opens in a pink version of the room I'm in. That's how I know I'm dreaming, the pink. All the Black Watch plaid has turned to rose velvet, pink satin sheets, and billowy blush-colored curtains that float like clouds from around the open window. Birds are singing. A warm summer breeze flits through the room.

The door to the bathroom opens and Connor emerges, totally naked, wings out. Now I'm sure this is a dream. He looks at me like I'm his next meal, stalks toward me. His eyes sparkle as he prowls up the bed, all golden skin and lean, corded muscle. What have I done to attract the attention of this god, of this dragon?

"What do you want from me?" I ask him. "Really? Tell me the truth."

"I want you. Just you," he says. "You are my mate. Our being together was written in the stars."

"Now I know you're lying. You can't want me for me. You could do so much better." I touch my scar, expecting my fingers to connect with the shirt I wore to bed, but they hit rough and thickened skin. I'm naked. My fingertips coast over the dreadful, discolored ridge that spans my torso.

He kneels on the bed near my feet, his insanely large cock hard and jutting toward me. I remember wrapping my hand around it in his pants. The size is almost overwhelming. He grabs me by the knees and pulls me toward him. I slide along the silk sheets until the back of my thighs meet the front of his. He's hovering over me, that massive erection extending to my belly button.

"Say you're mine, Fiona," he demands.

God, my entire body aches for him to the point it's almost painful. I reach between my legs and stroke myself. He grabs my wrist and pulls my hand away. I squirm, needing release.

"Say it, Fiona. Say you're mine."

"I can't. I am no one's but my own." I won't give in to him. I can't. I can't trust another person to be there for me, not after my sister. Not after Roman. Not after Connor wasn't completely honest with me. The only person I can trust, the only one who will ever be there for me, is me.

"You're wrong about that," he says, reading my mind again.

"Please," I beg, lifting my hips, wanting him in me.

He reaches between us, starts rubbing me just the way I like it. "I've got you," he says in that same growly voice he used before.

Knock, knock, knock. I come awake with my hand between my legs, soaking wet and near orgasm. I'm back in the blue room. I yank my hand away and glance over to the leather chair, but Connor didn't sleep in here last night. I locked the door. I'm alone.

"Yeah?"

"Breakfast is served, Ms. Morrow," Zaire says through the door. "Will you be joining us?"

"Uh, yes." I can't stay in here forever. I need to learn more about this strange connection I have with Connor and about this secret battle he has with the Order. My mind flows back to the dream, to the ache between my legs.

"Whenever you are ready."

I hear his footsteps pad away and throw an arm across my burning face.

Chapter Seventeen

CONNOR

Fiona told me what she needs from me last night, and I plan to give it to her. She wouldn't say my name, wouldn't say she was mine because she doesn't trust me. She wants to know the truth. Maybe I deserve that. I did try to influence her by using the information I learned from listening to her thoughts. I should have been honest about that. Which means there's only one way for me to win her back. With total honesty.

Starting today, no more secrets.

This has to work. My mating sickness is worse. I'm burning up with it. And that appetizer last night was like gasoline on an already-blazing fire. I need her. I need her soon and for real. Which means I need to open up to her. The faster I can break down the barriers between us, the sooner we can be bound together in the way the universe wants us to be, in the only way that will heal me.

While she eats her breakfast. I take Bones out and

play fetch. We find a good stick, and I toss it down the trail I cleared this morning when I was up at the crack of dawn, feeling like I could die from the chills and the shakes. I've instructed Zaire to invite her to join me when she's done but not to make it sound like a command. Time together is exactly what we need, but it has to be her choice. Her initiative. She can't feel manipulated, or I'll be back at ground zero again.

I'm relieved when she appears at the door in the red Canada Goose parka and Sorel boots I bought for her. Bones lopes over to her with his stick and drops it near her feet, a huge, lolled-tongue smile on his face. She grins and rubs his head enthusiastically, then picks up the stick and throws it for him. My heart clenches at the normalcy of it.

"He's a good dog," she says without making eye contact.

"The best. Would you like to take a walk? I want to talk about last night. I owe you an explanation."

She frowns slightly but gives a nod of agreement. We set off on the trail. Bones picks up his stick and bounds alongside us.

"How's the writing coming?" I ask, although I know damn well how it's coming.

"Unbelievable," she says breathlessly. "It's like the floodgates have opened and the story is pouring out of me."

"You're welcome."

"For what?"

I glance her way. "Last night you told me you thought you couldn't trust me. You thought I was manipulating you because I didn't share the entire truth about hearing your thoughts."

She nods once. "You were manipulating me. You were in my head—"

"You're right. I thought I was justified because you couldn't handle everything at once, not when you were sick and considering... what you'd been through. But I'm promising you now, no more secrets."

She narrows her eyes. "You'll tell me the whole truth?"

I look toward the sky. "It would take me years to tell you everything there is to know about dragons and the Saint's Order, but I promise you that what I tell you from this day forward will be as truthful and as accurate as possible."

She studies me, her steps slowing as she considers that, then quickening again. "I want to believe you."

"Well, then let me start with this. It was me in your dream the other night. I helped you break the chain around Alex's ankle and work through your writer's block. That's why you're able to write again."

Her eyes widen, her expression turning livid. "Oh my God. Are you saying you were actually there, participating in my dream?"

I nod. "I won't do it again without your permission. I did it once to make sure you were telling the truth about Roman and the Order."

Her cheeks flush red, all the way to the tips of her ears. "And what about this morning?"

I shuffle to a stop, my smile broadening into something truly wicked as I take in her blush and connect the dots. "I was not in your dream this morning, Fiona. I have to be physically near you to dreamwalk, and I was in my own room. Why? Did you dream of me?"

She walks faster and I catch up.

"What exactly was I doing in this dream? Why are you blushing?"

"So you're saying that when you went into my dream, you fixed my writer's block?"

I don't miss how she completely changed the subject, and I inflate at the idea that she had a sex dream about me. Fuck, do I wish I was actually in that one.

"It's also the dragon energy. It's why Zaire chose to become my Firetender. Being near me will naturally increase your creative abilities."

She scoffs. "I know your ego is big, but you can't possibly be taking credit for the pages I've written."

"Wouldn't dream of it. I don't create the art—I simply boost the creative energy inside you."

The corners of her mouth curl downward.

"That makes you unhappy?"

"I don't like the idea. I don't want to be dependent on you. What if the writer's block returns once I leave here?"

"Then don't ever leave."

The glare she shoots me arrows straight through the heart.

I swallow, schooling my features into the most serious expression I can muster. "Most likely the writer's block won't come back. Creativity is like a faucet. Once the water is on, it won't turn off just because you leave me. Something powerful has to turn the handle."

She lifts her chin. "Good."

"I really wish you wouldn't leave me though."

"I'm your hostage, remember? You can't exchange me for information if you don't hand me over for what you want."

My dragon stirs and everything feels dark. "I don't care about the information. The whole fucking world can burn for all I care. I'd burn it down myself to make you mine."

That seems to unsettle her. She looks away, into the trees as if she can't handle my intensity.

"Will you go back to him once you're free?"

"Initially. We have unfinished business."

"What if you find out he was responsible for Lucy's murder?"

"Then I'll leave him and go on with my life."

Alone she means. I see it then, what I'm really up against.

She studies me for a moment. "I know you say we're mates, whatever that means, but neither one of us has committed to anything. We don't truly know each other."

"I want you to know me," I say. "I want you to know who I am."

Bones brings me the stick, and I throw it for him again.

"Why did you name him Bones?" she asks.

Finally. A crack in the door. She actually wants to know something about me, and this one is easy. "My restaurant is in Manhattan— Hell's Kitchen. We toss our garbage in a dumpster out back at the end of the night. Something kept getting in there. Everyone thought it was rats. Thing is, we compost most of our food scraps, so the only thing food-related going into that dumpster is bones. Anyway, we couldn't figure out how anything was getting in under the lid and out again. I found this guy one night with his head and front legs in the bin and his hindquarters braced between the fire escape and the edge of the dumpster. His face was so dirty it looked like he was wearing a mask like a burglar, and he was so thin you could see his bones through his skin. When he heard me coming, he pulled his head out, his mouth jammed full of bones. I just started laughing because it's not like there aren't other restaurants in Hell's Kitchen. I'm sure there were more substantial scraps to be had, but he'd rather have bones from my dumpster than spaghetti at Luigi's. I took it as a compliment."

She laughs, and it's the most beautiful sound I've ever heard. So beautiful I have to stop because I forget how to walk.

"Anyway, I named him Bones because you are what you eat."

"I'm glad you took him. There are people out there who would have called animal control."

Bones lopes up to her and drops the stick again. She picks it up with her gloved hand and tosses it up the trail. We start walking again.

"Believe me, I was tempted. He was so dirty I thought he was a Labrador, and he smelled like three-day-old fish guts. But I said, 'Get out of there and come over here.' And I'll be damned if that dog didn't obey like he understood every word. Came right to me and sat in front of me. Once I got him cleaned up and on a better diet, he turned into the menace you see before you."

Her smile fades. "I never had a dog. My twin sister Marion and I were left at an orphanage as babies. They never allowed pets, and once we moved out and into our own places, I was too busy surviving to have one." She smiles, but it doesn't reach her eyes.

"You're a twin?"

Bones drops the stick for her, and she throws it again. "Not anymore. She died a little over a year ago."

"I'm sorry," I say. Her eyes shutter. Down the bond, I can feel this is a painful memory for her. I don't push it.

We walk in silence, stopping to watch a doe grazing in a nearby clearing.

"So...," she starts, seeming to struggle to form the right words. "Dragons have been at war with the Saint's Order since the time of Saint George?"

I give a deep sigh. "Fifty years ago, a Zodiac Brother sacrificed himself. He traded himself for a peace accord."

"Traded himself?"

"Allowed himself to be captured and kept prisoner. For humans, being near a dragon sparks their creativity and increases their health, prosperity and longevity. In exchange for him allowing himself to be captured, for the past fifty years, we've enjoyed relative peace. That's why this thing with Lucy Vale is so serious. To be sure, dragons *are* occasionally slain by Order members, even under the accord, but never publicly like Lucy was. Never so egregiously."

"Fifty years." She studies me again. "How old are you?"

"Thirty-eight. I'm thirty-eight." I chuckle. "The peace accord happened before I was born."

"Oh." She licks her lips, seemingly pleased to hear that. "I thought maybe you were like thousands of years old or something."

"No. We can be, under certain circumstances, but I'm not." I wonder if I should explain that the circumstances are an accepted mating bond, but she moves on before I have a chance.

"You mentioned that dragons other than Lucy have been killed since the accord. How is that possible if you're not at war?"

"Because under the accord, if we trespass on each other's private property, the rules ... change." This is a sad conversation, not where I wanted this walk to go. "When my nephew Mason was in elementary school, my sister Carolyn confided in a fellow mom that she was a dragon. She'd known this woman for most of the year, and the woman had reported behaviors in her child that were consistent with being a hybrid. Dragon genes are present in many humans, and if two humans with dormant genes get together, they can have a child who manifests as a dragon. It's not common, but it's happened. Anyway, the boy showed many of the signs, or at least it seemed so based on the mother's concerns, so Carolyn confided in her out of compassion for her son and to prepare the mother in case the boy eventually shifted. The mother seemed grateful. Weeks later, the mother invited Carolyn to her home to work on a project for the school. One thing dragons rarely do is go to a human's home because the one way the Order can justifiably capture or kill us is if we set foot on their property. But Carolyn trusted this woman, checked the register of Order properties we keep for the address, and decided to go. When the husband came home, she saw his Order ring. That's when she knew it was a trap."

"Oh my God! What happened to her?"

"She was captured, and the Order planned to auction her off. These billionaires buy dragons when they come available and imprison them in their office buildings or factories to inspire their workers. And because my sister was mated, she was even more valuable."

She blows out her cheeks, then releases her breath. "I'm not following. Why would that be?"

I remind myself she knows nothing about my kind. "Mated dragons live exceptionally long lives. Without a mate, we age more quickly and eventually go up in flames around our hundredth birthday. Mating grants both mates prolonged life." I take a deep breath, remembering that horrific time. "As long as my brother-in-law stayed alive, they'd have a dragon slave in their possession."

"That's *horrible*."

I nod. "So my brother-in-law was a warrior, a Zodiac Brother like me. He traded himself for my sister. The Order agreed. They couldn't pass up a chance at weakening the brotherhood. He chose the hunt rather than the auction."

She swallows. "The hunt?"

"The terms of the accord require the Order give every captured dragon a choice—auction or hunt. Auction means the dragon is sold to the highest bidder for life-long imprisonment. This is a boon for the winner who gets to exploit the dragons energy. But dragons can also choose the hunt. In that case, they set the dragon free in a magically contained area and hunt them to the death for sport. Normal human weapons can't kill dragons, but Order rings are enchanted with magic that, in weapon form, can slice through dragon scales like a hot knife through butter. The magic can also be used to make cuffs and chains that bind us and drain our power. Roger died from an enchanted lance through the heart when Mason was just eight years old."

"Oh my God!" She clutches her chest. "When Roman shot at us, those bolts were made with this same magic, weren't they?"

I nod slowly.

"Jesus. You took a huge risk taking me the way you did. If one of those bolts had hit you..."

"He could have killed us both."

"I'm so sorry. That's sick. It's twisted. The Order needs to be stopped!"

A dark laugh scrapes up my throat. "I agree, obviously. This is why it's so important I confirm that Lucy's death was brought about by the Order and not a rogue member or copycat. If the Order broke the accord, thousands of dragons' lives could be at stake if they are no longer abiding by the rules. If they've broken the accord, we need to take more steps to protect ourselves and our kind."

"They could slaughter you before you even knew you were at war. Jesus Christ. That doesn't seem like a very fair peace accord." She frowns.

"It's better than outright war. It's better than being hunted by the Order and every human they can sway against us. Most of us lead normal lives now. We have careers. Human friends. Human mates." I slant her a knowing look, but her eyes are cast away from me. "The Saint's Order is powerful. They have more money than any of them could spend in a lifetime and plenty of members in powerful positions. But we have something as well now, a legion of humans we've inspired to do things better, faster, more brilliantly. We have the artists, the craftsmen, the engineers. The creator sent us because there's no replacement for people, for relationships, for love. The Order thinks there is. The Order believes that everything is about money and power, ownership, control. They're wrong. And as long as we're here, there will be people who prove it every single day."

She's staring at me now, taking me in like she's seeing me for the first time. Bones chooses that moment to lope back to her with an even larger stick and nudge her hands with his nose. Turning away, she throws it again for him, and he bounds off after it.

"Looks like Bones volunteers to be your stand-in dog until you have your own."

She tugs at the cuff of her glove. "Who's running your restaurant while you're here... *guarding* me?"

"Guarding. That's a step up from keeping you prisoner. I think this walk is doing wonders for my reputation."

She snorts. "Don't let it go to your head."

"My manager and sous-chef, Carmen and Ezra, are

holding down the place. I usually take some time off this time of year anyway. I like to come here to disconnect."

She snorts. "Oh? How many women have you kidnapped and told they were your mate?" The edge is back in her voice, her fire rising. She's smiling, but it's not a happy smile. She's wondering if this is a yearly habit.

I shuffle to a stop. I'm sweating and nauseated, using all my energy to hold back my dragon from coming out to play. "Would you believe you're my first?"

"No." She turns her fire-filled stare toward me. "No one who looks like you makes it to thirty-eight without finding a mate. I'm sure I'm not the first woman to sleep in that bed." She cocks her head toward the lodge. "And isn't it a little convenient that your mate just happens to be the fiancée of your sworn enemy?"

"Believe what you want to believe, but I told you the truth last night. I had no intention of taking you that day. I was there to investigate Lucy's murder. That's all." I look up at the crisp blue sky and decide to lay it all on the table. "The moment I saw you, the world stopped its rotation and the air changed. You were the only thing making it flow in and out of my lungs. You were the center of the universe and the reason for the tides."

She rolls her eyes and tips her head, but I continue, closing the space between us.

"Deep inside, I already knew that I was yours, your mate. You called to me. You begged for help. You wanted someone to save you from that altar, and I heeded your call, not because I'm some hero who could plainly see you were making a mistake but because I knew, Fiona, from the beginning you were mine. My mate."

Her throat bobs on a hard swallow, my reflection looming in her widened pupils. "People sometimes have cold feet," she says weakly. "I might have thought those things in my head, but I didn't act on them and I didn't ask you to act on them."

I reach behind my head, grab the back of my Henley, and pull it off. "Keep telling yourself that, sweetheart. But one thing I know for sure—I've never felt about anyone as I have about you. Never." I reach for my belt buckle.

"What are you doing?" She eyes my bare chest as tendrils of steam roll off my hot skin.

"No secrets, right?" I unbuckle my belt and unzip my fly. "I take time off this time of year because it's my alignment. I'm an Aries dragon and the sun is in Aries. When a dragon is in alignment, they suffer from mating sickness. When we don't have sex and don't have a mate, we burn with fever." I toe off my boots.

She's shaking her head. "If this is some kind of tactic to get a replay of last night—"

"You keep confusing me with a human man." We're at least two miles into the woods, in the clearing where I've led her for a purpose.

"Connor—"

"I am no human. You still don't understand, so I'm going to show you. I'm going to make you understand." I'm naked now, and the cold feels great against my feverish skin. *Show her!* my dragon growls.

"Your eyes!" She backs up, her boots landing in the snow. "Wh-what are you doing?"

Bones circles excitedly. He loves when I shift.

I move toward her, my dragon surging, desperate to show the other side of our true self. One more step and the shift overtakes me. My arms extend, my hands transforming into two scaly black paws. In seconds, I'm towering above her. I spread my wings, showing off for her, then tip my head back and breathe fire for her, straight up into the Wyoming sky.

The smell of her fear becomes an acrid stench in my nose. She backs farther away from me. Fuck! Terrifying her was not my intention. I wanted her to know me. I wanted to show her my last big secret.

Fiona needs to see all of me so that she can fully accept our bond, knowing exactly who and what I am. We are fated to be together, our mating written in the stars. But her face has paled, and she's staggering backward, bracing herself on a tree as if she needs it for balance. I've overwhelmed her.

To comfort her, I lower my head to her level, my breath blowing back the hair that extends out the bottom of her hat. I nuzzle her neck with my nose.

She stops, shivers, and gapes at me, unblinking. I lick up the right side of her face.

There. Now we've bonded and—

I curse as she turns and bolts into the woods, not along the path but through the tightly spaced trees. I can't chase her like this. Not unless I'm willing to do some serious damage to the forest. *Fuck, fuck, fuck.*

I shift back into my human form and pull on my clothes again. Then I look at Bones and gesture with my chin in the direction Fiona's run.

He takes off.

"Find her, buddy."

I follow behind, easily chewing up the distance between us. By the time I catch up to her, she's struggling and exhausted. Her human body has had enough. Bones stops in front of her, wagging his tail. She looks over her shoulder at me.

"Don't make yourself sick again, Fiona. I only wanted to show you what I am."

"You're a monster," she blurts.

"No. I'm a dragon. One who would never, ever hurt you, in human or dragon form. I'd do anything to keep you safe." I catch up to her and easily sweep her into my arms. She doesn't struggle. "You're my mate. You can accept me and save me or reject me and doom me. But don't make this less than it is. You feel the bond as much as I do. And now you know exactly what I am."

Chapter Eighteen

FIONA

He's not human.

It should be an anticlimactic realization or else no realization at all. After the first time I saw his wings, I believed he was a dragon, whatever that meant. But believing something in your mind and really experiencing what it means are two very different things. Connor is a black as slate, size of an airplane, claws and teeth the length of my body, fire-breathing dragon! His wings in his human form are the least strange thing about him. I watched him transform into a creature of nightmares. A creature that could swallow me whole but didn't.

Of all the Stephen King-worthy, twisted and terrifying plot turns I thought my life would take, having a prehistoric fantasy creature experience some kind of animalistic love at first sight and take me back to his lair King Kong–style was not one of them. And the craziest part, the part I'm trying to fight with everything in me, is that I feel it too. This bond he says we have, it's there, undeniably. I've been attracted to men before, physically attracted. I've taken lovers. Once, in my twenties, on my own for the first time and missing my sister so much I could barely breathe, I went home with a man I met in a bar and had the most intense sex of my life. His name was Brayden, and it was the beginning of a six-month relationship.

My attraction to Brayden is a raindrop compared to the tsunami of desire I feel for Connor. The magnetic pull is a ground-shaking, all-encompassing, fire-blazing, breath-stealing sensory overload. It's like there's a wire binding my sternum to his, and someone is cranking it a little shorter each day.

I should be afraid after what I just saw, after what just happened between us. Or if not afraid, at least curious. How does shifting work? How does that giant dragon even fit inside this large but much smaller man? Where do shifters come from? Have they always lived among us? So many questions should be at the forefront of my mind. But if I'm honest with myself, I didn't run away from his dragon form because I was afraid of it. I ran because I was confused. I was confused about why I *wasn't* afraid. Because when I saw Connor shift, I definitely felt something.

I felt relieved.

I felt aroused.

I felt safe.

And given the circumstances, none of those feelings make sense.

Perfectly content in his arms, I watch him while I let those thoughts, the reality of this situation, further sink in.

It's all so confusing because he did kidnap me. From my wedding. To a potential murderer. Technically I'm still engaged to Roman. I barely know Connor. Am I becoming one of those women who always goes for the wrong guy? Because I am falling for him. Inexcusably, inexplicably, falling.

Connor kicks open the door, and Bones jogs in. He shoulders it closed behind us and sets me on my feet before helping me out of my coat. "Are you cold? Do you want some tea or something?" He kneels down before me and helps me take my boots off.

"No. I'm fine." I watch him hang up the coat and hat. "Are you angry that I ran? Are you going to lock me in my room now so I don't run away again?" My voice is light, as if I'm making a joke about what happened, but there's a real question there.

He glances up at me. "It's twenty-four degrees outside, and you're exhausted. Do you want to run away again?" He stands and reaches for the doorknob, holding it wide open. An icy blast hits me in the face.

"Uh, no."

He closes the door and gently adjusts my windswept hair. "I'm not angry. I'm proud that you handled it so well. And you won't find the doors in this house locked. You've always been welcome to go anywhere on the property you please." He traces my jaw with his knuckle.

For some reason, I can't seem to move. Alex Rogue would know what to do in this situation. She'd never quit trying to escape. She'd run to her room and lock the door, then make a plan to shimmy out the window and steal the housekeeper's car. Or, if she thought she needed Connor's help to solve a case, she'd take him as a lover and not think twice about the ramifications. But I'm not Alex, and I don't want to go anywhere.

"Do you want some tea or something?" he asks again.

His eyes are stormy blue again, his pupils round, not the green slitted ones of his dragon. "Does it hurt when you shift?"

"Only when I do it too fast."

"And the fire breathing... does that happen a lot?"

"Only when I need it to." His expression turns sheepish. "Or am trying to impress a mate."

"It *was* impressive." I glance down at my toes, my head spinning with questions. "So... how much control do you have when you're, um?" I gesture awkwardly at the door as if that version of him is still outside.

He steps in closer and runs his hands down my arms. His voice is low, rusty, as he says, "I've never had a problem with control." Somehow he makes it sound sexual, or maybe it's the tension ratcheting up between us that makes me feel that way. Suddenly what happened between us last night feels like an appetizer.

"I should get back to work. I have a book to finish," I say weakly.

"You can't put me off forever. You know it's true. You feel it. You're mine."

He's so close I can feel the heat coming off his skin. My gaze falls on his lips, and I'm so tempted.

"I need... time. This is..." I shake my head.

He nods. "Okay."

"Aren't you a little hesitant? After seeing my scar or because I'm a washed-up novelist who almost married your nemesis?" I laugh at how ridiculous it sounds that this Nordic god of a man is even interested in me. "I'm honestly nothing special. Nothing to go to war for."

He brushes my hair back from my eyes and tucks it behind my ear, shaking his head. "How is it that you can't see how beautiful you are, Fiona? You're breathtaking. Do you think your scar was what distracted me when I helped you change your first day here? Hell no. Seeing you naked, I almost swallowed my tongue. You're the sexiest woman I've ever encountered."

I swallow hard, backing away from him. I don't know what to say. I'm not sure what to think.

He draws back. "I'll tell Zaire to bring you that tea."

I nod and then race for the safety of my room.

Chapter Nineteen

FIONA

We fall into a pattern after that. Every morning, Connor has a gourmet breakfast waiting for me and then we walk Bones. We walk and we talk. He tells me about culinary school, which sounds like a completely normal and human experience. And then about training to be a warrior in a place called Cardinal Island, which he explains is another world, only accessible by dragons.

I tell him about the orphanage, our failed attempts at living with foster families, and my not-so-secret Taylor Swift addiction. His taste in music is eclectic. I'm not familiar with his favorite band, a group that his brother Seb just recently signed, an alternative rock band called Apples Fall. He plays a few songs for me and I dance around the living room to the album after he leaves.

And he does leave, every day after our morning walk. I see him sometimes chopping wood out back, his skin

179

steaming. Other times he looks pale, his skin clammy. Is this the mating sickness he mentioned? The fever?

If it is, he doesn't try to ease his symptoms with me again. A week goes by, and to my chagrin, he doesn't try to kiss me or anything else. I guess I asked him for time and he's giving it to me no matter how much I secretly wish he wouldn't. And I'm too much of a coward to do anything about the growing ache within me.

Every afternoon I return to my room where Alex is already there in my imagination, her arms spread wide. She's still wearing a maid's uniform. *You'll never believe what happens next, Fiona. After weeks working as a maid in the Milk Cult's headquarters, I find so many clues but I still don't know where they're hiding the girls.*

"Yeah, yeah. I'll figure it out. Give me a minute," I say to no one.

I open my laptop and get to work. I write like I've never written before, pages and pages flowing out of me like my brain is plugged into the keyboard.

I never hear anything more from either Roman or Vivian.

Every afternoon, Zaire brings me tea and an array of fruits, cheese, and vegetables. I barely notice. Alex is sleuthing in the Milk Cult's boarding house, then being chased by a group of thugs whose eyes glitter from the mood-altering drugs they're on. She's so close to the big reveal where I show the reader why the girl was murdered and why it all bothers Alex so much.

In the evenings, Zaire brings me dinner. I don't even taste it. I'm too wrapped up in the story. Only when my head starts to bob over my keyboard do I sleep. And when I do, I dream, always about Connor.

Twenty days into my stay at Dragon Lodge as I've come to call it, I wake genuinely excited to see Connor. Excited for our walk. But when I enter the kitchen, Zaire tells me he had some business to attend to and will be back in the evening. A pang in my chest has me rubbing the spot. I miss him. I miss him so much it hurts.

I play Apples Fall on repeat while I wrap up the day's work, realizing I'm only a handful of scenes from finishing *The Milkmaid*. Maybe three more chapters and it's done.

Tonight though, my thoughts of Connor outweigh the demands of Alex's voice. I crack my fingers. I've never written this fast in my life and I know it's because of him, because I'm living with a dragon. I know something else too. I want him.

I've been here almost three weeks, and I have no idea what will happen next. I certainly no longer have any desire to marry Roman. But this situation can't go on forever, can it?

It's out of your control, Alex says. She's back in her military fatigues, drinking a beer inside my head. *What you can control is tonight. Having the experience you want to have. And you can control your reaction to wherever you end up.*

I know Alex is me. I created her. But sometimes she gives great advice.

I shower and slip on a casual dress I find in the closet. It's soft and stretchy in a deep green that brings out the color of my eyes. When I think about Connor picking it out for me, I wonder if he chose it because he likes the color or because he thought it would be comfortable for me. He bought me an entire wardrobe. Everything fits and everything is comfortable. I can't help but compare it to my horror of a wedding dress, and that was made with me standing right in front of the designer. Which means Connor saw me more clearly in one day than Roman saw me over weeks and weeks.

I coil my hair up the back of my head, fastening it with a clip, then slide my feet into some leather slippers. A few turns in the mirror and I exit the room. Only I can't find Connor or Zaire anywhere. I search the kitchen and the dining room, and then I hear someone singing near the back of the house.

The hall is dark, but I can see a light on at the end of it, a bright natural light, and as I get closer, I know it's Zaire singing. I step into the room and instantly feel transcendent. The painting Zaire is working on takes up most of the wall—I'd estimate seven by five feet, but it's hard to tell because it comes off as much larger. The modern piece is constructed of red, purple, and blue splatters with other colors dripped and dribbled in. It's a rainbow of total chaos. Until you look at the negative space.

"Oh my God, it's you," I mumble, recognizing the pattern of white among the color. Up close, the painting is nothing but splotches, but taken as a whole, Zaire smiles from the tangle of color.

"It's my self-portrait. My first actually," he says, grinning proudly at me. "I'm relieved you saw it for what it is. You are the first to view the finished product."

I place a hand on my chest. "I'm honored. It's glorious, Zaire. Truly, this is a masterpiece. So many layers. So much dimension!" Art isn't my forte, but any amateur could see this was an exemplary accomplishment.

He bows. "Thank you, Ms. Morrow."

"Please call me Fiona. I should have asked you to call me by my first name a long time ago."

"Fiona. No matter, we are all still getting to know each other."

We stand there in companionable silence, taking in the painting for a few minutes more, until I can't put off the inevitable. "Zaire, do you know where Connor is?"

His smile fades. "Out back, chopping wood I'd guess. The cold helps with the symptoms."

"Symptoms of the mating sickness?"

He looks at me and gives a heavy sigh. "He's told you about it?"

I chew my lip. "Briefly."

"The dragons call it *appetency*," Zaire says. "For Connor, this is the worst I've ever seen it."

I squint at him. "So, it's a true physical ailment? When he told me it caused a fever, I assumed he was being metaphorical and it was more, um, psychological in nature. But I've noticed he hasn't been well."

His dark features take on a melancholy quality. "It's very much physical, I'm afraid. Dragons suffer a fever every year during their alignment. Now that he's nearing forty, the fever is accompanied by flu symptoms that worsen each year. It's caused by the beast within calling for a mate. Each year older he becomes, the more effort the dragon puts into the search and the hotter they burn.

If a mate isn't found, they will eventually die of the affliction."

"He mentioned that too." It wasn't something I wanted to think about at the time. "So, he just needs to get laid and he's cured?"

Zaire shakes his head but never cracks a smile. "It's not just sex, although he's told me the act does ease the pain of the fever. Before he met you, there was a woman who would visit this time of year to help him with the symptoms."

Jealousy rises within me, and I'm surprised at the sharpness of its bite. It must show on my face because Zaire raises a hand. "It was only a relationship of convenience and necessity. But of course, once he saw you, he told her not to come. A dragon can only bond with a true mate, and that mate is the only one who can stop the fever." He begins cleaning his brushes. "I would have thought he'd have explained this to you. He seemed sure you were the one."

The way Zaire looks at me wrenches my heart. The entire time Connor cared for me through my illness, he was suffering his own. "I... I am his mate, I think. He says so, at least. And I do feel a bond. I feel something. An affinity for him. But it's awfully fast. I don't know him in the way someone should know another person before they... *mate* with them."

He nods. "Only you would know for sure." He puts his cleaned brushes away and washes his hands in a sink fashioned in the corner. "Now if you'll excuse me, I believe I'll be preparing dinner tonight. If Connor is still outdoors, it means it's a particularly bad day."

I follow him from the room and toward the kitchen, but as I'm passing by one of the guest rooms, I see him. I step into the dim room and up to a large window overlooking the backyard. Connor is shirtless, his red flannel tied around his waist, his jeans low slung on his hips, exposing an impressive vee of muscle. He positions a log on a stump, hauls an axe over his shoulder, and chops. The wood splits, the impact causing his golden skin to quiver over the hard ridges and tight valleys of his body. My stomach flips at the sight, a sigh breaking the boundary of my lips.

Not for the first time I wonder at his godlike appearance. No one would argue with the comparison. But now that I know what I know, I see the steam coming off his flesh, the way his mouth is drawn as if he's in pain. I see the sweat at his temple. The sun is setting. It's cold out there. Bones is running circles around him. Connor just looks miserable.

If you don't fuck him, I will, Alex says in my head.

Go to sleep, Alex, I think. *We'll talk in the morning.*

Chapter Twenty

CONNOR

Two hours of chopping wood in forty-degree weather and I still feel like I'm burning up. I'm miserable. If I don't convince Fiona to be with me soon, I'm not sure I'll make it through the month. I'll be the youngest dragon to die of mating sickness.

My phone vibrates, and I set down the axe to answer it.

"Uncle Connor." Mason's deep voice comes down the line. He sounds excited.

"What's happening, Mason? Aren't you supposed to be training on Cardinal Island or making wedding plans with that girl of yours?" Mason mated Reagan last month. Reagan was raised human, and Mason intends to marry her in a human ceremony this summer.

"Actually, in an indirect way, that's why I'm calling."

"Huh?"

"We found the ring."

"Reagan's engagement ring? I've already seen it—"

"No. Not that ring. *The* ring. Her father's ring from when he was initiated into the Saint's Order!"

"No fucking way!" I lick my bottom lip. That ring is a major boon for the Zodiac Brotherhood. We've never gotten our hands on one before. The Order usually guards and retains them after a member's death. Reagan's father was an unusual exception.

Richard Bailey knew that Reagan's mother was a dragon and that she was killed by the Order, yet he still allowed himself to be seduced by the power the society offered him. He traded his daughter for membership in the Order. Reagan was a dormant until the Order used magic to force her shift. Her dad had planned to buy her back at auction, but she chose the hunt. Mason and I barely got her out alive.

Just days after his initiation and Reagan's escape, he committed suicide. He'd removed and hidden the Order's ring prior to his death and no one had seen it since. Once the mansion transferred ownership to Reagan, we searched every inch of the property for it. I'd assumed the Order got to it first.

"Where did you find it? I thought you guys searched everywhere."

"We thought we had too, but we decided to remodel her father's office because it holds bad memories for Reagan. When we demoed the bookcases, we found a secret room behind them. It was no bigger than a closet, Connor, but he kept a bunch of her mother's things in there. Reagan speculated that he also kept his wedding ring there because we found her mother's. He left the Order ring next to it on the shelf."

"Wow. This is big." I rub my chin.

"The biggest. Only we have a problem. Neither one of us can touch it. Burns like a son of a bitch. Reagan's friend Imani helped us move it to the safe. Obviously I can't take it to Cardinal Island. Even if I could devise some kind of carrying case, who knows what effect it would have on the portal or even if the ancient magic protecting the island would let it in."

"I agree. It's too dangerous."

"So what do you want me to do with it?"

Of course. That's why he's calling. For one more week, I'm in charge, which means he's looking to me for next steps. "Keep it in the safe for now. We'll need to find someone who can analyze the magic. I think Morwyn has an alchemical researcher on staff. Or we might be able to find a human witch to help us, although they're hard to come by these days." Witches are a secretive sort. I knew one in my early twenties in culinary school, but we've long since lost touch. "We've never had an opportunity like this. It might take some time to find the right person to analyze it."

"Maybe you should come get it? I hate having this thing in the house. Reagan has enough on her plate having just buried her father and inherited his company and the mansion. Neither of us is sleeping well. If the Order knew we had this, I don't even want to think about the danger Reagan could be in. They know she's a dragon and she's sitting on the board of his company. She's too exposed."

I glance toward the house. Fiona is watching me through the window. Our eyes lock. My mouth falls open, and my hand holding my cell phone drops away from my ear as I drink in the look of longing on her face. Before I can truly revel in it, it's gone. She retreats into the shadows.

"Connor? Connor?"

I bring the phone back to my ear. "Yeah."

"Are you coming for the ring?"

"Can't. I'm sorry. Brotherhood business. I can't leave my current mission."

"Is this about the bride?" Mason's voice rises. It's not like the Pisces to go from zero to sixty in the anger department, but any dragon that feels like his mate is threatened can get dangerous fast. "I think protecting your nephew's mate is more important than personally babysitting a hostage that the Order doesn't seem to give a shit about."

"Hey, watch it. You don't know what you're talking about. And how is it you know about her anyway? It's confidential."

"I'm a week out from filling Solomon's position. Seb told me as a matter of business."

"Her name is Fiona, and she wasn't involved with the Order in any way. She barely knew Roman."

"Oookay. More of a reason to cut her loose and help me with this ring situation. It's been weeks. Clearly she's not the means to the end you wanted. Wipe her mind and send her on her way."

My growl resonates loud enough to make my phone vibrate in my hand.

"Creator fucking hell!" Mason snaps. "Is your dragon targeting the human bride of Roman Cifarelli as your mate?"

"They were never actually married."

His deep, rich laugh comes down the line, reminding me so much of his father it almost breaks my heart. "Oh hell, this is too good. Connor, Aries dragon of the Zodiac Brotherhood, is mating a human! I never thought I'd see the day."

I frown. "You may not see the day."

"She's not going for it, huh?"

"Not yet."

"Have you talked to the Oracle?"

The back door opens, and Fiona is standing there in her coat and boots. Our eyes meet and hold. "I've got to go, Mason. I'll ask Seb if he can take the ring."

"Thanks, man. Good luck with, uh..."

"Fiona," I say, as much to her as to him.

"Yeah. Good luck with Fiona. I hope it works out."

"Me too," I mumble. The call disconnects, and I drop the phone into my pocket.

She approaches, never taking her eyes off mine, and stops inches from me, her hands in her pockets. "You missed our walk this morning."

"Wasn't feeling well," I mumble.

"Yeah, I noticed you haven't been feeling well a lot lately."

Bones runs up to us, tail wagging. I look at him and just feel tired. "He has an endless supply of energy."

Her voice is soft as she says, "Will you walk with me now?"

I busy myself putting on my flannel. "Of course." I could be missing one leg and bleeding from the eyes and couldn't deny her if she asked.

Her hand lands on my arm, and her expression turns soft. "I never told you, the day you shifted for me, that your dragon is beautiful. I've never seen anything more fiercely stunning."

I preen, loving the way she keeps hold of my arm. We've grown closer these past weeks, but we haven't touched much since she told me she needed time. "I could let him back out if you want a better look."

She raises her chin. "Not tonight. It's easier to talk to you like this."

I can't help the smile that overtakes me. "In that case..." I reposition her hand around my elbow and lead her toward the back trail. There's a full moon and just enough light to guide our way. "How's the writing going?"

"You always ask me that, and it's the one question you already know the answer to." She smirks. "I'm almost done. If I stay here much longer, I'll have to start another book."

"Why not five books more?" I slant her a hopeful smile. "You can write from anywhere, right?"

She snorts. "I can now."

"I finished your series." I've been waiting to tell her that, and I love the way she swells when she hears it. "I loved it, but I have a question."

"Yeah? What's that?"

"Does Alex ever get together with Henrik Angel? Not just for sex but for good?"

The glow of her smile rivals the moon. "An author never tells."

She releases my arm and shoves her hands into her pockets. "I think this is the longest we've gone without arguing about something."

"Fire on fire," I say. "It could be good under the right circumstances."

She flashes a witchy smile. "More fucking and less fighting?"

My dragon rumbles in my chest at the thought, and I know Fiona can feel it on the inside. Feel it down our bond. "I would be the most attentive mate to you, Fiona. You know I would be. I've cared for you for weeks. But more importantly, I know you. No one can ever love you like me because no one knows you like me. You need a challenge to feel alive. Every book you've ever written has made that clear, and yes, I read them all. The characters you create don't shy away from trouble, and neither do you. I inspire you, not because our relationship is easy but because the fire in me calls to the fire in you. Other men, they might appreciate your beauty, and creator, I do too. You're stunning. But you are no hothouse flower. Even when you were sick and it would have been so easy to assume you were fragile, all you gave me was fire. No one will ever appreciate how brightly you burn as an artist or how far you've come on pure grit." I hate the raw need I hear in my voice. I've lost all sense of my Aries self, all my fight gone. All that's left is this bottomless pit of need for her. I need her like I need air. Like I need nourishment. "I've seen inside your head, and this bond between us means I feel your strongest emotions. We were made for each other." I rub my chest where it's started to ache. "You fill in all my empty spaces. And I'll tell you one thing for certain—I don't regret stealing you off that altar for a second. I'll never feel remorse for it. Say yes and you will never want for anything. Say you're mine and I will show you what it feels like when stars collide."

She stumbles and I stop talking to catch her, hauling her upright. It was too much. I think I've overwhelmed her.

She rights herself, lashes fluttering. "I have some questions," she says breathlessly.

"Shoot." This is good. She has questions. I have answers.

"Your kind, do you mate with humans often?"

An easy one. "It happens, but not as often as with each other or hybrids of our kind. For our safety, we have to make sure a person isn't associated with the Order before we reveal what we are. Once they know, they target us. That limits how many humans we can get close enough to for a mating bond to form."

She looks off into the trees, contemplative. "You mentioned before that you're suffering from mating sickness..."

"Yeah."

"Zaire told me that you had someone who, um, helped you with that before."

I lift a brow. How exactly does she think this works? "If you're asking me about sex, yes, I've taken lovers before to help me with the sickness. The fever is uncomfortable without it. But that was before I met you. Before

I had a mate. Mating is more than sex. Dragons choose only one mate, and when we mate, it's for life."

"For life?" She swallows, her voice rising in pitch. "You want to claim me as your mate for life?"

My dragon rears inside me, my blood heating instantly. When I speak, my voice is ash and cinder. "Would you rather I only wanted to use you? Are you looking for a human fling? A one-night stand with someone whose name you might forget?"

"No, I—"

"Let me be clear," I growl. "I will take whatever you offer me. I am starving for you, Fiona, and I will eat sawdust if that is all you feed me, but that's not what I want. I want all of you. I want forever."

Chapter Twenty-One

FIONA

S‌*tarving for me. He's starving for me.*

I reach for him in the dark, my fingers finding buttery-soft flannel. "In that case, I wonder if you can help me with something." My voice trembles and my heart stutters.

"Anything," his deep voice rumbles.

I pull Roman's engagement ring out of my pocket and hold it between us. "Get rid of this for me. I don't want it anywhere near me."

His mouth twists into a grin and he plucks the ring from my fingers. Turning away from me, he draws a deep breath into his lungs. When he exhales, his breath ignites into a blowtorch of fire that jets across his palm. The blaze is intense enough that I feel its burn against my cheeks. My mouth falls open as the gold melts, dribbling through his fingers. When all that's left is the diamond, he hurls it into the woods, the garish stone whistling through the air until it plunks, with one last moon-reflecting twinkle, against a tree in the distance.

I can't restrain my laugh. "I had no idea you could breathe fire in this form."

His expression turns wolfish. "Just one of my many useful tricks."

Relishing the moment— the lightness and the warmth between us— I run my hands up his soft plaid shirt and encircle his neck, pressing myself against him. This close, I can feel his fever, the heat coming off him like hugging a radiator.

"You're burning up."

"It's the mating sickness."

"Zaire said this is the worst he's ever seen you."

"It gets worse each year, until we eventually go up in flames."

"Or find a mate."

He gives me a savage look and I want him, want him in a way that makes every other relationship I've ever had feel artificial. I've lived in a land of CGI, but I'm finally in the real world where things have texture, scent, and taste. Three dimensions.

I must be projecting my thoughts again because he sweeps me into his arms. His stride chews up the path to the house, and before I know it, we're back inside, Bones trotting in behind us.

"Find Zaire, Bones." Connor gestures toward the studio, and the dog lopes off.

Connor helps me out of my coat and then kneels to remove my boots.

"I can undress myself, you know," I say through a

smile because the truth is I'm enjoying this. "I'm not a child."

He runs his thumb along the arch of my foot, and the warm pressure feels like it runs straight up my inner thigh to my core. When he smiles at me, it's all dragon, hot and consuming, his penetrating gaze seeming to stir something deep within me.

"I don't help you undress because you can't do it yourself," he says. "I help you undress because it gives me an excuse to touch you."

His hand drifts up the inside of my ankle, along my inner calf to my knee. But when I look down into his eyes, I notice the neck of my dress has slipped and my scar is showing. I haven't had sex since the accident. Even a few nights ago, when we made out in the dining room, I was mostly dressed. I know Connor has seen my scar—he saw it when he dressed me my first night here—but my stomach tightens into a ball of nerves when I think about him seeing it again now. The skin along the scar feels thicker than the rest of me. How will it feel between us? The idea of being fully naked in front of him is intimidating. From what I've seen of his body, he's too perfect to be real.

"Fiona..." He stands and cups my face gently.

"Oh fuck! You're reading my mind again, aren't you?"

He shakes his head. "You're projecting. I can't help it. It's like you're screaming down the bond."

"Oh hell." I pull away from him and pace into the living room, crossing my arms against the deep discomfort of having my most intimate insecurities out in the open.

"You're not the only one with scars."

"Oh? Because I saw you with your shirt off, and there wasn't a single imperfection on your body."

I turn around and he's there. One of his paddle-sized hands comes to rest in the small of my back and I sigh as he pulls me against him. He points to the scar through his right eyebrow. Funny, I've always known it was there, but it's easy to lose sight of it when you're blinded by the glow of his overall attractiveness. I roll my eyes. "If anything, that one makes you look even hotter. It doesn't count."

The sexy smirk he gives me sends my pulse skittering. "It counts. I almost lost my eye."

"How did that happen?"

"I told you about my brother-in-law trading himself for Carolyn when she was captured."

I nod.

"It was my job to get her out of there while the Order took him away in those glowing blue cuffs they use. Separating mates never goes well. She became a menace of claws and teeth. We weren't off Order property when she shifted. The Order attacked, and we had to fight our way out. I had to shift in order to overpower her dragon form and carry her out of there by the neck." My eyes must pop because he adds, "It sounds worse than it is. She wasn't hurt, but I met the business end of one of their swords as I fought our way out. Morwyn saved the eye, but I have this."

For some reason, revisiting this story makes me tremble. The wrongness of it. The pain the Order caused. All at once, I realize that Connor saved me from a terrible mistake when he carried me from that altar. I never actually knew Roman and I'd been rushing into something that could have destroyed me. I've refused to fully face it until now, but I know deep in my heart that all Connor has told me about the Order and about Roman is true. And I know now, as if the clouds have parted and I can finally see the clear blue sky, that I hate Roman. Hate everything the Order stands for.

"I'll start a fire. You're shivering."

I grip him tighter. "No. I'm fine. God, you're like a million degrees." I press a hand to his cheek. "I just.... It wasn't fair what happened to Carolyn."

"At least I have my sister. The fever started again after Roger's death, but she's survived long enough to see Mason mated. That meant a lot to her."

"She deserves that."

"Tell me how you got your scar." It's a command, not a question. "Only fair. If we're trading secrets, it's your turn."

I lick my lips and fist his shirt, pulling him closer. "Wouldn't you rather pick up where we left off?"

Leading me deeper into the room, he sits in one of the leather chairs and pulls me into his lap. I squirm against the hard length of him under me, wanting him to kiss me again, but when I lean in, he draws back. "This scar of yours..." He traces it through the fabric of my dress, his touch sending another shiver through me. "...it's an important part of who you are. I want to know everything about my mate. I want no secrets between us when we become one. No reason for you to believe I haven't accepted every part of you. It's why I showed you my dragon when I did. Now I need you to show me the hidden part of you. I can wait for this."

The way he's looking at me makes my stomach flip, but I see in his eyes that he needs to know my secret before we can take the next step. Maybe it's time I shared my trauma with someone else. My heart beats faster with anxiety, but I won't deny him this. "I was in a car accident a little over a year ago. My twin sister, Marion, was driving. The scar is from my seat belt." He smooths a comforting hand along the back of my head, down my spine. I've never told a single soul the entire story. "Marion was wearing her seat belt too, but she had the steering wheel in front of her. When the airbags went off, the force, along with the crash, killed her instantly. I had more room. That's what they tell me anyway about why I survived and she didn't."

He winces, I sense he's feeling what I am, down our bond. It's intensely intimate. "To lose your sister like that and then have to recover physically while you were grieving..." He shakes his head.

I take a deep breath. This is a depressing conversation to have when only moments ago all signals pointed to us getting naked. But Connor is right—it's better if we can share the things that made us who we are. Marion is part of that. If he wanted to, he could enter my mind and see it all for himself, but he's asked me to willingly share it with him. It means a lot, and if he's brave enough to listen, I need to be brave enough to share. My voice comes out strained as I continue. "More difficult because we'd only recently reunited. We never knew our parents.

We were both abandoned at a religious orphanage as babies."

"You'd recently reunited?"

"Three years after we graduated the orphanage, Marion joined a convent. She became a nun with the same order of sisters who ran our orphanage."

"No shit? A nun?" He looks perplexed, which I get because no one was more perplexed than me when Marion took her vows.

"Yes. A Catholic nun. One of the Sisters of Mercy." I catch myself trailing my fingers through the scattering of ash-blond hair on his arm. I stop petting him, but he makes a disappointed rumble deep in his throat and I start again.

"The convent is why you lost touch?" he asks in a low, gritty voice. "I don't know many nuns. Their way of life is a mystery to me."

"She was a cloistered nun. They take vows to live a life separate from the rest of society and rarely journey beyond the boundaries of their abbey. When they join their order, they leave their families behind and consider the other sisters their new family. As you can imagine, that was particularly difficult for me as her twin. She was all the family I had. When she chose them over me, she was orphaning me all over again. I don't remember my parents giving me up. But I remember Marion leaving me."

Pain lances through me at the memory.

"But you reconnected."

I can tell he's trying to puzzle it all out, and I don't blame him for the confusion furrowing his brow. The truth is I've spent years trying to understand her choices. I take a deep breath and continue. "About two years ago, she called me. One of the things the sisters were allowed to do is take long walks on the property where they'd engage in prayers and meditation. My sister found a sliver of land adjacent to the abbey's property that she felt repeatedly drawn to, a spiritual connection she couldn't explain. She thought it was... angelic. I know that sounds weird, but it was part of her belief system."

Heat radiates off him in a wave that goes straight to my core. I shift in his lap and feel his nose brush the skin behind my ear as he says, "Dragons believe in angels, both light and dark. They're part of our mythology as celestial beings. Was the angel speaking to her?"

I sigh, leaning more fully into him. His hand lands on my inner thigh, just above my knee, and holds me in place. I hear him swallow. He's holding himself back, giving me time to share everything. "More like guiding her," I continue. "The wooded acres were home to a small chapel and a cemetery, all of it run down and long overgrown from lack of use. Marion didn't even know the land wasn't owned by the abbey until a For Sale sign appeared. Some steel magnate had died unexpectedly. The family hadn't even known the property existed until his death, and they sought to unload it quickly.

"Marion wanted it, but nuns aren't allowed to own things individually. I'm not sure what she'd tried before she called me, if she'd asked the Mother Superior to obtain it or simply wanted it for herself, but one day she reached out. Begged me to buy it for her. The sheer desperation in her voice... You would have thought it was life or death. I hadn't seen her in almost a decade, and she was weeping on the phone, asking for my help. So I helped her. I bought it, under my name, for her. I made the payments. She still had no money, of course. The Alex Rogue series had taken off. But one thing was still missing in my life, and it was her. I wanted my family back, so I bought it for her under one condition."

"What was that?"

"On the days she was allowed to walk and pray, I required her to meet me on that land. We met every Tuesday afternoon for over a year."

"In secret, I presume?"

"Oh yes. She was breaking her order's rules by meeting with me. Anyway, one afternoon she wanted to show me something. She said it was important, and at her insistence I allowed her to drive. To make a long, painful story short, we... crashed. She died. And I got this." I run a finger over the scar. "Between my medical costs and not being able to make my deadlines because I was recovering, I am officially broke and in danger of losing the very property I bought for her."

Our eyes lock. Connor's rapt attention is focused on me with an intensity that makes my breath catch. Marion's death holds so many questions for me. If I'd told her no that day, or if it had been me behind the wheel. My memory of our last meeting is wrapped up in guilt and confusion. But Connor seems to accept all of it. I adjust myself on his lap, my lips only a breath away from his.

"So that's how Roman sank his claws into you. You were lonely and desperate."

Anger sparks and surges in my veins. This again!

Fuck, the way he says it so matter-of-factly, as if it's a forgone conclusion, is utterly insulting. "Lonely and desperate?" I shove against his chest and leap to my feet. "Oh, I forgot. You're sure I was marrying him for his money! Fuck. You."

I whirl, my hands balling into fists as I stride for my room, but he snags me around the waist, his rough whiskers scratching my neck when he pulls me flush against his chest and growls into my ear, "Oh no you don't. Not this time."

Chapter Twenty-Two

CONNOR

Fiona struggles against me, kicking and trying her best to squirm from my grip, but it's not happening. Not today. Not after she finally shared her darkest memory with me. Down the bond, I felt her need to share that memory of her sister with me and also fear, slick as black ice in her mind. But I know my mate. That chain I saw in her head that stifled her creativity for so long, it came from that accident and her telling me just now was necessary to free her from another set of chains, ones that were keeping her from giving herself to me completely. Now that she's opened up, I won't let a few careless words ruin this. I wrap my hand around her throat and hold her to me, my cock hard against her backside with the need to claim her. I won't force her, but I won't let her cower from it this time. Not now. Not when we're this close.

"Stay with me," I growl into her ear. "You're safe with me, Fiona. I'm sorry. I didn't mean for that to come across the way it did."

She swallows, and I can feel it against my palm.

"Let me go." I set her down immediately. She whirls on me. Shoves me with both hands. "Why do you have to be such a brute?"

I narrow my eyes, the fire rising in my blood. "You're not pushing me away this time. Not over something like this."

"Something like this?" she hisses.

"A misunderstanding. When I said you were desperate, I wasn't suggesting you were a gold digger. I only meant that your financial problems made you vulnerable. I know you'd never marry someone for their money."

She shakes her head. "Damn you. Damn you for suggesting it."

I reach for her again, but she dodges my grip. My eyes narrow on hers, my finger pointing at the floor between us. "I don't think you understand what it does to me to think about you with him," I grit out. "It makes me jealous as hell. It makes me burn to claim you. It makes me wonder what he has that I don't."

Her breath comes in pants, and her brows knit together. "You're jealous... of Roman?" She scoffs.

I nod twice, slowly. "The idea of him touching you enrages me. The idea that he had you and I... don't... is intolerable." I turn my back to her, unable to watch her walk away one more time. For what seems like two full minutes, I stare into the cold fireplace.

"You never intended to trade me for information from the Order, did you?" Her voice startles me, as does the hand that lands on my back. "If Roman had agreed to meet with you about Lucy's murder, you would have never let him take me, would you?"

I catch her eyes over my shoulder. "Never."

Her expression softens and I turn, drawing her to me once more, and this time she doesn't fight me. "If you accept me as your mate, I will be loyal to you and defend you to my dying day. I'll always put you first. My soul will be yours. My dragon will be yours to command. You'll never have to question it. A mated dragon is biologically programmed to serve his mate. Our union has been blessed by the creator, fated, destined in the stars." I swallow. "You can reject it. I won't force it on you. But if you say yes, I'll make it my mission to love you the way you need to be loved. And I'll tell you one thing, no fucking scar or story about how you got it is going to convince me you are any less of a goddess."

Her heart flutters and her eyes go wide as dinner plates. "Oh," she says breathlessly. "Is that all you have to offer? Just a lifetime of love written in the stars?"

Another wave of sickness comes over me, and I close my eyes as my stomach pitches.

"You've been patient to wait for me. That's not what Aries are known for."

"No." I take a deep breath, fighting against my instincts to grab her. To claim her.

"And if I left you right now, you'd let me go?"

I open my eyes again, pain like I've never experienced

before slicing through me. A lump forms in my throat like a fist. "Yes."

Her hand presses into her chest and she draws a shaky breath. She feels it too, down the bond, the deep sense of dread, the awful black hole at the thought of being apart. "I've never truly been your prisoner, have I?"

I shake my head and my voice is trashed as I admit, "Never. If you ask to leave, I'll allow it. If you ask me to take you, I will fly you home myself. I can't deny you anything. Maybe I never could, not anything I thought you truly wanted. You do understand that when I took you, I believed it was what you wanted."

She licks her lips and moves a baby step closer to me. "When I was standing there in that ridiculous wedding dress, I never dreamed a love like yours was possible for a woman like me. A woman could get used to being loved like that." She reaches behind her back, and I hear her zipper.

My breath halts its flow in my lungs. I'm afraid to breathe. Afraid to say a word. Afraid my reality will shift and she'll pull away again.

But she keeps going, unzips her dress, then lets it fall off her body. I keep my hands by my sides as she draws near and brushes her lips against mine. "You don't have to wait anymore, Connor," she whispers. "Claim me. I accept you as my mate."

With a growl that rattles the paintings on the walls, I sweep into her, lifting her feet from the floor as my mouth crashes down on hers. Fire meets fire. She's already open. Already welcoming me in, her tongue stroking against mine in a breathless tangle of repositioned heads, nipping teeth, and bruising kisses.

"I can't be gentle. Not this time," I warn her, the words sinking into her mouth, swallowed by our need.

She draws back a fraction of an inch to unfasten her bra and tosses it onto the chair, then goes to work on the buttons of my flannel.

My dragon surges, sending scales flipping along one arm and disappearing beneath skin a breath later. "Faster. I'm not kidding."

She eyes the place on my arm where we both saw the partial shift, fists both sides of my shirt, and rips. Buttons fly and I shrug the scraps off me, my heart pounding in my ears. My wings unfurl.

"Jesus Christ, you're beautiful," she says, reaching up and stroking along the edge of one.

My answering purr makes her heart pound faster, and the scent of her arousal blooms between us. I hook my fingers in the sides of her panties and drop to my knees, taking them down with me. She kicks them aside.

Entirely naked now, she meets my gaze as I eye the scar she kept from me so vehemently, such an important part of her, a badge of honor for surviving her past. I lay the flat of my tongue on the place it starts at her hip and lick the length of it. Slowly, ever so slowly, I worship this thing she's been so afraid of, this piece of her she's guarded, still guards, from me. I end with a swirl around the nipple of her right breast.

Her breath stutters. My purr thunders in our ears. I know she feels it because she closes her eyes and her breath quivers. I grip her thighs and spread her feet, the scent of her arousal coloring all my senses, making everything bright and sharp and real. Her hands land in my hair, her nails digging in. I run my nose along her slit, breathing in her scent. It's pure fire in my veins, and when I lick up her center and hear her gasp of pleasure, it unleashes the last bit of restraint I had over myself. I penetrate her, then drag my tongue along the side of her clit.

"Oh fuck, Connor. My God." Her breath comes in ragged pants.

"You like that, my mate."

"Yes. More." She digs her fingers into my scalp.

My growl grows in intensity, vibrating against her clit, and I pick up the pace, lapping her pussy and spearing her with my tongue. If I weren't so desperate to be inside her, I might slow down and savor this. But I feel her pleasure building down our bond and can't rein in my enthusiasm. I replace my tongue with my fingers, massaging inside her while I tease her clit with the pad of my thumb.

"Come for me, Fi." The power in that command flows down the mating bond and lights her up from the inside.

Her body jolts and spasms, her hands landing on my shoulders as her legs give out. I catch her and lower her to her back on the rug in front of the fireplace, unzipping my jeans and shoving them and everything underneath down and off. Kneeling between her feet, I run a hand over her stomach and between her breasts, my wings fanning out over us both. My cock nestles into her crease, weeping to find a home there, and I brace myself on either side of her head.

I meet her amber eyes, knowing my own are glowing green from the light that dusts across her face, but I hesitate.

She arches, a moan breaking her lips, flashes her wicked smile, and kisses me in a way that has my dragon heating another notch. Into my mouth, she asks, "What are you waiting for?"

Chapter Twenty-Three

FIONA

Never in my entire life have I felt more wanted by a man. Connor is over me, that enormous cock of his nudging my drenched pussy. The orgasm he gave me still rings through every inch of my body, bolstered by that purr vibrating against the inside of my skin. I want him in me so bad I could cry.

I grab his ass and arch against him, but he stays insufferably where he is.

His forehead lands on mine. "Say my name, Fiona. Tell me you're mine."

I breathe deeply of his scent, soaking in the magic of being the center of his universe. *Say my name.* We're back to this, just as before. Of course he wants to hear it. After everything, he wants me to see him. To see him and to accept him the same way he sees me and accepts me. Why have I hesitated?

I look into his eyes and tell him the truth because he

deserves to know. "It's terrifying to be on the brink of having everything you ever wanted." Emotion chokes off my voice until some of the words are only breath, but I suspect he can hear me down our bond. It's like that connection is opening between us. I can feel his desire for me loud and clear. And so I project my feelings toward him. He has to know I want him too. "I've been alone a long time. The only one I've trusted is myself. Having you for forever is both a dream and a nightmare. Now you're inside my heart, and if I lose you like I lost Marion, there will be nothing left of me."

"You won't lose me, Fiona. I'm hard to kill, remember?" He squeezes his eyes shut like he's in pain, and I feel a surge of heat come off his skin. Down the bond, I feel him begging me. *Please.*

My next words, I make damn sure he can hear. "I love you, Connor. Claim me. I'm yours."

"I love you, Fiona," he says, and he enters me in one hard thrust. His lips brush my ear, his purr rumbling through me as he growls, "You're mine."

Stars become supernovas inside me. A million shooting fireworks fill my internal workings, and all I can do is lie back and absorb it because he's moving, holding me in place as he thrusts so deep inside he seems to take up every bit of space under my skin. It's almost too much, balancing on a thin line between pleasure and pain.

I think he can't possibly go any deeper, not without splitting me open, but he hooks my legs over his shoulders and finds a way. Holy fuck, I'm stretched to my limit and completely full, his thrusts pounding into the core of me as if he could touch my soul from the inside. Maybe he can. I have no other explanation for the connection I feel to this man.

Our eyes meet and hold. This is beyond physical. We're like two live wires twisting around each other, being fused together into something new.

Everything in my life has led up to this. Everything is right and meaningful and purposeful because I am here and he is here, finally together, our souls perfectly aligned.

I feel whole.

I feel loved.

With barely a nudge, I coax him onto his back, my hands on his chest as I ride him until my body is humming, balanced on the edge of another orgasm. His purr rumbles through me once more. His eyes glow brighter, that inner dragon staring up at me as I arch my back and grind against him. "By the creator, Fi, I've waited for this for so long. The way we fit. I never want to be without you again." He reaches between us and thumbs my clit. I throw my head back and tumble over the edge, collapsing onto his chest.

My body still rings with pleasure as he flips us over and flaps his wings. We lift off the floor. I reposition my legs, locking my ankles behind his hips and clinging tight to his neck with my arms as another orgasm slams into me, knocking me into oblivion. Inside, he lengthens, thickens, and I feel him coming too, giving me what my body so desperately wants. Hot jets fill me. Liquid fire that feeds the flame within. My orgasms come one on top of the other until I don't know where one ends and the next begins. My body milks his, taking everything he has to give me.

When we finally descend, he lands on his back on the floor, wings splayed. I'm lying on top of him, both of us panting, deeply connected. Skin to skin. His wings rise to wrap around us, swaddling me in their ridged velvet. I rest my head on his chest and kiss the underside of his jaw.

"I feel like a burrito," I say.

"Are you too warm?" he mumbles sleepily.

"No, surprisingly. I think you're cooling off." I hold a palm to his head.

"Fever's fed," he mumbles, his eyes drooping.

It suddenly dawns on me that we're in the middle of the living room. "Um, should we move to the bedroom before Zaire gets an eyeful?"

"He's been in his room watching a movie with Bones since we came in from outside."

"How do you know that?"

"He's my Firetender."

"You have a psychic bond with him as well?"

"Yup." His hand covers his mouth as he yawns. "Sleepy. Give me ten minutes."

"Ten minutes until what?"

He pops an eye open, now deep blue again. "Round two," he rumbles.

"Oh!" I grin, resting my head and feeling completely content. After a few minutes, his breath evens out and I'm pretty sure he's asleep.

I should have some anxiety about what just happened. I bound myself to a creature I never knew existed until three weeks ago. Bound in a way that I'm pretty sure is a bigger commitment than marriage. And as if that isn't the most illogical decision I've ever made, we didn't use protection. Strangely though, I'm not worried about it. The idea of having Connor's baby doesn't scare me at all. I can picture it actually, as clearly as I'd pictured him in my imagination before we met when I created Henrik. A little boy with Connor's blue eyes and my auburn hair. I never thought I'd want that, but I do. I imagine holding him on my hip, watching Little League games, his father teaching him to fly.

Lips press to the top of my head, and I'm suddenly aware that Connor is no longer breathing evenly. In fact, his enormous cock is rock-hard again and jabbing into my stomach. The pounding of his heart is a steady thump against my chest.

"That was barely a minute," I whisper, fluttering a kiss along his jaw.

"How do you expect me to sleep with you projecting images of our would-be child into my head?" Somehow, although it seems to defy the law of gravity, he flexes his wings and we rise together, me cradled in his arms. He walks me into his bedroom. "All I can think about now is putting a babe in your belly."

Heat creeps from my jaw to my hairline. "You heard that?"

"Loud and clear." He throws me down on the duvet, and I bounce once before settling into the mattress.

"You're so good at reading my mind." I roll onto my hands and knees, then crawl to where he stands at the end of the bed, spreading my thighs as I sit back on my heels. I wrap my hand around his massive cock and stroke from base to tip. Leaning forward, I run my tongue around the ridge, reveling in how he hisses when I draw him entirely into my mouth. He tastes of me, of us, and I hum in appreciation. "What am I thinking about now?"

"Creator Blessed, Fi, what you do to me." His hands are in my hair, gathering it into a ponytail behind my head.

I send him images of what I see, what I'm feeling. What he looked like to me the first time I saw him. The brightness of his smile as we walked in the sun. The feel of his hand on my face. The relief I felt when he unchained Alex. I parade out one happy thought after another as I hollow my cheeks and suck him deep. He growls his appreciation, but it's that mating purr I feel inside me, like vibrating silk being threaded through the tapestry of my inner workings. Our souls are weaving together ever tighter, with every minute we touch. Every stroke of flesh on flesh.

He slides out of my mouth and reaches down to haul me up his chest, his mouth finding mine. I wrap my arms around his neck and my legs around his hips. He slides into me easily, smooth and hard as slick steel. It's only been a few minutes since our first joining but having him inside me again is a relief. Why did I wait so long to do this?

He starts to move, his fingers lifting me by the thighs as he braces a foot on one of the leather ottomans for leverage. My nails are in his hair and then scraping along the strip of flesh between his shoulders where his wings join his back. His purr grows louder. He loves it when I stroke his wings. I follow that feeling, gripping one of the talons that hook from the apex and stroking the edge of his opposite wing. His hands circle my waist and he unleashes himself, lifting me and sinking into me, driving an impossibly fast rhythm.

This time my orgasm doesn't bloom but explodes. It rocks through me, and I toss my head back and cry out. Everything is gone but a shower of stars, and then I'm on my back on the bed, my inner muscles squeezing as heat fills me again and his growl of pleasure rings in my ears. We're both flying, our souls bound together in some endless tunnel of light while our bodies remain tethered to the earth.

It's a long time before we come back down again.

"I am covered in you," I say a while later, glancing down at the evidence of our lovemaking all over my lower belly and inner thighs.

"As it should be," he mumbles through a lazy smile. He sweeps me off the bed and carries me into his adjacent bathroom, sitting me on the edge of the tub while he adjusts the knobs.

"I'm going to forget how to walk if you keep carrying me around like that."

He kisses away my smile. "I'm okay with that."

I watch the water rise in the enormous tub, and my thoughts settle back to earth like spindrift on the needles of evergreens.

"What happens now?" I ask, suddenly feeling breathless.

He smiles. "Now we get in the bathtub and clean you off, and then I'll make you something to eat."

"No, I mean…" Fuck, I can't fathom not sharing openly with him, not after what we just experienced together. "I don't think I can go back to my life after you, Connor," I say softly. "I'm trying to picture what happens next. Do I go back to my apartment in the Bronx? When we leave here, we'll have to go our separate ways, at least for a while."

"Why?" he rumbles.

"Because we've known each other for less than a month. Because I have a home and a career and so do you. Because it's not like we're married."

"What were you going to do before?" He runs his fingers through the water, not looking at me.

He means what did I plan to do if I married Roman. "Well, I had plans to let my lease lapse."

"Then do that. Let the place go. Move into my Manhattan apartment with me."

"But…"

"Marry me. If you want to be married the human way, we'll do it."

I think about it, how crazy it all sounds, how anyone might cringe at how fast I've moved with Connor. How I don't give a damn.

"Okay," I say softly, offering him an intimate smile.

"Okay what?"

"Okay, I'll marry you and move in with you." I laugh at the absurdity. Oddly, I have no qualms about this plan.

His mouth spreads into a smile that takes over his entire face. "Problem solved."

"Wow." I stare at him for a second, taking him in. "I

didn't know how the mating sickness was weighing on you. When you smile now, it's like..."

"I'm not in pain anymore." Slowly he sinks into the warm water, then helps me in and settles me against his chest, tucking my head under his chin. The silky feel of the water, the heat, his skin, all feel like a balm for what's been broken in me the past year.

I close my eyes. "Neither am I. It's so strange. All of this feels like the most natural thing in the world. Shouldn't I be more worried about taking this step? I'm beginning to think your dick is magic and you've fucked all my apprehensions out of me."

He barks a laugh I feel against my cheek. "Well, my dick is magic, but I think what you're feeling is our mating bond. Don't be surprised if you experience other changes."

"Like what?"

"Difficulty being apart, especially during my alignment. Extreme jealousy if you see me with another woman—"

"Why would you be with another woman?" I ask, suddenly feeling a wave of that jealousy.

He laughs. "I do run a restaurant."

"I'm a fan of an all-male waitstaff."

"You won't say that once you meet Carmen. You're going to love her."

I turn my face to kiss along his neck, feeling more alive than I've ever felt before, and in that perfect moment thinking about nothing else.

Chapter Twenty-Four

CONNOR

Once I finally get Fiona dried off and back in my bed, I curl around her, exhausted. There's nothing I'd enjoy more than celebrating our mating all night long, but it's been weeks since I had a full night's sleep due to the mating sickness. Tomorrow will be better. Now that I've claimed Fiona as my mate, I'll never have to suffer the effects of mating sickness again. My mind immediately jumps to the Oracle. I'll have to ask her to bless our union so that I can bring Fiona to Cardinal Island.

I frown. I angered the Oracle when I took Fiona. I pray to the creator that when she sees how this has all worked out, she'll forgive me. Mason's ascension is next week. I'll see her then and plead my case.

"There's something I don't understand," Fiona says.

"Hmm?"

"You know how you told me over dinner that one of

the Zodiac Brotherhood's warriors sacrificed himself fifty years ago in exchange for the peace accord?"

"Yeah?" I'm barely awake, but I'll do what I must to answer my new mate's questions.

"If he suffers from mating sickness like you, wouldn't he have died by now? He must have been twenty or so—"

"Eighteen. Donovan was young for a warrior. He'll be sixty-nine this fall."

"Donovan? Donovan is the dragon who sacrificed himself?" She laughs. "I met him."

My eyes open more fully. "You met Donovan in person? How is he?"

She looks flabbergasted. "Fine. More than fine. He goes everywhere with Stefan. They're never apart. Actually, I assumed they were a couple at first because of the way they'd stand together, almost touching. Roman told me they were close friends."

I balk at that information. "Are you saying you met Donovan at a social event? One unrelated to the Order?"

"Um, yeah. We had a casual family dinner with them."

My mouth slackens. "How did he seem?"

Her shoulder lifts toward her ear. "Not like a prisoner. He smiled and laughed with us all evening. Ate and drank at our table. Looked fondly at Stefan often." She licks her lips. "Honestly, I'm baffled right now to learn he's almost seventy years old and their prisoner. He only looked about fifty."

"Dragons don't age like humans. We remain relatively young until the day we die."

"But wouldn't he be close to death from the sickness? You were terribly ill, and you're thirty-eight."

"Donovan is a powerful warrior. He'll fight the sickness as long as possible. He likely has another thirty years."

"But eventually... You said unmated dragons live to be around a hundred. What happens to the accord after he goes up in flames?"

"The accord is written to extend beyond his lifetime. That was part of the deal."

She stares up at the ceiling. "So weird. I would have never guessed he was a prisoner."

She snuggles into my side, warm and sleepy. I kiss her temple. But as I lay my head back on the pillow, I wonder why Donovan hasn't responded to our urgent messages if he indeed enjoys the kind of freedom she described. And I also wonder what it means that no one from the Order has come for Fiona.

Chapter Twenty-Five

FIONA

After the most intense sex of my life, I should have been out until morning, but I wake around four a.m. with Alex in my head, demanding I finish her story.

That woman I'm friends with at the Milk Cult's headquarters, she's not a victim. She's one of the organizers! You have to write how I outsmart her and free the girls.

At first I try to ignore her, but she just gets louder and louder until, with a sigh, I slip out of Connor's bed and pad down the hall into my old room. Taking a seat at the desk, I flip open my laptop and navigate to my work in progress. I start to write again, and holy shit, I'm reminded that Connor is a veritable dragon muse. The words fly out of me. And as the hours tick by, Alex double-crosses the woman in charge, pretending to be her friend and confidante, before flipping on her once she knows the location of the trafficked women. She frees them all with the help of Henrik Angel, who shows up just in time and still looks a hell of a lot like Connor. I end the book with Henrik stealing a kiss from Alex behind the police station and daring her to go on a real date with him. I smile as I type The End. The fans are going to love that.

I pop open my email and message my editor with the subject "Better late than never." I attach the manuscript along with a quick note and send it on its way. It's like a huge weight has been lifted off my shoulders. The sun is rising, light is streaming through the window, and I'm ready to celebrate. I'm going to crawl back into bed with Connor, make love for three days straight, only stopping to hydrate and eat gourmet meals we prepare together, and plan the next phase of our lives.

I'm closing my mail app when the text message bubble pops up on my dashboard and three dots appear next to Roman's icon. My stomach descends into the pits of hell. The bottomless pit. Two words.

Roman: *Be ready.*

Fear floods my system, my blood turning cold as ice.

Me: *What do you mean?*

There's no reply.

I read through our previous exchanges. *All in time.* That's how he'd replied when I asked why he hadn't done anything to get me back. Was he planning to come for me now?

"Fiona?" I look over my shoulder to find Connor standing there, rubbing his chest.

I swallow, my face feeling cold, as if all the blood has rushed from it. Slowly, because I can't speak, I raise my hand and point toward the chat box.

He strides to my side and reads the entire interaction. I don't even consider hiding it. He can feel my fear down the bond, for one, and I don't want to be the cause of anything happening to him if Roman does something stupid.

"I'm sorry," I say. "Zaire gave me the Wi-Fi password, and I sent it before…" He gives me a sharp look and I stop talking. *Before I realized I love you. Before you became my new center of gravity.*

A muscle in his jaw twitches. Fuck, he's angry. I feel it like my face is too close to the fire and I draw back, tears slipping from the corners of my eyes.

"I'm sorry," I squeak. Does he think I deceived him? That I truly want to be rescued by Roman?

He does a double take, then turns to me, taking my hands between his own. "I'm not angry at you, Fi, just the situation," he says softly, brushing my hair out of my eyes. "I told Zaire to give you the password."

"What?" I'm both relieved and annoyed at that revelation.

"I told him to give you the password so that you could see for yourself that Roman hadn't reported you missing. I also thought, since he wasn't responding to us, maybe he would respond to you. We still need the Order to answer for Lucy's death."

I gape. "You let me believe I tricked Zaire into giving me your supersecret Wi-Fi password, and all this time you meant for me to have it? How did you know I wouldn't use it to contact the police or the FBI?"

He sits on the bed beside me, his elbows resting on his thighs. "You've been here three weeks. The door has never been locked. Not a single minute since you arrived. If you walked to the end of the driveway, you'd find a road that would lead you to town. There's a phone, a landline in the kitchen you could have used at any time. If you'd asked Zaire for help, he'd have given it to you. You've never been my prisoner, Fi. I knew you wouldn't leave, and I knew you wouldn't contact the police the same way I knew last night would eventually happen. Your soul called to me. You called to me from that altar, and I answered you."

I think back. The door *was* never locked unless I locked it. The phone is exactly where he says it is, but I never tried to use it. I could have gone outside anytime I wanted to. I was left alone almost every afternoon and never tried to escape. I'm no damsel, and I wasn't waiting for Roman to save me. But I was waiting. Waiting for my mind to catch up to where my soul already was.

I meet those stormy blue eyes, now so familiar. My very own Viking dragon, complete with wings. "Well, your plan worked and it sounds like Roman is coming for me. What are we going to do?"

"You're safe here. I'll make sure of that. I'll call in a few of my brothers. We'll figure something out." He rises from the floor and kisses my head. "Try not to worry about it. How about pancakes? You want some pancakes?"

"Try not to worry about the psycho I almost married 'rescuing' me from the man I eternally love? I'm not sure that's possible," I say through a tightening throat.

He turns and starts for the door as if he's not worried

at all. "Pancakes, Fi. You are underestimating the power of carbs dressed in real creamery butter and maple syrup."

I rise to follow him into the kitchen, wanting to match his optimistic vibe, but a lead ball forms in my stomach at the memory of how Roman looked at me when he had me sign our marriage license. He's a man used to getting what he wants. Since the moment I arrived here, I suspected he'd come after me, if for no other reason than he hates to lose. If Roman says to be ready after all this time, I have no doubt he's got a plan, and I can't help but worry about all it might entail.

Chapter Twenty-Six

CONNOR

He can't have her back. I'll kill him before I let him put a hand on her. I pull my phone from my pocket and dial Seb.

"How good of you to check in, brother. How can I be of service for the next six days, eight hours, and thirty-seven minutes?"

"I need to call an emergency meeting of the four at my lodge. There's been a development."

"There has? Did you hear something from Donovan?"

"No."

"Then what's going on?"

I glance at Fiona over my shoulder. "I have reason to believe Roman is coming for Fiona. Soon. She needs protection."

"Protection." Seb quiets on the other end of the line. "Wasn't that the plan? He comes for her and we get our answers about Lucy and the peace accord."

"Not going to work anymore, Seb." My words rumble out, wrapped in a growl.

There's a long pause as Seb interprets every nuance of that growl. "You've got to be fucking kidding me. Already? Like you've sealed the deal?"

"One hundred percent sealed."

"Shiiit."

"Yeah."

"Fine. I'll wrap up what I'm working on and be there by tonight."

"Thanks. By the way, did Mason talk to you about the ring?"

"What ring?"

"Never mind. I'll tell you when you get here."

"Biting my nails in anticipation," Seb drawls.

"Wait! Can you call Ellison?" All I hear is a laugh and then the line goes dead. I guess that's a no.

"How many dragons are you inviting here?" Fiona sits down at the table in the nook, dressed and ready for the day in jeans and a sweater. I squelch my disappointment. I'm in the sweats I pulled on when I went into her room this morning, and I was really hoping to get her back in bed after breakfast. I still will, but every article of clothing on her looks like an obstacle to me.

I turn back to the mixing bowl and crack in an egg. "The rest of the four will be here tonight. They'll be able to assess the threat and keep you safe."

She's watching me intently, and all I feel down our bond is a sort of vague anxiety. She's worried.

"I promise he won't get his hands on you."

I bring the phone to my ear and dial Remus. A quick

rundown about what's going on, and he quietly agrees to join us. I heat the skillet while I beat the pancake batter and ring Ellison. I don't want to do it, but I'll do anything to keep Fiona safe. He's not as accommodating.

"I'm partner of a law firm, Connor. I can't take off at a moment's notice because your plan is finally coming together. Meet with him. Find out what we want to know and give him back his woman."

"She's not his woman. Not anymore," I snap, and that possessive growl resonates down the line.

"Fuuuck. Is that a mating growl? That sounds like a mating growl."

"Yeah."

"How long?"

"Recent."

"Fine." He sighs. "Count me in. You are one colossal pain in the ass, Aries."

"One you only have to deal with for another six days."

"Fucking bastard." He hangs up.

I toss my phone on the counter and pour a scoop of batter into the pan. "You want bacon?"

"Are we going to talk about this?" she says softly.

I do a double take and feel the tightness in my chest where the bond between us lives. The spiderweb that used to connect us is now a fiber-optic cable, and her rising apprehension is barreling into me. I pretend not to notice. "I can make sausage if you prefer."

"I'm not talking about breakfast meats." Her frown is a powerful cloud in an otherwise sunny room.

I turn back to the pan and flip the pancakes. "Then what are we talking about?"

She sighs. "You took me for a reason, and I can still serve that purpose."

Everything slows. My inner dragon is on high alert, and I grind my teeth against a growl before turning to her again. "Maybe we should talk about the breakfast meat."

She holds up a finger. "Don't you growl at me like that, Connor. Tell your dragon to back the fuck down because I am not having it."

My inner dragon recoils and buries its head under its paws. I don't roll over quite as easily though. This is too important. "How exactly do you intend to serve the purpose, Fi?"

"Trade me for the information you want."

"Fuck no!"

"Roman isn't going to hurt me. He thinks he's in love with me and has no idea I'm mated to you. If you allowed me to go with him, I could act like I've been your prisoner. I could send you information from the inside." She holds out her hands to me like it's the most natural thing in the world for her to suggest she pretend to want to go home with my mortal enemy.

I scoff and look at her through narrowed eyes. "And what happens when he wants to pick up where he left off? Will you marry him?"

"Of course not."

"What if he wants the honeymoon he's been denied?"

"I'll say I'm too traumatized."

I take a step toward her. "And how long will you stay with him and allow him to tend to your trauma?"

"As long as it takes."

"As long as it takes to what?"

"To find out as much as I can about the truth behind Lucy's murder. I'll stay until I know I've collected enough information to tip the war in your favor. I'll stay as long as it takes to ensure Vivian's safety and yours, and then I'll leave." Her eyes are sharp, confident, but her voice trembles slightly. The thought of doing what she's suggesting scares her, but in her mind she thinks it's for the best. She thinks she'd be doing it for me.

"Do you really think he'll just let you go?" I smell the pancakes burning and flip them onto a plate, turning off the burner. I leave them on the counter and take a step toward her, studying her with my full attention.

"I was his fiancée, Connor, not his hostage."

I don't miss the jab she takes at the circumstances of our meeting. "And you believe nothing has changed. He left you here for weeks. Why suddenly does he want you back? What if he's expecting you to supply him with the secrets you've learned here?"

She levels a deadly stare at me. "Unlike you, he can't read my mind, and I'm a very good liar. I'll make him believe me."

I'm in front of her chair, barely noticing that I've pushed the heavy walnut table aside with one hand to reach her. Our eyes lock, and when I speak again, my voice is menacingly low. "What will you do, Fiona? Will you let him touch you? Will you kiss him? Will you hold him and whisper that you love him?"

All the fire drains from her face, and her eyes fill with tears. It's probably new to her to feel what I'm feeling down the bond, the despair, the hopelessness at the mere thought of her enduring Roman's presence.

"Of course not," she rasps through a tight throat. "I'd never do that to you." She places both hands on my stomach, hooks her fingers into my waistband, and pulls me toward her.

I tuck a knuckle under her chin. "Do you think I could stop my dragon from coming for you? Even if it meant starting the very war I've been trying to avoid? Even if it meant my probable death? If I thought you were in harm's way for even a second, I'd come for you with teeth and claws and fire. I would not stop until I had you in my arms."

"Connor…"

I bring my face close to hers. "To be mated to a dragon is to have your finger on the trigger of a six-ton, fire-breathing weapon. I won't be able to stop myself, Fiona. Do you understand what I'm saying to you?"

She swallows, pulls my face down to hers, and then kisses me softly. "I understand." She places a hand over her heart as if it aches.

I slowly break a wicked smile. "Do you think that's enough? Shouldn't we make up after a fight?"

She answers my smile with her own. "What did you have in mind?"

My wings flare, and I sweep everything off the kitchen table, ignoring the shattering vase and the salt and pepper shakers clinking across the tile. I have her out of her chair and spun around in the next breath. I fold her over the table until her stomach is flat against the wood. Her hands land near her shoulders and I stretch them above her head, one and then the other, pinning them in place. My lips brush her ear as I lean over her and grind my erection against her ass. "I was thinking something like this."

The filthy look she shoots me over her shoulder makes my cock twitch. "I like this idea. We should make up more often."

I trail a hand down her spine to the waistband of her leggings. "Oh, I suspect there will be plenty of opportunities."

In a flurry of frantic movements, I strip her lower half and thrust into her before she has time to take her next breath. She's wet and ready, bucking against me. No way can I hold myself back when she's like that. I fuck her hard and fast, the table scraping across the floor as flesh slaps flesh. It's like we're both underwater and the only way to reach the surface is an orgasm. We're fucking like we need it to breathe.

She cries out. Her orgasm is a lightning strike that triggers my own. I collapse on top of her, resting my forehead on her back and bearing my weight on my elbows as we both catch our breath. After several minutes, she nudges me and I help her up.

"I'm covered in you again," she says, fluttering kisses along my jaw.

"As it should be." I fucking love it.

"I'm going to take another shower." She swipes her pants off the floor and moves toward the hallway. "And then I want those pancakes. I'm starving!"

Chapter Twenty-Seven

FIONA

By the time I'm cleaned up and finally eating Connor's pancakes, I'm absolutely ravenous. And sore. Every second of making love to Connor is worth it, but my lady bits have taken a beating. I shift in my seat a few times before putting another bite of pancake in my mouth.

"Is sex always going to be like this?" I squirm again. "Don't get me wrong. I love it. But every time with you has been fucking intense. I'm pretty sure we left bruises."

Connor's cheeks lift with his crooked smile. "I keep telling myself I'm going to take my time with you, but whenever I touch you, it's like…" He just shakes his head.

"A forest fire," I say. "All the kindling goes up at once and the heat is too overwhelming, impossible to control."

"Fire signs. I warned you." He laughs. "Next time. Next time we'll take it slow."

I bite my lip. "For the sake of my human flesh. Please."

He takes a sip of his coffee. "If you do have bruises, they won't last long. Dragon energy has healing powers. The longer you stay with me, the stronger you'll become. Human mates are rarely, if ever, sick, and when they do catch something it's usually because their dragon mate has been away."

I stop eating, the implications hitting me directly in the solar plexus. "Are you saying my fibromyalgia—?"

"No," he says quickly. "I'm sorry. I shouldn't have given you false hope. Dragon energy heals, but fibro isn't like an injury. It comes from within. My presence will help you recover faster and be more resilient to your triggers, but it won't cure you."

"Oh." I can't help the disappointment in my voice, but then he's a dragon, not a magic wand.

He reaches over and brushes a knuckle along my jaw. "Hey, there's not much data on this specific scenario. Maybe it will be better. Less frequent."

I frown slightly. "Better is good."

We're interrupted when then the front door opens and Bones bounds toward us. Zaire calls from the foyer, "Is everyone dressed? If I spend another minute outside with Bones, I'm going to need a tent."

"Yes!" we both call in unison.

Zaire glances between me and Connor as he loads his plate from the tower of remaining pancakes. "Please just wait until I'm done eating."

It's all I can do to stifle my laughter.

THE DRAGONS ARRIVE AT NINE, STARTING WITH A TALL, DARK, AND stylish man whom Connor introduces as Seb. I learn that Seb owns a record label with offices in New York and LA. Unlike Connor, who has a sort of rugged and wild quality about him, everything about Seb is highly groomed. Not a single dark hair betrays its marching orders, and the midnight-blue velvet jacket he wears falls smooth over a long, lean physique. There's something lethal about him for sure. The dragon occasionally manifests when his conversation with Connor becomes heated, but he's less stocky than my mate, more ballet dancer than bouncer, and from the moment he shakes my hand with a smile so smooth it gleams, I realize that physical grace extends to his personality.

Remus is something else altogether. The tattoo artist slips into the room like a shadow and gives me a quiet smile when we're introduced. His brown eyes twinkle with a kindness that belies the devil tattoo laughing at me from his biceps. And when he joins the others in the living room, he doesn't sit but lingers near the fire, easily overlooked next to Seb's flashy and illustrious presence.

Ellison arrives last, and I immediately feel the tension his presence causes Connor across our bond. It's easy to see why. His suit and tie are freshly pressed although it's late in the day, as if a wrinkle wouldn't dare to crease the man's clothes. He's uptight and formal. When he briefly shakes my hand, he seems hurried and a bit cool. Oddly, I don't get the sense that it's anything personal. My intuition tells me he's just an asshole to everyone, a villain in Versace, a demon to anyone who dares oppose him.

When he enters the room, the entire mood changes, from a happy reunion to a formal meeting. Seb starts to fidget. That muscle in Connor's jaw is jumping like someone plugged it in. And Remus, although I wouldn't have thought it possible, blends even more into the shadows beside the fire.

I cross my arms and pop out a hip. I've dealt with men like this before. Ellison Weber will not succeed in intimidating me. I station myself in the archway between the foyer and the living room, outside the circle of dragons, and wait for them to start.

"Maybe we should go somewhere more private," Ellison says, tipping his head in my direction. "After all, this is an official meeting of the four."

"Anything you tell me, she'll know anyway," Connor says. "She's my mate. She stays."

Glances are exchanged but no one challenges him. I stay put.

"Right," Seb eventually mumbles. "Congratulations."

Remus nods in my direction.

"Yes, congratulations," Ellison adds, brushing invisible lint from his sleeve. "As happy as I am for you, I presume this mating has caused some complications?"

Connor recaps what's happened and the message exchange on my laptop.

Ellison speaks first. "Let me get this straight. He's contacted her and told her to be ready. Nothing more? No instructions or time frame?"

"Exactly," Connor says.

"That doesn't give us much to go on," Ellison says. "My advice is to move her. Hide her somewhere else. Take her off-world if you have to."

Seb smooths his jacket. "He can't take her off-world, not without the Oracle's permission. And he can't get that permission while she's in seclusion."

"Roman has eyes everywhere. If he's traced the connection and knows she's here, he's probably watching the place. It's not safe to move her," Connor says.

"Sorry, Connor, but it's not just about keeping Fiona safe," Seb interjects, leaning forward in his chair with a gleam in his eye. "This is our opportunity to lure Roman or one of his cronies onto dragon property. If we do that, we can capture and question him. We want information. He has it. Fiona is the perfect worm to catch that fish. When will we have another chance like this?"

Connor tenses. He does not like them referring to me as bait, but he holds his tongue, although I sense the strain it takes to do so. Part of him must know that it's a good strategy, although every instinct in his body hates the idea.

Remus clears his throat, and they all turn to look at him. His hands are in the pockets of his dark jeans, his white T-shirt glowing in the firelight. "It's the best thing we've got. Stefan hasn't responded to our ultimatums, Donovan is MIA. If Roman tells her to be ready, then he's coming or sending someone for her soon. No one has died since Lucy, but everyone's on high alert. I'm hearing stories from dragons in my shop about humans getting real personal all of a sudden. There's something brewing, something we're not seeing."

"Real personal, like they're trying to determine if they're dragons?" I ask softly. Connor nods.

Ellison crosses his legs at the ankle. "The problem we're facing is that vague feelings of being targeted are not a violation of the peace accord. And we still have no proof that Lucy was killed by the Order. What we *do* know, what the Order has evidence of..." He points at Connor. "...is that you stole the man's fiancée. Legally, we broke the accord. Luring him here and capturing him isn't going to go over well."

Ellison's tone isn't unkind but it is terse. I get the sense that he's simply interpreting the letter of the law as it pertains to the accord, but everyone, especially Connor, bristles.

Connor waves a hand through the air dismissively. "You know damn well that if they didn't kill Lucy, we would have been given an explanation by now. They've gone dark because they're guilty."

Seb raises both hands. "All of this is moot. It is what it is. We're here, and as Remus suggests, we've no better option. Now that Connor has mated her, we need to protect her, and if Roman is dumb enough to step foot on dragon property, it would be stupid for us not to seize the opportunity, accord or no accord."

"This would be a great time for the Oracle to come out of seclusion," Remus mumbles.

Ellison groans. "So, what are we looking at logistically? Should we take shifts? A few days each? I'll need to work around my cases." Ellison pulls his phone from his pocket and starts thumbing through his calendar.

"You'll stay as long as it takes!" Connor barks. "I don't give a fuck about your law firm. You're a warrior first. This is her life we're talking about."

"And the peace accord between humans and dragons," Ellison retorts like he believes everyone in the room is losing sight of that fact. "We're going to protect her, Connor, but unlike your restaurant, I don't have a staff that can take over all my cases in my absence. There are practicalities—"

I push off the wall and take a step toward them, spreading my hands. "Why don't I just respond to his message and find out when he's coming?" I offer, because I sure as hell can't stand by while the tension continues to grow between these two. Connor's in charge, and if it was up to him these three would be guarding me twenty-four seven. But I'm not their only priority. Each of them has a life outside the brotherhood as well as an entire species to protect.

Connor growls, the bond between us going taut with his annoyance.

When all four dragons are looking at me, I say, "I can ask Roman for more details. Tell him to hurry. I mean, if you want to use me as bait, it won't hurt to chum the water."

"You'll have to be careful how you word it. He'll be suspicious," Remus says.

I shrug. "Let's just do it now." I turn to go get my laptop and Connor is behind me, following me into the hall and all the way down to my room where we left it.

"What are you doing?" he asks.

"Going to get my laptop."

"You know damn well that's not what I mean."

I grab the laptop off my desk. "Then what do you mean?"

"You're involving yourself. Putting yourself in danger."

I roll my eyes. "Roman is not going to jump through the screen, Connor. All I'm doing is messaging him back."

He grinds his teeth. "I don't like it."

I push past him. "It will be over soon."

I stride back into the living room with my dragon mate hovering behind me and lift the screen. After logging in, I navigate to the message that says to be ready. With four dragons looking over my shoulder, I type: *Please, Roman. I can't stay a prisoner here any longer. I'm going crazy. Please tell me you're coming soon.*

"How's that?" I ask.

Remus rubs his chin. "Tell him you don't know how long you'll have access to Messenger. If you don't respond, it's because you've been caught or are dead."

"Good idea." I add that to my message and hit Send.

We wait. The three dots appear.

"Jesus, that's fast," Seb says.

"It's his personal phone."

The message comes through: *Can you reach the southern border of the property at 4pm tomorrow?*

I'll try, I respond.

"Fuck," Connor says behind me.

"What? What's on the southern border?"

"The lake. And it'll be the damned hardest to defend," he says.

"Why?" I ask.

Ellison gives me my answer. "We need for Roman, or whoever he sends for you, to touch ground on dragon property in order to be justified in taking them prisoner. Water is neutral territory. If he comes by boat, we can't do a thing unless he docks and comes inland."

"Hmm. Then for this to work, I'll have to lure him to shore somehow." I'm about to share some ideas I have to do just that when my body is yanked out of my seat and thrown over Connor's shoulder.

"Meeting adjourned," he grits out.

Chapter Twenty-Eight

CONNOR

No one says a word as I haul Fiona to our bedroom, but the look Ellison shoots me is pejorative to say the least. His eyes roll toward the ceiling. I don't give a fuck if he thinks I'm wasting his time. Some things are more important. I close and lock the door behind us before lowering her from my shoulder.

"What was that about?" She shoots daggers at me, hands on her hips.

"You're still not getting this." I reach for the hem of her sweater and start to pull it over her head, but she stops me.

"Oh, I get it. You think just because we're mated that you can control me. You think you own me now. Well, I have news for you, Aries." She says my sign through her teeth, like my possessiveness is strictly due to my star sign's propensities, and pokes a finger into my chest. "No one decides for me but me."

Rage heats my blood. "So you'd endanger yourself just to prove your independence from me? This has nothing to do with me being an Aries, Fi. It has to do with me loving you. What kind of man would I be if I dangled you for Roman to snap at? Why would you want me to treat you like that?"

She waves a hand. "No one is dangling me. We're devising a plan. It's not like I'll be anywhere alone. There are four of you to keep me safe."

"I don't trust him anywhere near you. If he touches you, he dies." No part of me would hesitate to separate Roman's head from his body if he came within an inch of her. I hate the fucker because he's a leader of the Order, but when I think about his hands on her, my intentions go beyond hate. I want to rip his throat out.

"Oh, look at you, throwing threats around like he can hear you. Roman doesn't care about your threats. If he did, he would have already responded to your ultimatum. The only person he seems willing to talk to is me. So if you want answers about Lucy's death, you'll swallow your pride and let me help you!" Her voice is sharp, her eyes full of fire.

I stalk toward her, my wings flared. "You want to help me."

She backs up a step and then another.

"You think you can fool Roman into believing you need him? Into believing you *want* to be rescued?"

Her back hits the wall, and I bring my face as close to hers as I can without touching her. Close enough that my world is her scent. Even now, she wants me. She aches for me.

I lower my voice. "You think he won't know the moment he lays eyes on you that you're mine? A blind man could see it. One look in my direction, one brush of our hands, and he'll know."

"So we'll stay apart," she says weakly.

"Oh, but he'll know the moment he makes eye contact with you. He'll try to find himself in the depths of those enchanting amber eyes of yours, but all he'll see is me." My lips are so close to hers that we're sharing the same air, but I won't kiss her, won't close that space when she stopped me before. This time she has to initiate it. "I can't risk losing you, Fi. My life would be ruined if he got his hands on you. I don't want to end up like my sister, destined to walk this earth without the one person who makes it worth living."

Her eyes are trained on my lips, and I watch her throat bob on a swallow. "Okay."

"Okay?"

"I'll stay behind. I'll stay in the house while you guys intercept Roman. I don't want him touching me either. But we need to make sure we get Vivian back, Connor. He's still got her. What will he do with her when he realizes he's lost me? She'll lose all value. From what you've told me, they aren't the type of people to issue an apology and put her in a cab."

I brace my weight on an elbow against the wall above her head, leaning in. "Consider it a priority."

She licks her bottom lip, and then she breaks. Leaning forward, she captures my mouth with her own. A moment ago, my blood was heated by anger. Now my temperature rises for a much more pleasurable reason.

Her hands land on my stomach, then go to work on the buttons of my red flannel.

Again I reach for the hem of her sweater, and this time she raises her arms above her head, encouraging me to take it off. I oblige. I fold in my wings, then take off the flannel and the T-shirt I'm wearing beneath it. She's already working on my belt, my fly.

I'm surprised when she hooks a finger into my belt loop and leads me over to the bed. She sits on the mattress in front of me and tugs at my pants. I help her take off the rest of my clothes. I'm hard as fuck, which seems to be a given around her, and I've barely stood back up before she's taking my cock in her mouth, sucking me deep.

She gazes up at me with raw possessiveness in her eyes as she wraps her lips around my cock. That look is warranted. She owns me, in every sense of the word. My fingers land in her hair, my hips thrusting gently until I hit the back of her throat. Her eyes fill with lust and she moans, drawing back and taking me in her hand.

"Whose reflection do you see in my eyes right now, Connor?"

"Mine," I growl.

"As it should be." She echoes my earlier words back at me and swirls her tongue around the head. The feel of her warm mouth on my cock along with the way she's looking at me turn on every light in my house. My dragon is purring, my hands are in her hair, and the excitement down our bond has her hollowing her cheeks and finding a rhythm. This connection between us, it's a feedback loop. She feels my pleasure and gives it all back to me. She winds me tighter and tighter.

Her teeth scrape against my skin.

That's all I can take. I empty myself down her throat, watching her swallow me down like she relishes every drop. When she finally falls back on her elbows, the smile she gives me is deliciously dirty.

"Creator blessed, Fiona, I'm going to lose my mind loving you." I reach for her pants and start pulling them down her legs. "It's like I've finally found the missing half of myself. For the first time, I'm whole and understand who I am in the universe." I shake my head. "Fuck, I'm not making any sense."

"I'll tell you when you're not making sense. Everything you've said makes sense to me. I feel the same way."

I finally get her naked and spread her knees. "Touch yourself. Show me what you do when you're thinking of me."

She reaches down between her legs and starts working her clit. Fuck. There's no hesitation. No shame. Her hand skims up to her breast. And I watch her pleasuring herself while she thinks of me, projecting memories and fantasies into my mind that make my wings twitch. She arches off the bed as her pleasure crests.

I'm over her. In her. Moving with her. Joining in her pleasure in a slow, sensual dance, my only goal to draw out the ecstasy she's experiencing. This time, finally, I'm unhurried. I dress her in soft kisses to her inner elbow, the crook of her underarm, the underside of her jaw, the tips of her fingers. I explore every inch of her until she's writhing again and I give her exactly what she needs.

Chapter Twenty-Nine

FIONA

When I wake the next morning, I can hear Connor and the others talking in the kitchen. I can't hear what they're saying, but his mood feels calm and determined down our bond. I take that as a good sign.

After a quick shower, I pull on yesterday's clothes because I still haven't moved my things into Connor's room and then make my way down the hall to where I was staying before. I run into Zaire along the way. He does the little bow thing he always does when he sees me and smiles bright as the sun.

"Good morning, Ms. Fiona. Would you like me to move your things into the primary suite? I presume you'll be staying in there from now on?"

I nod, my cheeks warming with the admission. "Yes please."

"I'll have it done by this evening."

"No rush."

He gives another little bow and advances down the hall. Once I'm changed, I join Connor in the dining room where the dragons have gathered over a breakfast suitable for a small army. Remus has a stack of sausages on his plate that could feed a family of four, and Seb is downing a plate of what looks like a dozen eggs. I select a croissant and some bacon and take a seat at the table.

"So what's the plan today?" I ask when they all grow conspicuously quiet.

Connor speaks up. "Remus and Ellison will man the southern border, while Seb and I patrol the rest of the property in case Roman tries to get creative. Once one of us has visual confirmation of his arrival, we'll converge, lure him onto the property, and capture him. You'll stay here with Bones and Zaire."

"How do you plan to lure him onto the property?"

Remus stops eating long enough to call out, "Roman! Roman! I'm here. I need your help!" He sounds *exactly* like me. Not like an impression. Like a recording.

"That's incredible," I say.

Seb grins. "A Gemini talent that comes in useful now and again."

"Seems like you have it figured out." I take a bite of my croissant. It's for the best that I'm not involved. After last night, I know I'd only be a distraction to Connor. The last thing I want is to be the reason he's injured. Or worse.

"What's the plan for you and Connor now that you're mated?" Ellison asks, sounding somewhat bored. He's focused on his plate like he's only asking to be polite.

"I'm going to move into his place. My lease is up anyway."

"Sounds like a recipe for mated bliss," Ellison says, and I can't miss the bitterness in his voice. He looks older than Connor, and I wonder if the mating sickness is getting harder for him. I wonder if his abrasiveness, at least in part, is fueled by jealousy.

I smile sweetly and say, "I certainly hope so."

Seb seems to notice the tension rising in the room and, just like before, defuses it by changing the subject. "Connor, about the ring Mason found…"

"Did you get a chance to talk to him?"

"Briefly, on the way over. He still has it in his safe, but none of us can touch it. Exactly what do you want me to do with it?"

Connor scratches his jaw. "We need to find a witch who can analyze the magic. We know they use dragon blood, but the other ingredients in the spell are a mystery. If we could find someone who could reverse engineer the spell, maybe we could find a way to protect our people against it."

"And you think I can find a witch why?" Seb asks.

Connor shrugs. "You work in the music industry. You know a lot of people. A lot of really odd people."

"Okay. I know *of* one," Seb says, as if he's reluctant to admit it. "I've never actually met her in person, but I'm aware of her from Full Throttle."

"Sorry, what's Full Throttle?" I ask.

"My record label," Seb says. "She's the lead singer for a band called Raven's Wish. We've been following their growth on social. Honestly, I don't know if her witchy vibe is just a marketing ploy or the real thing."

"Wait, I know her," Remus says. "I tattooed a tree of life on her calf at Venomous Ink. She told me she's been a practicing witch for almost fifteen years, since she was in high school. Her mind was strong, and I could sense her power. I think she sensed mine too because she told me during one of our sessions to stay out of her head." He gives a quiet laugh.

"Do you think you could approach her about the ring?" Connor asks, directing the question at both of them.

Remus shakes his head. "I have a very strict privacy policy for my clients. I don't even keep their contact information after the job is done."

Seb groans. "I might be able to use my position to facilitate a meeting, but it's a delicate situation. Honestly, from what I've heard, Raven's Wish isn't ready for the big time. Leading her on to get what we want could backfire, and I don't need to tell you how bad it would be to have a witch as an enemy."

Connor grins. "So use that persuasive Taurus charm and convince her to help us with no strings attached."

Seb shovels in another bite of eggs and groans. "Fine. I'll come up with some ruse to get her to do what we want. Let me think on it."

"You could just be honest with her," I suggest. "Instead of trying to manipulate her, maybe just ask her for her help."

Seb stops eating, his fork poised over his plate, and

looks at me like I'm glowing green. He scoffs. "Never work," he mumbles.

I don't argue with him.

The rest of the morning goes by quickly, the dragons acting like they're preparing for war. After breakfast, Connor moves the table and rolls back the carpet in the dining room to reveal a trapdoor. Inside is an arsenal of weapons the likes of which I've never seen before. Guns, daggers, and other weapons are doled out and passed around. I learn they don't need communication equipment thanks to the dragons' abilities to communicate psychically. The guys all change into black leather armor designed for fighting. Even Ellison, who takes on an entirely different vibe when he's not wearing a designer suit.

I picture Roman rowing up to shore in a rented fishing boat and being absolutely annihilated by these four. I know that's not how it will happen. And I know Roman is more dangerous than he looks. But what could be more lethal than four fire-breathing dragons?

At three, all four of them head out to begin their patrol of the property, leaving me, Bones and Zaire behind. Worry for Connor has me pacing the floors. Finally, I grab my laptop and settle into one of the velvet chairs near the fire in the living room, hoping to distract myself with some writing. Bones curls up next to me. I can hear Zaire humming to himself as he works in the kitchen. It's all very peaceful, but my muscles are tense, ready. I can hardly concentrate. I wonder again how all of this will impact Vivian.

I've written my next Alex Rogue pitch when a notification pops up from my editor. She loved *Milkmaid*. They're moving forward with it. I give an internal squeal. I can't wait to tell Connor. I'm back, and he's the one who got me here. He's the one who inspired me. I do a little dance in my chair.

Then another bubble pops up. Roman's chat. I glance at the clock. Four p.m. sharp. Is he texting me from the boat?

All it says is "Stay down."

Bullets rain through the glass windows at the back of the house and I hit the floor. Bones barks viciously at something, but I can't see what because I'm flat on my belly behind the chair. I abandon the laptop and peek around the base, through Bones's paws, into the foyer and adjacent hall. I gasp when I see Roman, gun in hand, step over Zaire's fallen body, eyes locked on me. Bones attacks. Roman doesn't hesitate.

I scream.

But Roman fires and Bones falls, whimpering, to the floor.

I can't breathe. I stare and stare as Roman walks right up to me, his black eyes guarded and inaccessible, and hooks a hand around my biceps, pulling me to my feet. How is it that I never noticed how empty his expression is, how waxy, as if his entire countenance is a mask? The corner of his mouth tugs up as he silently ushers me out the back door and onto a helicopter that seems to come out of nowhere and land on the back lawn. We're on it and in the air before I can process that Bones and Zaire were shot.

He buckles me in, then kisses me hard on the mouth. "Hello, wife."

Chapter Thirty

CONNOR

"*It's a trick!*" Seb yells inside my head as the boat we've all been watching approach the dock on the southern border, abruptly veers and speeds away from shore. "*That's not Roman.*"

We know we've been duped when we hear the spray of bullets and the sound of a chopper in the distance. Fear swarms down my bond with Fiona and knocks the breath from my lungs. He's come for her, but not here, not where he said, not where his lookalike lured us.

Fuck, that's why he chose the southern border. It's the farthest from the lodge, more than a mile of wooded acreage. I can run fast, but I won't make it in this form. I shift, exploding into the sky, beating my black wings as fast as they will carry me.

I see the helicopter, Fiona strapped into one of the seats, looking absolutely terrified. Roman stands braced in the open side door with his crossbow glowing blue and aimed at me. In that moment, I don't give a shit if I live or die. I only care about Fiona, about saving her from whatever horrors the bastard has in store for her. I fly faster. I can't blow fire for fear of hurting her, but if I can catch the helicopter in my claws or teeth—

A blue bolt flies from Roman's crossbow. I bank right, but it pierces my lower wing. I roar and speed faster toward my mate, my mind going dark. All my human words melt away, replaced by pure instinct. Another bolt flies. I roll out of the way but I'm hit, the point imbedding deep in my chest, near my left shoulder. Pure agony tears through me, the icy poison branching through my scales. But I don't stop. A crack forms in my consciousness, and a high-pitched sound bleeds in. A scream. Fiona's scream.

I see her behind Roman, her hands over her mouth, her eyes red. I'm not *hearing* her scream. I'm feeling it down our bond. Fuck.

Roman takes aim again, his soulless eyes locking onto mine, that crossbow of his leveled at my head. I attempt an evasive dive, but my injured wing is completely locked from the spreading poison and won't move. The bolt flies. My eyes widen as I accept that this could be the end.

A flash of green comes from my right, and I'm knocked out of the way as the bolt flies right through where my left eye had been. Talons grip me, and I tumble through the sky, carried by another dragon, one with dark green scales. *Ellison.* My brain is producing words again.

Yeah, it's me, fucker, he thinks back to me. *You're hurt, but I've got you.*

We land behind the lodge and shift back to our human forms. His transformation is graceful. Mine is not. The entire left side of my body feels like barbed ice is being forced through my veins. I roar and try to rise. I have to get to Fiona!

Ellison takes my hand, his eyes still slitted like his dragon's. "Seb already called Morwyn for Bones and Zaire. He's on his way. I've got you. I've got you, brother."

Those are the last words I hear before the pain is too much and darkness swallows me whole.

Chapter Thirty-One

FIONA

Roman curses and lowers that crossbow of his, the way it glows blue reminding me of its dragon-killing magic. I gasp in horror as it morphs back into his Order ring. At least two of those bolts hit Connor. Is he dead? Frantically, I search for the bond deep within me. Nothing. No. No. No. No. But then, as if someone throws a switch, I feel him. Pure agony pours into me and I have to white-knuckle the seat to keep from curling in on myself. Connor's hurt, but he's alive. My breath comes in pants as Roman sits down beside me and buckles in, thumbing that deadly ring.

"You look pale," he says through his teeth, and I know one thing for certain in that moment: I absolutely can't allow him to know what Connor means to me. "Something upsetting you?"

I see the question for what it is—a test. "Of course I'm upset!" I grab his hand. "I've been a prisoner for weeks, and a dragon almost ate our helicopter. Are you sure it's gone?"

He studies me for what feels like a very long time. "It won't be back. Those bolts I shot it with are poisonous. With any luck, it's already dead."

I look away from him, out the side of the helicopter, to hide my eyes. I'm fighting back tears with everything in me.

He threads his fingers into mine. "Relax, Fiona. I have you now. We're going home."

I force a grateful smile onto my face and then hug him like he's my hero.

Alex appears in my head, slow clapping. *An Oscar-worthy performance. Keep it up. Connor's going to need all the information you can obtain while you're undercover.*

Days ago, I offered to allow Roman to take me. I wanted Connor to use me as a spy for the Zodiac Brotherhood. This wasn't what Connor wanted for me, and I wouldn't be here by choice. But now that I am in this position, I need to play the part until Connor finds a way to rescue me. He's not dead. I can feel him on the other end of our bond. And once he's healed, he will come for me. Nothing will keep him from me.

The helicopter lands at a small, private airport, and Roman leads me by the hand to his jet. I've flown with him before, but everything feels different now. We buckle in, and I go to work on plan *Make Roman Believe I Love Him.*

"What took you so long to find me?" I load my shaking voice with all the fragility of a damsel in distress.

He sighs. "Nothing about the property where he was

holding you is connected with dragons. Once you were able to get a message to me, I traced the IP address of that computer you were using and then narrowed the location down to that lodge in Wyoming. It took a few days to put together a plan. I knew if you were getting messages out, he was monitoring them. Sending them in the wrong direction worked like a charm."

I fight to keep the sadness and guilt from my expression. Connor gave me the WiFi password so that I could see that Roman hadn't reported me missing, and what did I do with that information but immediately message Roman. In doing so, I gave him a map to our door. Now that he knows about the lodge, Connor won't ever be able to use it as a safe house again. "But why didn't you just negotiate with them from the start?"

He doesn't answer me. The stewardess comes by and hands him a gin and tonic. She asks me what I want, and I say water. Alcohol is out of the question. I have to keep my mind clear.

"She'll have a chardonnay," he tells her.

The stewardess nods and brings me a chardonnay. No water. An urge to argue and ask again for water rises in me. Being with Connor has awakened a fire in me that desperately wants to burn. But old Fiona would never challenge Roman, and my life and my future with Connor depends on me proving I am the docile, obedient creature I was on that altar.

"Thank you," I say sweetly, as if I couldn't possibly expend the mental energy to know what I'd like to drink.

"Where's your ring?" he asks, noticing my bare finger.

I glance down at my hands. "He took it. I never saw my wedding dress again either after the first day."

"Did he"—his eyes trace me from head to toe—"spoil you?"

Spoil me. If he only knew. "Do you mean did he rape me? No."

"Good. Dragons can be brutes. You're lucky to be alive."

I sip my wine. "But Roman, if you knew that, why didn't you negotiate for me?" I wipe under my perfectly dry eyes and make my voice sound small and upset. "The dragon kept asking me about the Order and about a woman named Lucy Vale. I didn't know what to tell him. I thought he was going to hurt me."

Roman's eyes go darker still. "I told you, Fiona, I do not negotiate with dragons. As for the Saint's Order, I planned to tell you everything you needed to know once we were wed. It's sensitive information. You of all people know the importance of keeping a secret society secret."

"Of course I do, but—"

His phone chimes, and he raises it to his ear, mumbling a greeting as he unbuckles himself and disappears through a door to his office area. I don't see him again until we begin our descent.

It's late by the time we land and take a private car to a mansion on the coast of Rhode Island that Roman calls home. Although *home* is a strong word for one of over a dozen places around the globe where he sometimes stays. I once had dinner at his flat in Paris, but I've never been here. I now know that all those places are in the Order registry. If a dragon sets foot on this property, the

Order has the right to capture or kill them. That won't stop Connor though. Nothing will stop him.

The hair on the back of my neck stands on end when Roman guides me directly to a bedroom. "This is our room," he says. "Shower. I'll have the butler lay out fresh clothes for you. Then we can talk over dinner. I know you must have so many more questions for me." His gaze turns dark. "And I have a few for you."

I look around the room, at his things on the bureau, and ask, "Will we be staying together then?" We've never slept in the same bed before. He always claimed he wanted to wait until we were married.

He brushes my hair back from my face and tucks it behind my ear, and I smile wider to keep from flinching at his touch. "Premarital relations are forbidden by the Order. They make us vulnerable." I try to disguise the relief that I feel at those words. "However..." His fingers trail along my neck, down to my collarbone, and dip between my breasts. "I think after everything, we've waited long enough. Our not being legally married is a technicality that I plan to rectify as quickly as possible. We will share a bed."

I swallow and nod, my anxiety raging again. If it shows on my face, he doesn't ask me about it.

"Don't be long," he commands. I breathe a sigh of relief when he turns on his heel and leaves, whispering something to a maid who stations herself in the hall outside the room.

Slowly I close the bedroom door, shutting her out. I open one of the drawers. My breath trembles as I take in a tray of watches and cuff links. The enormous walk-in closet is full of his things. This is *his* room. A room he regularly uses by the looks of it. It stinks of him.

God help me, this is worst-case scenario. He wants me to stay in his room with him. Wants to make our marriage legal as quickly as possible. Wants to have sex. I swallow hard and try not panic at the thought.

I go into the bathroom and start the shower, stripping out of the clothes Connor bought me, the soft, warm and comfortable clothes that fit me exquisitely despite him not knowing my size. What I need is a plan. But after twenty minutes in the shower, I still don't have any ideas of how to get away from Roman and back to Connor.

Worse, when I try to feel my mate through the bond, I can't anymore. There's just... nothing. I tell myself it's the distance, or maybe he's unconscious. I refuse to consider any other scenario.

I shut the water off and wrap a towel around myself, finding the clothes the butler left for me in the adjoining dressing area. It's a cocktail dress and heels, because of course the thing you want to wear to a late dinner at home after traveling all night is a cocktail dress. I roll my eyes. The bodice is beaded, tight and unforgiving, strapless with a short, ruffled skirt that looks like it will end halfway down my thighs. I slide my feet into a pair of shoes with red soles and tall, skinny heels. I hope to heaven I can even make it to the dining room in these things.

When I finally clop out of the room, there's a woman in a black maid's uniform waiting for me. She shows me to the empty dining room and commands me to sit.

"The master will be with you shortly," she says as she fills the wineglass next to my water goblet, which is blessedly full.

I wait, sipping my water, for five minutes, then ten, then fifteen. I'm both grateful for the time away from him and annoyed. Every minute I sit here, my anxiety ratchets a notch higher. I'm starving and uncomfortable. I'm considering collapsing out of the chair and feigning illness to gain some power over this situation when he finally walks in.

He chucks me under the chin with his knuckle, then turns my face to the left and right as if he's admiring a doll. His gaze rakes down over the bodice of the dress. "You look lovely, Fiona. It will be a relief to put this entire thing behind us, wouldn't you agree?"

Because a person who's been held hostage for more than three weeks should immediately bounce back? I force the smile again. "I'll try, but I might need time to recover." I swallow hard, allowing my hands to tremble. If I can milk the trauma of my ordeal to maintain distance between us, it might give Connor enough time to come for me.

"Oh, I think the best thing for you is to pick up exactly where you left off." He taps my nose and then makes his way to the other end of the table, lowering himself into his chair.

"Speaking of, where is Vivian? I haven't seen or heard from her since the wedding day. I thought you said she was with you."

He scowls and unfolds his napkin, resting it across

his lap before reaching for a dinner roll. "Let's not ruin our first dinner at home with talk of Vivian."

"What do you mean, ruin dinner? Is she okay?" I'm a good actress, but I can't hide how upset I feel. If something's happened to her, it's entirely my fault.

He smiles in a way that chills something deep within me. "Perfectly fine and somewhere safe."

I nod and sip my water, forcing down the rising tide of apprehension and anxiety that almost overcomes me. Roman is a psychopath. I don't believe for a second that Vivian is perfectly fine. But I do sense she's alive. That's the important thing.

"I was also wondering if you had my purse and phone and things. I left it all in the dressing room at the château." It seems like the obvious first thing someone would ask for.

"We can check with the staff, but I'm sure there's nothing we can't replace. You won't need those things for a while anyway." He taps his thumb on the table twice, and a servant rushes into the room with the salads.

"Is that some kind of signal, the thumb tapping?" I ask casually, honestly perplexed by it. The woman flees like the dining room is on fire.

"You'll find the staff here is highly trained and serves me without question or hesitation."

Connor treated his dog better. I lift my fork and push my salad around my plate. No way can I eat. Not with my stomach churning like it is. Roman, however, has no problem enjoying his dinner and proceeds with neat, precise, efficient bites.

I gather my courage and ask, "If we're going to be

living here, can someone take me to my apartment tomorrow so that I can box up my things?" *And I can use the opportunity to run and hide.*

Roman stops chewing to look at me with flat, dead eyes. "That depends on how quickly we resolve our little problem."

"Problem? What problem?" I set down my silverware but toy with it and my napkin.

He sighs. "It's the oddest thing, Fiona. I watched you sign that marriage license, so imagine my surprise when the officiant informed me your signature wasn't legal."

I sip my wine, playing dumb even though I know exactly why it isn't legal. Flaring my eyes, I ask, "Why's that?"

He looks me over, seeming to weigh my words and expression. "You signed Alex Rogue instead of Fiona Morrow."

A rebellious laugh barrels out of me before I can rein it in, and I hope to God I haven't made a grave mistake. When Roman pressured me to sign that paper, something of my younger self bubbled to the surface. I signed Alex's name as an act of defiance. But Roman won't see the humor in that. "I'm so sorry," I say quickly. "I often sign her name in books and to get into her character. I was nervous that morning. Must not have been paying attention, but then you weren't either, considering you didn't notice."

He doesn't laugh, but a tiny, wicked smile turns his lips. "Easily rectified," he says. "I have new paperwork, and a judge—a personal friend of mine—lined up to perform the ceremony tomorrow."

"Tomorrow?" My brows pinch together, panic rising in my throat. "After everything that's happened, we can't possibly have a replay of our wedding tomorrow. Having a new dress designed and fitted will take weeks, and then there's renting the venue, the flowers, and the guest list. It can't be done." *Not to mention I have no intention of marrying you.*

"No wedding will be necessary. We'll just formalize the marriage and put this entire thing behind us." He raises his glass of wine to me in a silent toast and then drinks.

I draw a shaky breath. "You don't want a wedding anymore?"

"No."

"But a wedding like the one we planned has been a dream of mine since I was a little girl."

"And you had it, before you were abducted. It doesn't matter anyway. What matters is that we are legally wed as soon as possible."

I tilt my head and giggle lightly to diffuse the growing tension I can feel coming from his side of the table. "But why? It's not as if we've had a lengthy engagement. What's the rush?"

He taps his thumb on the table again, and the staff rushes in as if they've been hovering on starting blocks just out of sight. They take our salad plates and replace them with a main course of rare leg of lamb on a bed of vegetables and couscous. "Because I wish to be married to you." He says it like no other explanation is needed. "I've waited long enough."

The fire in me starts to rise again. I know it now for

what it is—a part of me that I squashed after the acci-dent. I was so beaten down and defeated I would have gone along with anything to ease the pain, and I did before. When I met Roman, I was an empty husk of a person, moving through the world like a robot. Roman loved that about me, loved having a Barbie he could dress up and control. And I didn't see how sick it actually was until Connor healed me. Not just of my writer's block, but of the remnants of my grief. Connor reignited that part of my soul I'd put out after Marion died. I don't ever want that fire extinguished again.

"Marriage is supposed to be about what both people want, and I want it to be special, Roman. Besides, I need the time to recover from everything that's happened. Maybe I should talk to a psychotherapist first. I don't want the trauma of my experience to come between us in our marriage." *Another excellent reason to delay until my mate can get me out of here.*

"It will be special. How could it not be?" He meticu-lously cuts off a perfect square of lamb and brings it to his mouth. "And as for your... trauma..." He scoffs as if he doesn't believe in the word. "I'll make certain you are safe from this day forward. The best thing for you is to fall into a regular routine. Our marriage will give you a purpose. You won't have time to wallow in those feelings."

Jesus, he's a psychopath. My palms start to sweat, and my pulse pounds as every door to freedom is slammed in my face. I rack my brain. There must be something I can use to stall this thing, some card I haven't played. I take a deep breath and it comes to me.

"If we're getting married tomorrow, I'll want Vivian there." He scowls across the table at me. "It's nonnegotiable. You have to allow me to see her tonight so I can ask her to witness for us again."

He sighs in annoyance but takes in the determined set of my jaw. "Very well. After dinner, I will take you to Vivian."

A bit of tension eases from my shoulders. If he's promising to take me to Vivian, she must be close and unharmed. I pick up my fork, and this time I take a bite of the lamb, proving myself to be the appreciative fiancée. It's flavorless compared to the meals Connor made me this month. But I chew and swallow.

"Now I have some questions for you, Fiona."

My stomach clenches, threatening to expel the small amount of food I've put in it. "Yes?"

"How many dragons did you meet during your captivity?"

"Just one," I answer immediately. "And his servant and his dog."

"What was his name?"

"He called himself Valentine."

"What did he look like?"

"Dark hair, thin. He changed his appearance though. It was never the same."

We continue like this, him asking and me saying the exact opposite of the truth.

When he finishes his questions, I say, "He told me a bunch of things about the Saint's Order, but I didn't know what to believe. Can you explain its purpose, Roman?"

His voice is soft but lethal when he answers. "The Order is the antidote to those secret societies you write about in your thrillers. That thing that took you, if we had our way, we'd end them all."

"You'd kill all the dragons? Sorry, this is all so new to me. The dragon who held me told me the basics but it was so confusing. Why do you want them dead?"

His brow lifts. "After being his prisoner for so long, I'm surprised you'd need to ask. They're brutish and wild, adhering to no rules or propriety. A world ruled by dragons would be a world of chaos with ever-shifting axes of power. The Saint's Order maintains stability. Our members have maintained a level of wealth that transcends generations. People like you—ordinary people— you play the game. You work your way from pawn to knight to rook to queen, and you think if you have enough of the things you desire that you've won, but the members of the Saint's Order have been ordained by God to own the board and all its pieces. No one makes a move we didn't decide for them to make. Dragons, if they have their way, would have each person designing their own set of rules, or perhaps not playing at all, simply existing and being happy about it. It's ludicrous. They are the creation of the devil."

God, he's sick. What a twisted way to look at the world. I nod, because I sense that's what he expects me to do, but my mind keeps circling back to the fact that he pursued me. He was going to marry me. And I can't stop myself from asking the obvious question. "You've always known then, that I'm just a pawn. Why did you pursue me? Why ask me to marry you?"

He takes a sip of his wine. "You are no pawn, Fiona. You are a queen. A stunning beauty. You are exactly what I deserve."

My disbelief must show on my face because he raises an eyebrow. "You don't believe you're beautiful? You are. Exceptionally. But you're correct to assume that I'm not the type of man to fall for a pretty face alone. Initially, I sought you out because you also have something I want."

My head starts to pound. He sought me out. In other words, our meeting was no coincidence. "I don't know what you mean."

"Oh, but you do," he says. "As it so happens, you own a very important piece of land, one that used to belong to the Order until one of our members died unexpectedly and his family sold it within hours of his passing."

An icy chill spider-walks up my spine. I shake my head like I don't know what he's talking about.

"A small but important property. One with unique qualities that must stay in our society's hands. One that would also be mine if we were married. We were supposed to be married by now."

Slowly my brain sifts through the timeline. It never made sense to me, how hard he pushed to marry me. How quickly he asked me. How he wanted me to sign that marriage license so badly. I stare and stare at him, and all the little pieces start clicking together. Roman pursued me, at least initially, because he wanted Marion's land. It feels like a punch in the stomach.

"What's so special about the property?" I ask, keeping my voice light. I remind myself that Connor will come for me, and when he does, the more information I can give him, the better.

He cocks his head and slants me a patronizing grin. "That is information for Order members only."

Of course it is. Bastard. A dark thought comes over me, and I clear my throat. "After we're married, the land will be yours. Will you still want to be married to me?"

He tilts his head, studying me. "Oh Fiona, so needy already. Take heart. While it's true that I initially pursued you because of the land, there were other ways I could have obtained it. When I realized who you were, the author of the Alex Rogue series, I knew you were wife material."

I sip my wine, digesting everything he's shared and drawing some conclusions. "You couldn't reveal your involvement in the Saints Order before we were married, but you knew through my books that I was capable of understanding your role."

He nods. "Not just understand it. Help to expand it. Propel it. Every grandmaster needs a woman to help with the day-to-day. Who would make a better grandmaster's wife than an expert in secret societies like you?"

Grandmaster's wife. Ice forms in my veins as I connect more dots. Connor said that Stefan and Donovan hadn't responded to his messages. My stomach churns and I swallow reflexively. "I thought your father was grandmaster."

"Not anymore." His smile is chilling and sends another tremor of fear through me. "That title is now mine."

"Congratulations," I sputter with all the enthusiasm I can muster.

"No more secrets, Fiona. If we are going to be man and wife, you must fully embrace the mission of the Saint's Order."

My skin crawls but making him believe he chose wisely with me is my best chance at survival. "You've always made the right choices when it comes to us. Now that you're grandmaster, I'll support you however you see fit. And you're right, we can't have secrets between us if I'm truly to be useful to you."

He stands from his meal and saunters to my side of the table, holding out his hand to me. "Then come, darling."

I allow him to help me out of the chair, suppressing a cringe at the feel of his touch, and then follow him as he leads me by the hand toward the back of the house. "Where are we going?"

"To see your friend Vivian."

Chapter Thirty-Two

CONNOR

I wake in a frothy white bed with the sounds and smells of the sea rolling through the open window. My head is foggy, but the salt air and sunshine tell me immediately where I am. Cardinal Island. A quick look around the room and I know I'm in the infirmary in the warrior camp. But why did they bring me here and not Morwyn's clinic?

Fiona! I roar and try to sit up, the memories of what happened to her flooding back. I'm off-world which means I can't hear anything down our bond. It's not impossible for an image or feeling to travel between us while I'm here, but it would have to be intense to cover the distance. Right now, the bond is quiet. Pain erupts in my upper left pec and wing. I inspect them both and find them bandaged.

A jingle comes from the far corner, and I follow the

sound to find Bones hobbling toward me, his front leg and side bandaged.

"Hey, buddy," I say softly.

He doesn't make it to me but flops down on the floor halfway between the dog bed and the adjustable I'm on. I work my feet over the edge of the mattress, and they clunk against the bedframe. Damn, I can't remember ever feeling this weak. I rub a thumb over my scarred eyebrow. Nope not even then.

The door opens and Morwyn rushes in. "Connor, if you get out of that bed, I swear to the creator I will put you back in it and drug you unconscious until your wounds are entirely healed."

"The Order has my mate," I say through my teeth. But I don't put my feet on the floor. In fact, I'm not entirely sure I can stand on my own. The room is spinning, and my head is pounding hard.

"Seb, Remus, and Ellison are tracking her. They won't let anything happen to her."

I close my eyes. "Zaire?"

"Alive but still unconscious. He's in the next room. If he weren't your Firetender, he'd definitely be dead. But that's why we're all here. You were very close to death when we brought you in. I don't think you would have survived to make it to my clinic." And if I had died, Zaire, cut off abruptly from our bond and my healing energy, would have likely died too. They did the right thing.

"Thank you," I grit out.

As pained as I am to be beyond the range of my bond with Fiona, Morwyn wouldn't lie about the severity of our injuries. He kept the three of us alive by using his key to open a portal and bring us here. The realm itself is healing to our kind. Cardinal Island is a place between places, a realm gifted to us by the creator for our safety and use, imbued with the celestial stuff we come from. I'll heal faster here. Zaire's and Bone's survival was far more likely here than anywhere else.

"You did the right thing," I tell him.

"Someone send a heater to hell because it has definitely frozen over."

"How long have I been out?"

"A few hours."

"And how long before I can go after her?"

"Two days," he says. "If you eat and drink and rest, you'll be ready to fight again in forty-eight hours."

I close my eyes. It's too long. "Twenty-four hours."

"This isn't a negotiation. You don't have a choice. I can't make your body heal any faster."

I lean back against the pillows, my eyes closing of their own volition. I'm wrecked. Forty-eight hours. *Fuck.* What might he do to her in forty-eight hours?

"Do I need to knock you out?" Morwyn asks, brushing an invisible piece of lint from his sleeve. He's capable, and it wouldn't require drugs. Despite the lab coat, he is as much a warrior as I am and has knocked me on my ass in the sparring ring a few times when I was perfectly healthy.

"No. I'm not going anywhere."

"Good. Because the Oracle wants to talk to you, so much that she's coming here."

My eyes pop open. "Here? Like today?"

"I'm supposed to send word when you're awake."

Never, in my recollection, has the Oracle ever left her temple for a personal visit, which means I'm probably in big trouble. Will she remove me from the brotherhood? I squeeze my eyes shut. I knew when I took Fiona that there would be consequences, but I can't bring myself to regret it. She's worth anything that comes. So I look on the bright side. Meeting with the Oracle might mean answers about Fiona, about what's happening to her, about how I can get her back.

"Tell her I'm awake," I say, "and honored she'd give me her time."

Morwyn reaches a hand out, and I grasp it. "I got you, Connor," he says softly. "You're not alone in this. *We* got you. That's why this is a brotherhood. Seb, Remus, and Ellison are already zeroing in on her location."

And wasn't that just my worst nightmare, to have to wait and exercise patience, to not be the one leading the charge? But I hold on to Morwyn a good long time. I want to rain violence on the Order, the likes of which they've never seen before, and carry Fiona out of there myself, but in lieu of that possibility, having my brothers do it is the next best thing.

Soon after Morwyn leaves, one of the Oracle's acolytes arrives. Dressed entirely in red, their face is masked by a red veil that's tucked into the high neck of their uniform so that no skin shows.

"Peace, warrior," comes a soft, low voice through the veil. "I am Nova, here to prepare the room for the Oracle's arrival." Nova heads for their bag, their tall, slender body breaking up the endless white and ivory of the room. Bones hobbles after them, wagging his tail, but ends up tiring quickly and returning to his bed.

All acolytes take vows of piety and abstinence before entering the vocation, and in exchange they train directly under the Oracle in divination and astronomy. One of them will eventually rise to replace her. The Oracle herself has a mate, but per tradition, her acolytes must remain celibate while in the position. Celibate and, to the outside world, genderless until they either rise to become Oracle themselves or leave the position.

I push myself up in bed, groaning at the pain that branches through me.

Nova mercifully stops what they're doing and puts another pillow behind my head. "Be at ease. She knows you are recovering and will require nothing of you physically."

"Right."

They return to their work, lighting the red candles and topping them with reflective domes that diffuse the light. They place a gold clock on the dresser across from me. It looks like something out of the Victorian era, all gears and glass with gold-and-pearl accents. Quiet ticking fills the room. Nova removes a black silk shroud from the bag and covers me and the bed with it.

The acolyte bows and exits the room, turning off the lights on their way out. Everything in the dim, candlelit room is black and red and gold ticking gears. My mind goes quiet in that space, my focus landing on the rhythm of my heart, my breath.

Sometime later, it might be a minute or an hour, the Oracle arrives, striding in with the posture of a queen. Although her size is diminutive, her presence would give even the strongest warrior pause. Rightfully so. She's powerful. More powerful than any of us. She holds her chin high, her wild, curly hair framing a face with olive skin, a hooked nose, and a smile with one slightly crooked eyetooth. She wears a simple white blouse and a long floral skirt with a wide belt and leather sandals. It's an outfit I might find on any older woman walking past my restaurant in New York. Nothing special. Nothing regal. But the power coming off her makes the hair on my arms stand at attention. And although I can't get out of bed, I bow my head.

"Such deference from an Aries," she says, moving closer. Bones gets up and hobbles over to her, wagging his tail. She smiles at him and rubs his ears. "Ah, an ambassador on your behalf. How persuasive he is. But I'm afraid you and I have unfinished business, Connor."

"Bones, go lie down," I command, and he does with an almost comical harrumph.

"I'll get right to it," she says. "Taking the bride from an altar in front of more than a hundred Order members was impulsive, irresponsible, and dangerous. You disregarded the direction of your appointed advisors, abused your position almost tyrannically, and in so doing, toyed with the lives of the brotherhood and our species. You had no idea what the fallout would be when you threw that woman over your shoulder, and here you are, injured and without the muscle to back up your decision while your brothers try to clean up your mess."

"You're right. I'm sorry."

"No, you are not."

"Okay. You're right and I'm not sorry."

"Now we're getting somewhere," she murmurs.

"The bride, Fiona, is my mate. She called to me, and I was unable to deny her."

The Oracle's pupils reflect the candlelight as if she holds an entire universe within her. "Has Fiona accepted your claim?"

"Yes. Just before she was stolen back by Roman. She is my true mate, the other half of my soul. Everything you accused me of is correct. I am impulsive and reckless, and I acted on my own without guidance from you or the rest of the four. But I don't regret it. I could no sooner leave her on that altar as I could leave my own head. Every single moment I spent with her was worth the rest of mine without her. I will never regret saving her from him. I will never regret taking her."

"I see." She rubs her palms together in tight circles as she paces the room, her footsteps and the ticking of the clock the only sound. "No doubt you are curious what punishment I'm planning for you."

I gulp. "It has crossed my mind."

She stares up at the ceiling, and the flames from the candles reflected there. So that's what the acolyte was doing. Normally, the Oracle meets with her subjects at the center of her sanctuary, where an observatory offers a clear view of the night sky. Here, the candles and reflective things Nova set up create an artificial view of the sky, one I have no doubt mirrors the actual position of the planets accurately. Her eyes glaze. "I've spent the past weeks in solitude, meditating on our predicament. Never in my thousands of years as Oracle have I seen the stars quite like this. And when you took her, I feared the path before us had become bleak, darker even than it would have been before. But it is easy to forget that the creator is always at work in the universe and that coincidences are often not coincidences at all. Was it a grand coincidence you met your mate when you did? Or did the creator place her in your path?"

"I'd like to think it was destined."

"Yes. Because of love. You think your love was destined. But the stars tell me she is more. She is much more. You should know that Fiona is human, Connor, entirely so. She's fragile. And while being with you will grant her health and prolonged life, she will never fly. She will never be a dragon."

"I know. I accept her as she is."

The Oracle paces in the opposite direction. "Different species. Different gods. Different ways of worshiping."

I scratch my jaw, wondering what she's getting at.

"Your mate, as it so happens, is exceptionally blessed."

"Blessed?"

The Oracle nods slowly. "Blessed with a gift from her god, one that may be our salvation."

"What kind of gift?"

The Oracle taps a fist to her chin. "It is veiled from me. The answers the stars give us are always shifting. They show me multiple futures, crossroads, possibilities. Fiona's light is bright. I see her clearly and that she was chosen to be your mate for a reason, but beyond that, the future is cloudy. What I can say now, with certainty, is that you were meant to be in that garden on her wedding day and you were meant to take her, and if we are going to be ready for what is to come, it is imperative you get her back."

A huge, relieved sigh leaves my lips. "Morwyn says I won't be well enough until the day after tomorrow."

"Listen to Morwyn." Smiling wistfully, she looks back at the ceiling, her fingers grazing her throat. "I see you with her. I see her in your arms." The Oracle inhales sharply, a look of horror transforming her face. Her hands fly to her mouth.

"What's wrong? What do you see?" I push myself up in a panic.

She quiets me with a raised palm. "The fires of change." She closes her eyes and shakes her head. "Heal, Aries, then go get your mate. You have my permission to bring her here for Mason's ascension when it is done." She turns to leave, looking forlorn somehow.

"Is there something else?" I ask, knowing in my gut she hasn't told me everything.

With a long deep sigh, she turns and looks directly at me, her dark eyes large and soulful in the candlelight. "Whatever happens, whatever you have to do to get her back, you must succeed, and do not blame yourself if there are unexpected complications. Some things are meant to be."

A soft smile warms her face as she turns and leaves. All the candles flicker out. The clock stops ticking. And her acolyte breezes in, turns on the lights, and takes it all away without another word.

Chapter Thirty-Three

FIONA

Roman positions me in front of him, and we descend a steep staircase too narrow for us to walk side by side. I wonder how this place can have a basement at all, considering it's built next to the ocean, but I learn pretty quickly that this is no ordinary lower level. After the last step, the carpet ends, revealing a metal grate for a floor and bolted steel walls. I'm descending into a submarine, a tankard, some sort of vault.

"Vivian is down here?" I ask, but I know the answer. She hasn't been his guest. This entire time, she's been his prisoner. If she had been his guest, she would have returned my messages and calls. Only now do I worry that *prisoner* isn't the term for what's happened to her, that it might be something more, something darker. "Is she still alive, Roman?" It's a brazen question, but we've passed tiptoeing around the reality that's right in front of me.

He snorts and places a hand in the center of my back, guiding me deeper into the dark depths of the room. A smell hits me, and I can't place it immediately; then I do. It's like a stairwell in a parking garage in the city. Dried urine, dirty human, and something medicinal like someone tried to cover it all with a spritz of Lysol.

A switch clicks. Long, rectangular fluorescent lights blink on along the ceiling, one after another, to reveal cages—no, prison cells. A filthy skeleton of a woman appears at the bars of one, blinking like it's the first time in a long time she's seen light.

"Vivian!" I run to my friend, grabbing her hands through the bars.

"Oh God. Oh God, Fiona. Oh no. Oh God." Her eyes are so wide and her voice is raw. But the way her skin hangs on her disturbs me the most. She looks like she's starving to death. This is torture. This is...

Alex pops into my head, those shrewd green eyes narrowing. *Do you want to wallow in the horror or figure a way out of this for both of you?*

I wipe my tears. "I've got you," I whisper, even though truthfully, I don't have anyone. Not even myself. I search her face and find bruises along her jaw, her wrists. There's a cut healing, like someone dragged the edge of a blade across her throat, just deep enough to break the skin.

Roman steps forward, sending Vivian scurrying away from the bars. "Vivian doesn't follow directions very well. I enjoy playing with her, but like a puppy, I can't trust her outside her cage."

Only then do I glance into her cell, where she huddles in the corner next to a filthy cot with a blanket that isn't close to warm enough for down here and a toilet that allows for no privacy. Worse, she's still wearing the same dress she wore at the wedding. He hasn't even given her a change of clothes. And she is so thin. Gaunt. Skeletal. Her eyes, her once-vibrant eyes, how hollow they've become. I can't stand it.

I whirl on Roman, fire rising in my blood, but it's doused immediately by the cold, merciless look in his soulless eyes. Unless I want to play Roman's painful game and end up Vivian's roommate, I need to become his sweet, obedient fiancée. "You're right. Vivian has never been good at following directions. But now that I'm here, I can help keep her in line. Will you let her out please?" I lay my hands softly on his chest. "I really would like her at our wedding, and I can't have her standing with me, looking and... smelling like that." I cascade my fingers toward the bars.

Roman seems to contemplate my request, then brushes under my eye, rubbing a stray tear between his fingers. "Not if she's going to upset you."

I plaster on the biggest, brightest smile. "I'm not upset. Those are happy tears, Roman. I'm happy to see her, just like I'm happy to see you."

He skims a hand along the outside of my arm, causing my stomach to pitch. "I'm glad you said that. Truly, Fiona, it's refreshing to be with someone who finally understands me." He strokes the back of my head like I'm his new favorite pet. "I have another surprise for you, and I think you are going to really enjoy this one." His smile is broad and beaming as he gestures proudly across the room at the neighboring cell.

It's all I can do to stifle a scream when I see Donovan strapped to a chair behind the bars, eyes closed and head hanging. An IV in his arm drains blood through a tube leading to a bag near his hip. He's unconscious and pale. So fucking pale. The last time I met the man, he looked about fifty—tall, fit, with brown hair and graying side-burns. Only a few lines marred the area around his smiling eyes to betray his age. But now he's barely recog-nizable. He looks old, like he's aged thirty years in a day, with sunken cheeks and sallow skin. All I can think is I'm looking at a death mask.

My gaze flicks up to Roman, and it takes all my willpower to keep my own mask in place. He's watching me intently. Watching me with a tiny smile of pleasure, as if he'd like to sop up any panic and disgust I'm feeling with a dinner roll like it's gravy.

"Why is your father's best friend in a cell?"

That tiny smile blooms into something fuller, wider. He backs me against the bars of Vivian's cell and braces his forearm above my head, leaning in way too close, close enough that the stiff erection in his pants brushes the front of my dress. In all the time I dated Roman, he never appeared aroused. Now I get it. This dungeon, with its blood and stink and suffering, is his kind of porn. Seeing Vivian afraid, seeing Donovan caged and bleed-ing, it's some kind of kink to him.

My skin crawls with the need to fight or flee, but then

he says, "All those times you wrote about dungeons and torture in your books, I bet you've never seen the real thing. I bet you've never experienced it, smelled it." He takes a deep breath like it's a warm day in spring, his enthusiasm for his dungeon radiating from him. "Are you taking it all in? This is gold."

Terror makes my stomach clench, and for a moment I think I might vomit, but I swallow it down and force my face to remain impassive. It's his comment about writing that gives me an idea. I disassociate and become an observer of this scene, as if this truly is research for a book and not real life, not the most horrific experience I've ever had.

Alex's voice pops into my head, *He's a psychopath. He gets off on pain and suffering. Don't show him any. A toddler won't play with a toy that doesn't work. Be as boring and sweet as possible. Go along with everything he says. Make him believe you're enamored with him.*

I force an appreciative smile, perfectly suitable for the Mrs. Psychopath he wants me to be. "It's all very intriguing." I gesture around the dungeon. "Exactly the inspiration I need, actually. But why are you draining Donovan's blood? He looks sick."

He taps the tip of my nose with his finger. "Have you figured out yet that Donovan is a dragon?"

I slowly shake my head. "No. You said he was Stefan's friend."

He laughs, and the sound is awful. The laugh of a maniac. I take shallow breaths. I count to ten inside my head.

"A necessary ruse. Donovan is a dragon, just like the

beast who took you. He's been my father's pet for ages, but since my father is dead now, I've decided not to keep him."

"Stefan is dead?" I'd wondered how Roman had risen to grandmaster so quickly.

He gives a low chuckle. "Sadly so. And Donovan, keeping him around has become problematic. Only, dragon blood is what fuels the magic of our rings. I can't let it go to waste." He holds up his right hand and thumbs the wide band of his Order ring. He told me once it was a class ring, and it could easily pass for one, with its wide platinum band and the Saint George's cross engraved on the face. I'd thought the etching around the edge was decorative. The font is tiny and hard to read. But now that I'm studying it up close, I realize it's the inscription—the same quote as was written in blood above Lucy Vale's head—*Astra inclinant, sed non obligant.*

"I saw your ring transform into a weapon before," I say, lashes fluttering.

"Would you like to see?" A dimple appears in his cheek, and the ring glows blue. With a twist of his wrist, it transforms into the crossbow he used to shoot Connor.

"That's... incredible," I say breathlessly. I try to make it sound like I'm amazed instead of terrified. "Do you ever run out of bolts?"

"That's the best part. Once I fire, they regenerate. It takes a few seconds, longer if my energy is low."

"It draws from your personal energy?"

He waves his hand, and the crossbow becomes a ring again. "It feels like a hard workout afterward. It's... rewarding." Of course it is. He probably loves killing.

"Did you use it to kill Lucy Vale?"

He leans in closer, sniffing the side of my neck, and it's all I can do not to sprint for the exit. "No. It can be whatever I want it to be. I prefer the crossbow because it's useful when your prey has wings, but Lucy—for her I used a blade. She didn't know what she was. She couldn't fly."

"Then why did you kill her?"

He draws back and raises an eyebrow. "I would have thought a mind like yours would have figured it out."

I study his face. He's a clinical psychopath with soulless eyes and a heartlessly flirty grin, as if this is a test, a test to see if I'm clever enough to figure out what he did. A test to see if I'm truly wife material, perhaps. Or maybe he likes my books and wants to feel like he's just as clever as one of my villains. "I bet you killed Lucy to attract the dragons to Europe. To Paris."

He smacks the bars above my head. "Yes. You truly are bright for a woman. I knew you would be when I chose you." He stares down at me, teeth gleaming. "Go on."

"I don't think your goal was for a dragon to kidnap me. That seemed to surprise you as much as it did me. But you did want them there for some reason. It couldn't have been about humans though because they don't know dragons exist. Plus, when I was taken, you told no one, which means you didn't want the humans to know."

"So close. You're almost there." His voice drops to a seductive whisper and he runs the back of his nails along the outside of my arm.

I flash him a dazzled look as if to say he's so very

intelligent, but then duck under his arm and start pacing the space between the cells like I need to walk to think. My ridiculous heels clack on the concrete as I rub my chin. What I'm really doing is scanning everything, every corner of this dungeon. "Since you clearly didn't care what the humans thought about the dragons' response to Lucy being murdered, you must have wanted someone else to notice." Quickly I put it all together like a plot I'm writing that is only now working itself out. "You wanted to convince the rest of the Saint's Order."

I turn away from Roman to look at Donovan, the only clue the dragon is still alive the rise and fall of his chest. "You needed a dragon to come to France so that you could blame the dragons for killing your father," I say softly as a chill comes over me at the supreme evil of it all. "Because if they knew you did it, they wouldn't elect you grandmaster. You went to great lengths to make sure you were standing on the altar in front of all of them at the time your father was murdered and Donovan went missing."

His hands land on my shoulders, and I can't keep myself from flinching. "Very good."

"And that means the Order thinks the dragons broke the accord."

He barks a laugh of surprise. "He told you about the accord? Your captor was certainly forthcoming."

Fuck. "Only to explain what he wanted from you. He said he'd taken me to force you to explain why you'd broken the accord by killing Lucy."

"Hmmm. I suppose I should thank him. So much easier for me to bring you up to speed." He clasps his hands behind his hips and rocks back on his heels. "You were right when you suspected my father and Donovan were together. Obviously he was more than a family friend. That was a ruse I came up with to explain why they were always... touching. But after you mentioned you believed they were partners, I discovered you were right. The two were mated."

I try to keep my expression steady. I'd suspected they were together, but mates? The implications madly rush through my head.

"Do you know that mating a dragon bestows a human with health and an unnaturally long life?"

I shake my head.

"No, of course you don't. But it's true. My father intended to rule the Order and remain CEO of Cifarelli Enterprises for as long as possible. I'd never have *my* chance to rule. He planned to steal my birthright from me. When I killed him, it started the clock ticking on Donovan. Now that his mate is dead, he'll start to age again. Eventually, he'll go up in flames during his alignment. He's almost seventy. I might have a few decades left to use his energy, but it's too risky to keep him around, considering he's the only one who knows I murdered my father. That's why I'm collecting his blood. We'll have enough to last the Order until I can capture another dragon."

He rests his hands on my shoulders, stroking the bare skin with his thumbs. For a few minutes, I can't move. It's like my blood has frozen in my veins from his touch. I stare at Donovan, watching his blood drip, drip, drip into the bag.

"So you murdered your father and blamed it on the dragons, who were there because of Lucy. Who did you blame for killing Lucy?"

"Also the dragons," he says with a dark chuckle. "They needed an excuse to legitimize their actions."

"And the Order bought it all?"

"Never suspected a thing."

"Wow, Roman." I shake my head as if I'm impressed when really I'm deeply disturbed.

"We should go to bed, it's getting late." His tone is eerily seductive, as if all this was meant to impress me. As if all of it were foreplay.

I lick my lips, then glance toward Vivian, whose eyes are enormous in her gaunt face. I'm walking a tightrope here and I have to be careful. I have one chance to prove to him that I'm as crazy as he is, to become Harley Quinn to his Joker. It's the only way I'll earn his trust.

I rest my hands on his chest and stare up at him through my lashes. "This is so impressive, Roman. Really. Your entire plan was nothing short of brilliant. I couldn't have written it any better in one of my books."

He seems to swell under the compliment and leans in as if to kiss me. I rest two fingers on his lips.

"But can I ask you for a wedding gift?"

He steps in closer, those dead eyes narrowing in on me. "You know I can give you anything you want."

"I want the dragon," I say through my teeth. I fist his shirt and pull him closer to me. "The one that took me. I want you to capture it so that I can keep it in that fucking cage after Donovan is dead, just like it kept me caged.

And I want to watch you burn the bastard with your ring whenever I feel like it."

Even saying that aloud, knowing I'm lying, makes me want to die, especially with Donovan within hearing distance, but I throw every bit of control I have left into the act. *You've got this*, Alex says inside my head. Indeed, Roman's pupils are wide and he's looking at me like I'm his favorite slice of birthday cake.

"I swear it on my father's grave," he says.

I nod. "It counts for more since you put him in it." I cackle like I'm entirely off my rocker.

"Come, it's late," he says, glancing at his watch.

I'm not wearing one, so I look at his. It's not just late, it's early morning. "No wonder I'm so exhausted. I can barely keep my eyes open."

He threads his fingers into mine and starts for the stairs.

I plant my feet. "Aren't you forgetting something?" I point at Vivian.

She tentatively takes a step toward her cell door, her eyes darting in Roman's direction. He blinks at me and shakes his head. "She knows too much."

"She won't tell anyone. She's my friend." I make eye contact with her and widen my eyes slightly.

"Of course I won't," she promises through a dry, raspy throat. I can see what saying it costs her.

"She realizes how powerful you are, Roman. We both do. Besides, if I'm going to be a proper grandmaster's wife, I'm going to need a friend I can confide in, one who knows how to keep a secret."

He scowls. "Your *friend* has not been cooperative up to this point."

I swallow down the bile rising in my throat and cup his face in my hands. "At least move her to a guest room. Feed her dinner and let her shower. Guard the room if you must but give me a chance to convince her to do it your way."

"Our way," he says softly, brushing a hand along my back.

Swallow, swallow, swallow. *Don't you dare puke right now, Fiona. Not until she's out of that cell,* Alex yells in my head. I meet his soulless black eyes and hold them. "Our way."

His cold lips meet mine in a kiss that makes me think of kissing a snake, and somewhere deep down, in that place where I can feel my bond with Connor, a place that's been silent for hours, I finally hear a roar.

Chapter Thirty-Four

CONNOR

The nightmare grips me. Fiona's in my arms, screaming as I fly her away from the helicopter to safety. But Roman is shooting at us, those deadly blue bolts whistling far too close to her pretty face. I twist and turn and fly as fast as my wings will carry me, but icy pain, so cold it burns, pierces my flesh, punches a hole in my wing. And then another. And then another. I'm twisting and dodging, but he's too fast, and before long, the membrane of my wings is tattered. Cradled in my arms, Fiona is weeping now, her creamy skin splattered with my blood. But I've protected her; I've saved her. Until the air starts to sing through the holes in my wings and I realize we're falling. Her eyes grow wide just before we careen into the earth.

I wake, heart pounding, and sit up in bed. Bones is at attention, ears trained on me. "Just a nightmare, buddy. Go back to bed." He rests his head on his pillow.

The first rays of silvery light diffuse through the window, chasing the moon from the sky. Morning. Tentatively, I stretch my wings and peel away the bandage where the hole had been. I can still see where Morwyn stitched it, but it's not as painful to move. Almost healed. I dig my fingers under the one on my chest. That wound is worse, still sporting blue veins that branch across my torso. They're fading but still hurt like hell.

"One more day," I mumble.

Carefully, I swing my legs over the side of the bed, my feet landing on the cold stone floor, my eyes on the attached bathroom. An image crashes down the bond that knocks the air from my lungs. Roman kissing Fiona. And I can feel her cringing. I can tell she doesn't want it. But he doesn't stop.

I roar so loud it shakes the walls.

A nurse runs in. I don't remember her name. "What's wrong? Do you need help?"

With hardly a glance in her direction, I tear the bandages from my chest and wing and stumble toward the dresser. "I need my clothes and my Cardinal Key."

She holds up her hands, clearly sensing that I'm not exactly safe in my current mood. "The doctor wants you to rest for one more day."

I dig in the drawers of the dresser, but they're empty. "I don't have a day. Bring me a set of fighting leathers and my key. Now!"

Chapter Thirty-Five

FIONA

The kiss goes on far longer than I want it to, and I don't engage with it, but I also don't fight it. I go somewhere in my head where Alex is drinking a lemon-drop martini and telling me all the times she had to do something like this to save the victim or nail the murderer. When he finally draws back, I pant. I'm sure it looks like I'm excited, when really I'm just trying my best not to be sick.

For his part, Roman's gaze veers toward Vivian and narrows. "I will give you this, wife, as a wedding gift. But if she causes any trouble, she dies, and I will punish you for your misstep. Are you prepared to endure the consequences if she's not worth your trust?"

I gulp and nod. I know better than to try to save Donovan. Even looking in his direction right now could jeopardize Vivian, and by the tears forming in her eyes, I know she needs out of this cell. "I'm prepared. She'll be agreeable." I turn to stare directly at Vivian. "Or I'll kill her myself."

Vivian has the good sense to look terrified, although she must know I'm acting.

When I turn back to Roman, he gives me a sidelong glance like a husband might if he was indulging his wife with some jewelry or a clothing splurge and then punches a code into the keypad. I memorize it. 8-8-3-6-7-8. I say it over and over again in my head. Maybe the code to Donovan's cell is the same. Maybe I can sneak back down here when Roman's not in the house and free the dragon. He runs a damn company. He can't stay here forever, can he?

The door swings open, and Vivian practically leaps into my arms. Her body is so thin it feels like I can wrap them around her twice, and she smells like she hasn't bathed in weeks. I squeeze her hard and then leave my arm around her waist even as I take Roman's outstretched hand and allow him to lead us up the stairs.

Vivian doesn't say a word as he leads us to the second floor and shows her to one of the guest rooms, one I see has an en suite bathroom. I catch the eye of a member of the staff who looks like he's trying hard not to be noticed. "She'll need food and a change of clothes," I say in a firm voice, then immediately turn to Roman. "I mean, if you approve."

He gives me another creepy smile. *Play the part. Just a little longer. For your friend.*

Roman glares at the man. "Do it."

Fine. Better than that cell. I meet her eyes and load mine with promise. I'll get us out of this, somehow.

The servant bows and then takes off toward the kitchen. Roman looks at Vivian, and there is death in his eyes. "Leave these rooms without my permission and I will remove your legs from your body."

I wouldn't think it possible, but Vivian pales even further before Roman closes the door between us, her wild, terrified eyes disappearing behind the heavy paneled wood.

Roman turns to me with a sigh, his hand stroking down my spine to the curve of my back. "Shall we?"

I nod, although I'm not sure what he means. Are we going to sign paperwork? Get married this very minute? I've been awake for almost twenty-four hours. Will he allow me to sleep?

He leads me to his bedroom, and the sight of the bed makes me long to lie down. My feet ache in the heels. But then what will he expect from me?

Behind me, I hear him close and lock the door, and then he approaches until I can feel the buttons of his dress shirt against my back. "You're trembling."

My eyes burn and my head pounds, exhaustion limiting what few inner resources I have left. "You said the Order requires we wait until we're married. Do you still want to wait?" My voice cracks and I pray it comes across as nerves and not dread.

His hand lands on my zipper, and I close my eyes as he draws it down my side. The red dress falls off me and pools around my heels, leaving me in scraps of lace that serve as a bra and panties. I almost break down when he unhooks my bra and slides it from my shoulders. It drops to the floor. When the cloth hits the carpet, it barely makes a sound, but inside my head, an explosion is going off. *I'm Connor's. I'm Connor's!* I don't want this man touching me. I don't want him seeing me.

He's still behind me, and I'm shaking hard now, hard enough I worry about tripping in the shoes.

"Arms up," he orders, and a whisper of silk falls over my body.

I look down to find myself in a black silk nightgown. I release a shaky breath.

"Lie down. You're exhausted."

Slowly I walk to the opposite side of the bed, remove my shoes, and climb under the covers. He strips down to his boxers and climbs in beside me. But he doesn't touch me, just closes his eyes.

I try to fight sleep. I want to fight it. I want to run. But the consequences if I did would fall on Vivian, just as I will suffer if she tries to escape. I'm only human and a physically weak one at that. My joints ache from the stress of the day, and I pray to God this doesn't throw me into another flare.

No, if I'm going to survive and escape Roman, I'll have to do it using my mind. I believe in my soul that if I give Connor enough time, he'll come for me. I don't trust Roman, and I want to stay awake, but in the end, the endless fatigue and exhaustion is too much. I fall into a sleep so heavy I don't even dream.

Chapter Thirty-Six

CONNOR

I pass through the lighthouse that marks the portal between Cardinal Island and Earth and dial Seb before I've even made it out of the building. My heart is pounding so hard I barely feel the ache of my wounds.

"Where is she?" I bark as soon as he answers.

"Morwyn said you'd be another day."

"Fuck Morwyn. Where is she, Seb? Were you able to track her?"

He groans. "Have you ever in your life followed a rule?"

"Seb! She's in trouble. I saw things down the bond. We have to get her out of there now!" I reach down the bond again but feel nothing. My dragon twists anxiously inside me.

Seb seems to hear the distress in my voice now because he says, "We've tracked them to his property on

315

the Rhode Island coast. But it's tricky. The place is defended like a military base."

"Give me the address."

"You can't go in there alone, Connor. You'll never make it out."

"Give me the address, Seb." He does, thank the creator. "Thank you. I can't ask for your help. It's too dangerous, and if I die, the brotherhood needs you to lead."

"Fuck off, you prick. I'll see you in Rhode Island as fast as I can call in the others."

"Creator bless us." I disconnect the call and grab my key, cloaking myself and launching into the sky. Pain branches out from my wounds, and I acknowledge that Morwyn was probably right about me needing another day to heal. Then I remember that fucker Roman kissing Fiona. Touching her. And when the magic of the key opens a portal to Rhode Island in the sky, I fly faster through it.

I find the house on a rocky beach surrounded by about five acres of heavily patrolled land. Blue-uniformed security guards with visible weapons pepper the property as the early-morning sun splashes across the saltbox architecture of the mansion. Even if we can use our camouflage to get past the guards, there's a lot of square feet of space in that house. No telling what's going on in there. I land on a neighboring rooftop and am relieved when Seb, Remus, and Ellison, dressed in their fighting leathers, appear beside me.

"What's the plan? Aside from admiring Ellison's ass

on the rare occasion it's not covered by a suit jacket?" Seb asks through a wry grin.

Ellison flashes him an obscene gesture.

I give a low growl. "There's no cover, there are guards everywhere, and we don't have eyes or ears inside," I say. "Oh, and this place is laden with dragon-killing weapons."

Remus grunts. "If we had more time, I could find some humans to bug the place."

"Not waiting. I'll go in the front door if I have to," I grit out.

"And be shredded to pieces the moment someone with a ring senses you through your illusion," Ellison says.

"Then I'll shift, bite the head off every guard, and burn the entire place down." My skin tingles, and I get to my feet, ready to be a one-dragon wrecking crew.

Seb rolls his eyes. "You do that and you're libel to kill Fiona. You have no idea what room she's in or if she's locked up or not. You start a fire or start knocking down walls and you could kill her."

"He's got a point," Remus says, rubbing his laughing-devil tattoo.

Ellison draws his phone from his pocket, thumbs the screen, then lifts his eyes to me. "Tell me I'm your favorite brother."

"Why? What did you find?"

"I'm waiting."

"You're my favorite brother, you filthy prick."

"Apparently Roman hasn't given up on marrying Fiona, because a friend of a friend says a judge is on his way here to perform the ceremony and pick up the license." Ellison grins.

"How the hell did you find that out?" I ask.

"Believe it or not, even judges don't like rich pricks paying them exorbitant fees to perform a marriage on demand. Disgruntled people talk. They talk to other disgruntled people in the legal profession. People like me. I only needed to roll some stones in the area to find this worm."

"Can we intercept this guy?" I scratch the healing wound on my chest.

"I think so," Ellison says. "I know what he looks like, and there's only one road in. Do you think you can hold an illusion strong enough if we find a way to… detain him?"

"As long as I need to," I say, though impersonating a human is more difficult than regular camouflage for a number of reasons. Voice, mannerisms—those are things that take time and practice to imitate. "How well does he know this guy though?"

Ellison frowns. "Let's hope not very well. If he's wearing a ring, we're in trouble."

I scowl. The Aries dragon in me isn't accustomed to thinking first and acting later. Aries are known for being daring, courageous, and dynamic. We're the ones who solve a problem before the other signs have met to discuss a plan of action. But for me, under stress like this, daring often turned to recklessness, courage turned to impulsivity, and being action-oriented turned to impatience. Everything is different now because of Fiona. I *had* to wait for her. I had to work for her. Even now, when my anger and bloodlust burn in my veins, I know I am capable of calculated action because of her, and if there's ever a time to use the control she's taught me, it's now.

"Fine. It's the best idea we've got. Let's find this guy."

As we set up the roadblock and transform ourselves to look like police officers, I try to remember the last time the Zodiac Brotherhood had to go on the offensive like this. We've trained. Some of us have performed rescue missions, like the day I helped Mason recover his mate, Reagan. But we've relied on the peace accord for a long time. We've trusted the sanctity of it.

And now that trust is gone. All communication between us and the Order is finished. They came onto my land and stole my mate. War is here. It is with some sadness that I wait for the black Mercedes and the judge driving it, knowing that we stand on the brink of dark days. Thinking back, I'd hoped I was wrong about Lucy. A small part of me wanted the Order to apologize and admit to a rogue incident. I would have rather we patched a rift than shred the accord. And now we're in unnamed territory. Fighting an undeclared war. A pit forms in my gut as I consider my mate will now have to live in a world at war, that we won't go home to the life of peace we've enjoyed so far.

"There," Ellison says, adjusting the brim of his cap and stepping out into the road to block the car. I take a good look at the man as Ellison pulls him from the car and pushes him up against the back doors, getting in his face so he can slip into his mind.

"Do you know who I am?" the judge says with a tip up of his chin. That defiance lasts only as long as it takes Ellison to invade his mind. The man's arms fall limp against his sides. Ellison really is a damned pain in the ass, but I'm glad the guy is on my side. Everyone needs at least one friend who challenges them, and he's mine. Not to mention his fucking mind is a weapon of its own. The judge slumps in his arms, asleep.

We check his hand. No ring.

I take one more look and transform myself into Judge Adam Burk. My chest aches as I do it, but when I'm done, Seb confirms it's a good likeness. I slide behind the wheel and peel out of there, back toward the house, watching my brothers and the real Judge Burk blink out of existence in the rearview mirror.

I'm coming for you, Fi. Hold on, baby.

Chapter Thirty-Seven

FIONA

A hand runs down my spine and over my ass, dragging me from sleep. I turn my head, the events of yesterday coming back to me in a series of images and memories when I see Roman watching me from the pillow beside mine. I yawn to hide the way my body bristles at his touch.

"I'm going to enjoy taking you apart and putting you back together," he says, those soulless eyes drifting over my bare shoulder before his fingers follow the trail over my skin.

"Wh-what does that mean?" My voice shakes, and the corner of his mouth curls.

"I've waited for you." His finger traces down the side of my silky nightgown. "Waited to sample the pleasures of your body. It's right to be married first. You're not a toy. I've had toys before, but they're so easy to break. You, on the other hand, you're indestructible. That mind of yours won't shatter like the others. All the ways you've written characters being tortured, we'll play out those scenes and so many more. Together we'll find your limits."

"Limits?"

He slides his hand to the hem of the nightgown, then drags the edge of his ring across the skin of my thigh. It hurts, and I gasp and jerk away from him. I glance down to see he's drawn blood.

He wipes the cut, then sucks the bead of blood from his finger. The way he watches me, it's like he's reveling in the small reaction he's elicited. "I can't wait to see what you look like when I make you scream." He doesn't mean in pleasure.

"And how long will I have to wait for that?" I scissor my legs and force myself to sound enthusiastic, but I'm trembling now, unable to hide my reaction as I did yesterday.

His gaze turns molten. He loves that I'm shaking. The sadist takes pleasure in my fear. He scoots closer on the bed. "I swear, Fiona, it's like God made you just for me." He kisses my shoulder. "The judge is on his way right now. You'll sign the license, he'll perform the ceremony, and he'll file the papers for us when it's finished. We'll be legally married by the end of the day." His hand smooths over my ass again. "Which means this will all be mine by tonight."

I flutter my lashes and press two fingers to his lips. "He's on his way now? I should get ready." I use the excuse to slide away from his touch and hop out of bed. "What would you like me to wear?"

He climbs out of bed, wearing nothing but his boxers and an obvious erection. God, he's human trash. He pads to the walk-in closet. "I picked this out while I was in Paris for you to wear on our honeymoon. It wouldn't be appropriate for a formal affair, but for this it will please me."

Paris. Did he buy this while he was there to murder Lucy? I swallow down bile and take the hanger from him before hurrying into the bathroom and shutting the door between us. Tears flood my face as I crumple to the floor with the dress in my hands. *Help. Help. Help me! Connor, if you can hear me, you have to come for me. Please come for me.* I project the words down our bond as forcefully as I can, sobbing silently.

I remember the poisoned bolts in his wings, in his chest, the way he dropped out of the sky. I flash back to Roman showing me his crossbow last night, the bolts magically enchanted to kill dragons, fueled, he said, by something made from dragon's blood. Not for the first time, I wonder how badly Connor was injured. Is he even in any shape to challenge Roman? If he comes for me, is it possible that Roman might finish him off this time?

I shake my head. I refuse to believe it. Connor's a fucking dragon, a god of a man who made me laugh, woke my creative light again, and stole my heart. I choose to believe he's invincible. And he's mine. He'll never give up on me.

I close my eyes on a silent sob. He'll come for me. He will. I just need to survive until he does. Only I'm not sure I want to live through what Roman has in store for me. But then I remember something else. I have to endure, because if I die, it's Connor's life too. If I die, his fever will return. His greatest fear was living a half-life like his sister, pining for a lost mate. I can't do that to him. I close my eyes again and clutch for my crucifix, but it's gone. I haven't had it since Esther removed it from my neck before the wedding. Still I pray; I pray for deliverance. I pray for a miracle.

At one point, I do think I feel something down the bond, but it's barely a whisper. Still, I cling to it. *Survive. All I need to do is survive.*

AFTER A LONG SHOWER, I FACE THE DRESS AGAIN. I KNOW I'M running out of time. I've been in here close to an hour. Roman won't wait forever, and the last thing I want is him coming in after me. The dress is hideous. It's white and lace, but those are the only similarities to a wedding dress. The spaghetti straps give way to a deep vee that reaches halfway to my navel, and the skirt lands midthigh. The lace is positioned over a nude slip to give the illusion you're seeing flesh peeking through the fabric. I pull it over my head and go look in the mirror, hoping it's not as bad as it seems on the hanger. It's worse. It looks like a negligee.

I close my eyes. *Hold it together,* Alex barks in my head. A scene I wrote in book three, *Devil's Wrath,* plays in my head. Alex was captured by a Russian spy, tortured for twenty-one days, and beaten senseless and still managed to survive. Survive, I tell myself. *Just survive.*

Slowly I open the door to find Roman standing there in his wedding tux. His eyes drift over me.

"Almost done." He grabs a pair of silver-white shoes from behind him.

Again, they're stilettos, uncomfortable as hell and no doubt meant to hinder my ability to move quickly. I slide my feet into them. He grabs my chin, turns my face this way and that, inspecting my hair and makeup. I've done the bare minimum, not wanting to please him but also not wanting to invite his wrath. He frowns a little but says nothing.

"Sign," he orders, pointing to the marriage license on the bureau. I do, and he tucks it into the inside pocket of his jacket.

I take a step away from him, toward the door, but he stops me with a hand on my elbow.

"Wait. You need jewelry." He opens a drawer and pulls out a diamond-encrusted collar. It looks like something a billionaire would buy for his dog. He fastens it around my neck, tight enough to be uncomfortable but not cut off my air. "There," he says, as if this ensemble could possibly look anything but gaudy.

"They took my ring," I say, remembering with some internal relish how Connor had melted the gold and hurled the diamond into the woods. I picture it buried beneath a pile of bear shit.

He scoffs. "We'll get you another. For today you can use this one."

He reaches into the same box and pulls out a diamond band. The engagement ring I'd once worn was part of a set. On our wedding day, Roman carried the band but never had the chance to slide it on my finger. I stare at it, again praying for Connor to come. He saved me that day. I never fully appreciated it before, what he knew, the level of the mistake I was making or the personal risk Connor took when he abducted me. I never fully appreciated the kindness and patience he showed me while I worked it all out.

"What were you thinking about just then?" Roman asks.

I blink away the memories and plaster on an insipid smile. "Our future."

He chucks me under the chin. "Judge Burk just passed through security. We're very lucky to have him. Not only is he a judge, but he's also trusted by the Saint's Order. He's not a member yet but has applied to be, and he understands Order business. He can marry us properly."

I have no idea what he means by that, but I don't fight as Roman takes my elbow and leads me out of the bedroom and through the hall to the back of the house. We descend a staircase and then walk down a long corridor. I worry that he's taking me to the dungeon again.

"What about Vivian?" I ask nervously.

"I've already had security escort her to the chapel."

"You have a chapel here?"

He glances at me. "Every Order member maintains a chapel in their residence. It's part of the vows we take."

What sort of medieval society is the Order to have their own chapels? I'm finally seeing it on the level of the Illuminati or the Knights Templar. I think back to the hours I spent researching secret societies throughout history, and my author's curiosity piques. I can't stop my voice from shaking when I ask, "Do you think killing dragons is your mission from God?"

We ascend another set of stairs and arrive at stained-glass doors. He pulls one open for me. "It's our mission from our god and the god of those who came before us." Our eyes meet, and his are darker than I've ever seen them. And then he ushers me inside.

The chapel is paneled in dark wood and lit only by candlelight and the ambient light filtering through the mostly red stained glass. My breath catches at a stained-glass representation of Saint George mounted on a horse. The saint is holding a spear stabbed through a dragon's head. It's not the first time I've seen this depiction, but it's the first time I've noticed the look of pride on Saint George's face and the way the dragon is at his mercy. The dragon isn't fighting back. George hasn't a scratch on him. He might as well have a spear through a dog.

Dragons were sent to inspire humans, I remember Connor saying. The Order slaughtered them for greed, to maintain their status and position. I'll never look at art like this the same way again, not as long as I live.

Roman tugs me toward the front of the chapel, his grip almost painful. There's an altar, but the cross hanging over it is strange. It's flanked by dozens of ivory candles, their dripping wax collecting on the wrought iron scrollwork of the candelabra. Vivian is waiting in the front pew, her traumatized eyes catching mine.

Physically, she looks a tiny bit better. She's clean and there's more color in her cheeks. She's eaten and rested. But her eyes are haunted. And she recoils when she sees

Roman. She's terrified of him, as well she should be. I am too.

Her gaze falls on the place Roman's hand grips the back of my upper arm. She frowns, her eye catching mine as she squeezes the back of the pew until her knuckles turn white. I know she wants to help me but I try to tell her silently not to try. It will only end badly for both of us.

Roman leads me up the aisle where a kneeler has been placed in front of the altar table. It's so quiet I can hear the candles burning. On either side of the altar, suits of armor stand guard, swords and shields in their hollow hands. It's an odd choice. Marion and I were raised attending churches with light-filled pews and candlelit statues of the blessed mother and Saint Joseph. The cross was always a crucifix. The symbol hanging above us now is strange—a cross with two bars instead of one and an infinity symbol at the bottom. I vaguely remember coming across the symbology before while researching one of my novels, but I can't remember what it's called or the historical significance.

"What type of cross is that?" I ask softly.

"A leviathan cross. It symbolizes the Order's role in maintaining the balance between the divine and the wicked." He still has me by the arm as if he fears I'll bolt if he lets me go, when the side door opens and an elderly man walks in. He's balding with a nose that's both crooked and hooked, but I can't take my eyes off him. The closer he gets, the safer I feel.

"We want the full sacramental rite," Roman

commands. He pulls the marriage license from the interior pocket of his tux and hands it to the judge.

I frown and bow my head, staring at my tangled fingers. There was no getting around using my real signature this time. Roman watched me carefully, even made sure it was legible.

Roman drags me to the kneelers and yanks me down with him. I fall hard and catch myself on the rail. *Easy*, I hear in my head. That's Connor's voice!

I raise my chin and stare at the officiant again. He's surveying the room like he's never been in here before.

"Now, Burk!" Roman orders. "I want it done and filed by end of day."

Duck, I hear in my head.

Faster than my eyes can track, Burk lunges for one of the swords in the suit of armor, draws the weapon, and swings it toward Roman's head. I drop to my belly, and the steel whistles right over me as the entire being of Judge Burk flies apart like scattered sand and leaves Connor in his place.

Just when I think Roman's going to lose his head, his ring transforms into a glowing blue sword of his own. The blade extends just in time to block, even before Roman seems to register the attack, as if the ring's magic is sentient and acts of its own volition. He's not entirely fast enough.

Connor's blow is so powerful the momentum carries around Roman's sword and the tip slices the back of Roman's head. Blood drenches his hair, but Roman is on his feet, attacking with all the psychotic rage I've seen brewing under his skin the past few days.

Connor's answering energy is death's swift vengeance. Swords clang again and again. Connor is stronger, and I can't understand why he doesn't have the clear advantage until I see his wing is bleeding. Oh my God. He's still injured from the bolts. And if his wing hasn't fully healed, his chest is probably bleeding too beneath the leather armor.

A hand lands on my back and I almost scream, but it's just Vivian, pulling me away from the skirmish. We back behind a pew just as the flat of Roman's sword slaps Connor's shoulder. He roars, the place of contact smoking like it burns, but he doesn't retreat. He moves closer to Roman, into the pain, and sends a sharp elbow into Roman's chin. Roman goes flying like he's been hit by a car. He crashes into the wall, his head thunking hard against the wood. He crumples to the stone, but then he's on his feet again, the sword transforming into a crossbow.

He levels it at Connor.

I race forward, positioning myself between the two of them, my hands raised. I lock eyes with Roman.

"Move out of the way, Fiona," Roman demands, lowering the bolt a quarter of an inch.

"No." I won't let him shoot Connor again. I won't.

His lips peel back from his teeth, his eyes narrowing to slits. "I had such high hopes for you. So disappointing." He fires.

A paw the size of a paddle knocks me aside, and I turn my head to see Connor throwing the sword in his hands like a javelin. Roman's bolt whistles between us, missing its mark, but the sword flies true. It impales

Roman through the chest and embeds in the wall behind him. I scramble to my feet, trying to reach Connor. He's bleeding, and I can't tell if it's from old wounds or new.

"Look out!" Vivian screams.

I whirl back toward Roman. Despite being pinned to the wall like a mounted beetle, he raises his crossbow and a second bolt flies. Connor dodges it, leaps over a pew, and slashes Roman's throat with one partially shifted hand. Blood sprays across wood and stone, the light shining through the stained glass washing my entire world in red.

"Fiona!" Vivian cries. She's suddenly hysterical.

I'm not sure why until I look down and see the fletching of a blue bolt protruding from the biceps of my left arm. Oddly, I feel no pain. No weakness. I reach around and yank it through my flesh, dropping it on the stone. Blood spurts from the wound, and I clap a hand over it.

"Oh my God! Fiona!" Vivian helps me into a pew as Connor's roar fills the chapel.

Chapter Thirty-Eight

CONNOR

Watching my claws slice through Roman's throat even as the sword I threw at him pins him to the stone makes my dragon surge with pride. All my Aries instincts feel satiated from both a battle won and the act of protecting my mate.

But when I hear Vivian scream Fiona's name, I whirl to find she's been hit, and my tower of pride turns to dust.

I rush to her side. Vivian's moved her to a pew. With her hand pressed over the wound, all I can see is blood seeping through her fingers, but I don't have to see the injury to know the poison is in her. I need to get her to Morwyn.

But she's smiling—smiling as bright as she did the last day we were together. "We've got to quit meeting like this."

She leans toward me, and I'm there, cupping her face

in my hands and kissing her. Creator, I can smell him on her and I hate it. I desperately want to make love to her, to mark her as mine, to reassure myself that I am not too late, that he didn't damage her in any lasting way. But she's hurt, and that will have to wait.

I pull back and say, "Fiona, as many times as you can dress up in these hideous dresses and pretend to marry this guy is the number of times we will meet like this."

"Considering he's dead, I think this will be the last."

I try to pry her hand off the wound in her arm to see what we're dealing with. "Let me see."

"I'm fine," she says, searching my face. "It's already feeling better. We should just go."

"It's not fine. Order weapons are viciously poisonous. We need to get you to Morwyn's to clean out the residue so it doesn't get infected." I tug on her wrist. "Come on. Let me see."

Vivian moves closer, her hands hovering near the wound. "Let us take a look, Fi. Maybe we should bandage it before we leave."

"You helped us before," I say because we've never officially met. "In France, thank you."

Fiona squeezes my hand. "Connor, this is Vivian." She looks at her friend. "Vivian, this is Connor... my mate."

"Your *mate*?" She eyes my wings. "You're a dragon like Donovan?"

"You know Donovan?" I ask.

Fiona's eyes go wider. "Oh my God. Donovan. He's here, Connor! In the dungeon. They're draining him. We have to get him out of here."

"Draining him?"

"I can show you where to go," Fiona says.

Vivian pales and has to sit down. She has serious bruises. I don't want to know how she got them. Not yet. First I need to get everyone somewhere safe. We can process the trauma of what happened to them then.

A shower of gunshots comes from the other side of the wall and then a scream.

Vivian covers her ears, her eyes filling with tears. "What is that? Are they coming for us?"

"That would be Seb, Remus, and Ellison. Sounds like they've incapacitated the guards, which means they'll join us soon."

"You brought backup," Fiona says, followed by a relieved sigh. Her gaze drifts over the wound in my wing and she winces.

"It's not as bad as it looks," I tell her. "Now let me see your arm."

Carefully, she peels her hand back and spreads the rip in the dress to give me a better view. "See, it's not even..."

We all stare at the pink pucker in her biceps. Her dress is stained with blood, there's blood on her fingers, but the actual wound isn't bleeding at all. In fact, it looks like it's healing at an accelerated pace, already knit together and slowly fading. I've never seen anything like it, and I gape in confusion.

She looks up at me, her brows rising. "I guess it's not as bad as I thought it was."

Seb chooses that moment to push through the side door into the chapel. "This is cozy in an I-worship-the-devil sort of way." He scans the room. "I see you've taken care of public enemy number one. Just so you know, we probably want to get the fuck out of here just in case one of the guards we took down called the cops before they passed out. Plus the real Judge Burk isn't going to stay asleep forever."

"We've got to get Donovan," I say.

"Donovan? Here?"

Fiona stands. "I'll take you to him."

But Vivian is shaking her head. "I'm not going back down there. Fi. You know I love you, but no."

It's too dangerous anyway. I turn to Seb. "Take them both out of here. I'll get Donovan."

"I'm going with you," Fiona says, clinging to me.

I shake my head.

"I'm the only one who knows the code to unlock his cell door."

"Then tell it to me."

"No! We've already figured out that bad things happen when we're apart, Connor. Let's do this. Together."

I stare down at her for a second, my fierce, flinty mate. Despite everything, she looks strong, healthy. There's a spark in her eye. She kicks off her shoes and pulls me toward the door that must lead to the main house while Seb ushers Vivian toward the side exit.

"Aren't you afraid?" I whisper as we exit the chapel doors and move into the rear of the house.

"Not anymore. I knew you would come for me. I knew you would never let that guy force me into marriage."

"But the stress, you're not feeling ill?" I study her, looking for any signs the fibro is back.

She stops in front of a door with a keypad and blinks at me. "Being in Roman's web was terrifying, but it could have been much worse." Her eyes widen. "Speaking of, do you still have that fucking marriage license?"

I remember the paper Roman handed to me when he thought I was Burk and find it in my pocket. She snatches it from my hand and tears it to pieces.

"Allow me." I take the pieces from her and, with a deep breath, blow fire across my palm. We watch the ashy remains of the paper float to the polished floors.

Stony faced, she lifts her chin high, then turns back to the door and punches in a code to unlock it. We descend into a metal bunker transformed into a dungeon, and when I see Donovan, a lump forms in my throat. He is sweating, pale, unconscious. A dragon very close to death.

I've never been the type of male to cry easily, but Donovan has always been a hero to me. Every Zodiac warrior knows his story and his sacrifice. Since I was a boy, training at my father's side, I've thought of him as an invincible force in dragon society, a peacekeeper, a guardian of us all. To see him like this, it crushes something childlike and innocent inside me. It mutes a tiny voice that still believes in purpose and destiny and the creator's gentle hand.

Fiona codes open his cell and rushes in, removing the tube that's draining blood from his arm and using a torn section of her dress to stem the hole the needle leaves behind. I move to his other side and slap his cheek to try to rouse him, then cup the back of his neck to keep his head from rolling to the side.

"Donovan? Donovan? Are you still with us?"

He doesn't rouse.

"I'm going to have to go into his head." I look to Fiona, and she nods.

"Go. I'll keep watch."

Drawing in a deep breath, I close my eyes and dive in. The familiar blackness meets me, and then I find myself sitting next to Donovan in an empty theater. Scenes flash on the screen in front of us, but I turn my full attention on the dragon beside me.

I grab him by his shoulders. "You've got to wake up," I say. "We can get you out of here, back to Cardinal Island where we can heal you."

Donovan doesn't even look at me. His eyes are locked on the screen.

When I still can't get his attention, I follow his stare to what's happening behind me. The scene playing now is of him and a much younger Stefan swimming in a pond. They're laughing, splashing. Then a picnic. Then a walk in the park. Two hands, fingers entwined. Two faces on the same pillow, whispering in the dark.

"Donovan?" I swallow as more images come. Quiet dinners. Stefan kissing the scar on his palm where the Order sliced him for his blood.

"He was my mate," Donovan finally says, his red eyes shifting to look at me.

"Was?" I swallow hard.

His eyes move back to the screen. Roman and Stefan are arguing about leadership of the Order while

Donovan frantically pulls at the blue cuff that keeps him prisoner, the cuff that makes it impossible for him to disobey an order from a member of the society. Roman draws a blade from a messenger bag on his hip. No, not a blade, a massive claw. A dragon claw. Ancient by the looks of it.

Stefan is confused and asks what he's doing, where he got it. But Roman's already swinging. The claw cuts through his father's throat, almost severing his head. Blood spews. Stefan's body collapses to the sound of Donovan's howls of agony and rage. The claw is gone, and then Roman removes the cuff on Donovan's leg.

A legion of guards enters the room in the next blink to find Donovan, uncuffed, covered in blood and hunched over Stefan.

Mate. Stefan was his *mate*.

"You judge me."

"No," I say. "I'm just surprised."

"It didn't start this way. We were enemies in the beginning. It's not always clear to us why the creator makes us love the ones we love."

My mind is a whirling vortex of confusion and emotions. He was a prisoner! He was a pet! How could he have loved one of our enemies? But I watch the video again, now replaying the quiet moments, the touches, the looks. Two lives intertwined. Two hearts that together brought our people peace for over fifty years. All love comes from the creator, and this one, this peace-bringing love, would have gone on forever if Roman hadn't ended it.

"I'm sorry." My voice is heavy with emotion as I think

about what I'd feel if the same was done to my mate, my Fiona.

He turns to look at me again. "The end is close now. You must leave and take the girl with you."

My eyes sting. "No, Donovan." I shake my head. "We can save you. You have to come back with me."

His gray eyes turn incredibly sad, and the screen starts to flip like we've reached the end of the film. "You know as well as I do that we go where our mates are. I am old, Connor, and my heart is broken. Under the best of conditions, I might have a few more decades before the creator called me home during my alignment. But Roman has bled me to the point of death."

"We can figure something out. If we move fast. Maybe a transfusion—"

He shakes his head. "No. I won't fight this. I want to go. My body is dying. You know what that means. Get out and protect your mate. I won't be able to stop it when it happens."

My eyes are wet now, and I don't care. I place a hand over my heart. "Thank you for your years of service to the brotherhood and your personal sacrifice." I stand and bow.

He bows his head. "It's up to you and the others now."

He means to protect our people. His death, Stefan's death, and now Roman's death—it means war. It means that everything changes.

I pull out of his head with a gasp and grab Fiona's arm. "We have to go. We have to go now!"

"Wait! What about Donovan?"

I don't answer, just lift her into my arms and start to run. She clings to my neck, trusting me completely although she has no idea what's going on. I hear the chiff of the flames coming to life behind us just as I reach the stairs.

"What is that sound?" she asks fearfully.

"Fuck." I plow through the door to the main house as fast as I can and throw my wings around her just as a mushroom cloud of fire blows us out of the stairwell. I howl and leap for the closest window, crashing through with Fiona wrapped tightly in my arms, tightly in my wings.

Shards of glass tear my flesh, but the injuries heal almost immediately. I keep running though. Keep moving as the entire house is consumed as if we'd detonated a bomb in its depths. By the time I reach the hill where Seb, Ellison, Remus, and Vivian wait, the house is completely consumed in fire.

"Donovan?" Seb asks.

I cock my head in the direction of the house. My voice cracks as I say, "He didn't make it."

I release Fiona and check that she's okay. She hugs Vivian, both of them sobbing now. My mate and her friend stand, arms around each other, watching the house burn. My brothers and I take a knee and bow our heads, our hearts heavy with the loss of a warrior, a brother, and our last hope for peace.

Chapter Thirty-Nine

FIONA

Bright sunlight warms my face, waking me from my slumber. We must have left the window open last night. Lord knows when we staggered in from the Compass Point, drunk and shedding clothes like they were burning our skin, we weren't worried about the window. At least the climate on Cardinal Island is pleasant. The salt air breezes in, blowing back the gauzy white curtains. I move to get up, but Connor's arm drags me back against his hard chest.

It's almost embarrassing how fast I settled into my new life with Connor. After watching Roman's house burn down, we took Vivian home. Connor offered for her to stay with us if she needed time to feel safe. But she insisted all she wanted to do was take a hot bath in her own bathroom, order Indian food from her favorite restaurant, and give herself time and space to recover. She promised though to keep Connor's existence a secret.

Neither of us are concerned. If Vivian has proved anything, it's her loyalty.

Connor's condominium felt like home the second I laid eyes on Zaire and Bones. Thanks to dragon energy and Morwyn's medical care, both are almost fully healed, although Zaire is still walking with a limp. I've started to incorporate my things with Connor's, bringing more of me into the Upper East Side apartment.

I love Diabolique and every member of Connor's staff, to whom he introduced me as his fiancée. They served us a welcome-home meal I will not soon forget, and Connor gave me a behind-the-scenes tour of the kitchen. I love that he can cook considering I've never been much of one.

I'm writing again, too. My editor thinks *Milkmaid* will be my most successful title yet. I've started my next book in the series, *Angel's Share*, and it's pouring out of me.

The fire, though, does make the national news. The authorities suspect arson because of the death of Stefan Cifarelli days before in his apartment from a similar fire. They're still identifying the bodies and have not confirmed the whereabouts of Roman Cifarelli, although we know they eventually will. We all watched him die.

I think about Roman at times, impaled on that sword, dangling from the wall. I think about his body burned to ash, and I can muster no empathy for him, no remorse. Vivian still hasn't told me everything he did to her, but I know it was bad. And I know she's just as glad of his death.

If all of that isn't blissful enough, Connor brought me

to Cardinal Island last night, to his other home, a seaside mansion in the warrior camp here. I've never set foot in a more magical place.

Behind me, Connor grinds against my backside, rousing with a deep inhale against my hair.

I laugh. "Hey, today's Mason's ascension. I need to get ready. The new human mate cannot be late to her first official dragon ceremony."

"Mmmm. I'll be quick then." Connor pulls me under him, his rock-hard erection nudging my entrance.

I press a long kiss to his lips. "Haven't you had enough, Aries? I think I'm still covered in you from last night."

"As it should be." He nuzzles the side of my neck, coaxing a contented sigh from my lips. "And no, I haven't had enough."

He rocks into me. No matter how many times I'm with Connor, sex with him is always grounding, like I've found the other half of my soul, my center, my guiding force. I feel it now as he threads his fingers into mine, moving over me in a rhythm of contented breaths and soft sighs of pleasure.

My hands explore his body, the scar on his chest where his wound has finally healed, the velvet-soft webbing of his beautiful black wings that looks purple when the sun shines through.

Soon he's increasing his pace, his mouth finding mine in a claiming kiss that leaves me breathless and on the edge of a heart-stopping orgasm. One more thrust and I feel like the sun itself, radiant heat, bright, blinding pleasure. Connor follows me over, his wings twitching as he empties himself inside me.

Fully sated, I smile at him as he rolls off me. "Now, I really do have to get ready. I bound out of bed and head to the bathroom. He follows behind me.

I turn on the shower. "I'm serious Connor. I want to make a good impression."

"It'll be quicker if we shower together."

I laugh, glancing down at his already recovering erection. "Why don't I believe that?"

He shrugs. I slide under the spray, and soon he's there, grabbing a loofa and lathering my back. I'm not surprised at all when he enters me again from behind and I find myself holding on to the shower wall as my mate gives me three more orgasms.

By the time we're dressed and stumbling out into the streets of Cardinal Island, I'm power walking to make it to the arena on time.

"Relax, they won't start without us," Connor says through a smile.

I flash him an annoyed look. Cardinal Island is the most beautiful city I've ever seen, with buildings painted the colors of the sunset. Coming from the warrior camp, we pass through the restaurant district where the smell of freshly baked bread makes my mouth water. "You owe me breakfast." I cast a wink his way.

He slants me a grin that seems to hold both an apology and a promise. "After the ceremony. I'll take you to my favorite place and then we can explore the arts district."

I can't wait. Cardinal Island is a thriving artists'

community. Last night, the shops were closed, but I spied impossibly delicate pottery, breathtaking sculptures, exquisite paintings, and every manner of fabric from silk to crochet in the windows. Today, the streets are full of both dragons and humans as the population makes its way toward the arena, musicians playing on every corner.

Up ahead, a red temple rises on a hill, with architecture that curves as if the wind carved it from the rock. And all around us, in the distance, behind the buildings, I can see the ocean.

"Will you miss being in charge?" I ask Connor as he takes my hand and leads me toward the entrance to the arena. His alignment is over. Seb officially rises to power over the brotherhood tomorrow.

"Not at all. I find I have better things to do with my time these days." His grin turns wolfish.

"You're insufferable." Something low within me heats, and his nostrils flare with his smile. He knows. He always knows.

"Seriously. I'm okay with Seb taking over. I like to lead, but it's his time."

I know what he means. Connor and I have worlds left to discover about each other and lifetimes to do it in. It will be nice to take a back seat for a while. And I feel so lucky, so incredibly lucky, to be his mate, to be part of this new, bigger world he's introduced me to. If I'd known this existed before, what love actually looked like from the inside, I would have never settled for less.

We follow the crowd into the arena. The shape reminds me of the Roman Colosseum with towering walls of polished marble and tiers of seating for viewing. The field, though, is breathtaking. Built to look like a compass, it appears to be made of sand of varying colors, and I wonder how they do it, how they keep the colors from mixing. Connor leads me to a viewing area on the east end of the compass, a section with the best view and special padded chairs. He leaves to join his brothers at the heart of the symbol.

There are nine empty seats around me. Reagan, Mason's mate, sits down in one of them, the curvy blonde as awed by our surroundings as I am.

"Is this the section for brotherhood mates?" I ask her.

"I think so," she says. "How's your head?"

I got to know Reagan last night over a few bottles of wine. "Surprisingly fine."

"Gotta love dragon magic." We both laugh.

A lanky, silver-haired woman on my other side offers me her hand. "I am Jada, Solomon's mate. I'm afraid this will be my last time in this section, but also my first time in a long while not sitting alone."

"Your mate is stepping down so that Mason can ascend?"

She nods once. "I'm so happy to see both Connor and Mason mated. Creator willing, I hope the trend continues. The brotherhood needs the steadying force mates bring, especially after what happened with Donovan."

Reagan grips the arms of her chair. "Does it truly mean we're at war?"

Jada frowns. "It means the peace accord is no more. Now, with Stefan and Roman dead, it's the Order's move.

Whoever rises to lead them will either reach out to negotiate a new pact or take the first shot."

I lean back in my chair and stare out across the sandy field at my mate and wonder what's to come. Unconsciously, I reach up to toy with the cross around my neck, one Connor bought me to replace the one I lost. We can never know the future, but maybe, with enough faith, we can accept whatever part we're called to play in it.

"It's starting," Jada says, staring up into the sky.

Quiet falls over the crowd. The moon arcs toward the sun and then slowly over it, darkening the sky. A roar comes from the north, and two enormous doors pull open.

"The Oracle," Jada whispers.

A massive red dragon walks into the arena, wings spreading until her shadow is cast across the compass, and the sands begin to shift, reordering the field into something else, something more.

"*In the beginning...*" The Oracle's voice reverberates in my head, coming from inside me like my mate's purr. When she pauses, I feel the ocean breeze on my face, smell the salt air, but I hear only her when she begins to speak again. "*The creator descended from our world and birthed man into being, blessing the earth with fruitful life. Of all their creations, humans were the ones, the only ones, with the power to build, to invent, to design, to make purely for the joy of creation. Art, music, dancing, acting, poetry, stories, and every other beautiful thing belonged not just to dragons and the creator any longer but to man.*

"*All was well until the destroyer saw what the creator had done. Jealous that they had never been able to create them-*

selves, they brought their own gifts to man: greed, pride, wrath, gluttony, lust, sloth, and envy. Some men began to destroy the creator's work, scheming for control and hiding the beautiful things from the world, keeping them only for their own pleasure. So the creator sent us dragonkind to inspire, to free humans from the chains of the destroyer, to spark again the creator's gift within.

"Today we continue the battle for human minds that was forged in our ancient beginnings, by naming these twelve warriors as the defenders of our race and our mission."

The sands shift, darkening to look like the night sky, and I gasp as constellations form on the field, the wheel of the zodiac taking shape before us.

"As Aries, Connor Drexler."

Wings out, Connor steps onto the constellation of stars winking from the north, right in front of the Oracle. The image of a ram lights up beneath him, encompassing him in light, and then fades away. My heart swells with pride, and when Reagan squeezes my hand, I realize I'm beaming.

"Sebastian York as Taurus."

Unruffled, Seb slides into the constellation to the northeast of Connor, releasing a dazzling grin as the symbol of the bull ignites around him.

"Remus Townsend as Gemini."

Remus's head is bowed, his tattooed arms coupled at the hands as he steps onto his constellation, the twins lighting up and disappearing.

"Ellison Weber as Cancer."

I chuckle as Ellison smooths and straightens his suit before taking his position in the crab constellation.

"Lucas Oliver as Leo... Morwyn Fitz as Virgo."

Memories of Morwyn coming to see me at the lodge warm my heart as the men step onto their constellations.

"Finnegan Bell as Libra, Quinn Adira as Scorpio, Hunter James as Sagittarius, Atlas Moore as Capricorn, Jordon Azzurro as Aquarius."

Reagan sits up straighter, and I squeeze her hand in support.

"And finally, dragon ascending, Mason Forge, son of Roger Forge, grandson of Beckett Forge of warrior blood, replaces Solomon Chirag in the position of Pisces."

As soon as Mason steps on to the symbol of two koi fish circling each other, the entire field lifts and rays of blinding light radiate in a pulse from the twelve. I blink when it hits me and I can feel it flow through me, hot and foreign but somehow familiar, as if I'd felt this power in some incarnation of a past self.

"Go forth, Zodiac Dragon Brotherhood. Your time is now."

Chapter Forty

CONNOR

The Sisters of Mercy abbey is an ancient brick building in upstate New York, four stories with white framed windows that watch us through centuries-old forest as we breeze by. It was Fiona's idea to visit Marion's chapel again. She still calls it that—Marion's chapel. I would have never suggested this visit, considering how raw Marion's death still is for my mate, but I'm glad she decided to go back. Roman originally pursued Fiona for the property. There has to be a reason, something about it the Order desperately wants back.

I need to know that reason. I need to know if the next grandmaster is going to come after Fiona. I'll kill as many Order members as I have to to keep her safe. But understanding what this is and why it's valuable to the Order is the first step in knowing where to direct my energy.

"You can park on the street here. We'll have to take a trail to the chapel. We can only get there on foot." She runs her hand along my thigh, and I pull my Land Rover over on the shoulder to park.

"You keep touching my thigh like that and I'm going to do something to you that shouldn't be done within driving distance of a convent." I flash her a lascivious grin.

She grabs my jaw and kisses me firmly. "I'm not against that idea, but let's explore Marion's chapel first. I have to get this over with while I'm feeling strong." She cocks her head toward the woods.

We both get out of the car, and she takes my hand and leads me along a narrow path. I don't think the rut we're following is human made based on the size and simplicity. More likely forged by the migration of deer. I walk behind her, pushing branches out of her way by reaching over her shoulders as necessary.

"You said Marion died in the car crash that gave you your scar."

"Yeah. She was driving and too close to the steering wheel. The impact from the airbag killed her."

I squint into the sun. "You met her here, all the way back here, once a week. Why were you in the car at all? And why was she driving?"

Fiona grows quiet, introspective. "The doctors tell me that my memory of what happened may not be completely accurate because of the trauma, but on that day, Marion met me at the car. She was afraid. Someone or something had frightened her to the point she was shaking." Her eyes meet mine, and the memory turns them dark and stormy. "I'd been driving, but she shoved me toward the passenger's side, and she was so insistent

I didn't argue, just shifted over. She said she had to take me somewhere safe and then she'd tell me everything. She floored it, and that's when we crashed."

"Crashed into what?"

Fiona frowns. "That's just the thing. I have no memory of hitting anything. They told me that it looked like the front of our car had wrapped around a utility pole, but there wasn't one. They found the car in the middle of the road, wrapped around... nothing. They believe it must have been a large animal that ran off after we hit it."

I'm glad I'm behind Fiona, because the story has left the hair on my arms standing on end. It's odd, and I wouldn't put it past the Order to have used magic to cause the accident if they wanted this land. Maybe one of them approached Marion. Maybe they threatened her. If both women had died that day, the land would have gone up for sale again. I keep these thoughts to myself though. It's in the past. It's done.

About a mile into the woods, we come to a clearing. Wild violets form a carpet of purple flowers around a small chapel whose white paint has almost completely chipped off. The roof though looks like it's made of slate and appears to be intact.

"Wait until you see. It was Marion's favorite part." Fiona leads me toward the doors, which look like they were once red, and enters. Inside smells of dust, candle wax, and wood polish, but it's in perfect condition. A plain wood cross hangs at the front above the altar. Hand-fashioned and polished wood pews line up on both sides of the stone-floor aisle. Candelabras, frothy with cobwebs, line the walls and front of the church. There's no statuary or stained glass, just plain glass windows, left dingy from age and inclement weather.

"Isn't it lovely?" she asks.

It is and I tell her so, but I feel no magic here. I can't see where this would invite Roman Cifarelli's attention. She gestures toward the front of the church, and we walk out into a small graveyard. The stones are so old the names and the dates are worn too thin to read. Still, we walk through the graves, noting the size and shape. A long rectangle of marble appears to mark the grave of a small child.

I reach out with my mind, with the essence of my dragon self, and find we're alone. I don't sense Order magic or dragon magic. This is only a sweet chapel with a graveyard that, by the looks of it, will one day be overrun by nature and the ravages of time.

"Nothing?" she asks me.

I shake my head.

"Maybe they only wanted it as a buffer between the estate and the abbey." She toys with the lock on the wrought iron gate.

"What's that?" I ask, noticing a partial stone fence in the distance.

"A well. It's in terrible condition though. All boarded up."

I stride to her side and kiss her on the cheek as I push through the cemetery gate. The well is indeed boarded up, the circular stone wall that surrounds it crumbling with age, but when I reach it and take a long, full breath, I can't hide my excitement. It smells of sweet water and sunlight, of something not quite dragon, but undeniably celestial. I start pulling up the boards and casting them aside.

"What is it?" Fiona catches up to me and looks down into the well.

"I'm not sure, but it's something. Something of ours, not of theirs."

Her eyes widen. "I can smell it now. Like sea air and... lilacs... spring. It's bright and fresh."

I look around the well and find a bucket and chain. The bar and crank once used to lower it are long broken, but it appears the bucket will still hold water. I lower it into the well and then pull it to the surface.

"Oh my stars. What is that, Connor?"

The water sparkles in the bucket as if it's infused with galaxies, and when I run a hand through it, it feels thicker than water and hums against my skin. "I don't know."

She dips her hand in, raises it with a bit of the liquid cupped in her palm. Fiona seems enchanted by the water, but when she moves to drink it, I stop her with a gentle hand. "Not without someone who understands magic analyzing what it is. I need to talk to Seb."

She frowns and pours the water out of her hand and back into the well.

I empty the bucket too. As I'm setting it aside, a feather blows up from below and catches on the edge of the well. Fiona plucks it off the stone and holds it up to the sun, her eyes narrowing. It's over a foot long and white as freshly fallen snow. When the light hits it, it sparkles.

Fiona gapes at me. "Have you ever seen anything like this?"

I run a finger along the feather and wonder at the hum of power that buzzes against my fingertip. "No, Fi. But this, without a doubt, is what Roman wanted."

Epilogue

ROMAN

The night of the fire...

Death, as it turned out, was not as peaceful as Roman had expected. The sword pierced his heart, Connor's claws ripped open his throat, and then the darkness enveloped him. Darkness and nothingness were a welcome release from the suffering. He went somewhere painless, peaceful. It was everything he wanted.

He had no idea how long he was dead until he heard a voice that said simply, "Rise."

It wasn't a kind voice, and when he jolted back into his body, he was seized by pain like he'd never experienced before, agony that no human body should experience. His eyes fluttered open, and he stared into the face of a fearsome and terrible beauty. The walls were burning and the air smelled of ash, but the woman

359

before him wasn't afraid. Behind her, two feathery wings as black as a raven's spread and lifted.

A hand landed on his chest, nails abnormally long at the end of slender fingers. The hand smashed him against the wall, then yanked the blade embedded in his chest until it dislodged from his heart and ribs and clattered to the floor. But the hand gave no comfort. It drew back, allowing his body to crumple. His head slapped the stone.

Pure torment crashed over him. Blood flooded his mouth. He was drowning in it, his lungs full from where the sword had punctured them. His head throbbed and his eyes burned from the fire and the ash. He flopped and spasmed hopelessly at the feet of the creature as the flames grew closer, scorching his skin.

"Relax. It's just your body learning it can't die," the winged thing said in a high-pitched, melodious voice. "Ignore it. You will endure."

Roman curled on his side and emptied his stomach. What left his mouth was mostly blood, but he noticed afterward he could breathe again. Air, hot and ashy, flowed in and out of his lungs. It hurt and it burned, but he was alive.

"Tsk, tsk, tsk," the dark queen said, her silver hair falling over one shoulder. "The dragons did a number on you, didn't they? But I need you, Roman. The Order can't reach its full potential without you. Your father was too soft. For too many years, the creator's abominations have bred like cockroaches on this world. You were the only one with any vision. The way you murdered your father for the cause was admirable." The thing's voice was smooth as a starless night. "Now rise, Roman. And hold your place as grandmaster."

Roman climbed to his hands and knees. He could move now, could breathe. But could he stand? He stared down at the wound in his chest. It was already healing. And the flames were licking his skin, but he wasn't burning. He put one foot under him and then the other. Slowly he rose and looked his dark angel in the eye.

"Better. Now leave this place. And if anyone in the Order questions your survival or your authority, tell them it is a gift bestowed on you by the destroyer."

"The destroyer," he repeated quietly. Roman bowed, and then he obeyed.

THANK YOU FOR READING DRAGON ASCENDING. IF YOU enjoyed this novel, please write a review wherever you buy books.

HE'S A DRAGON BOUND BY DUTY. SHE'S A MAGE FIGHTING her own demons. Together, they could save their world—or destroy each other.

As the newly ascended head of the Zodiac Brotherhood, Seb takes his responsibilities seriously. Like any Taurus dragon, he's stubborn, protective, and unflinchingly loyal. Using his position as an executive at Full Throttle Records, he's determined to shield dragonkind from their greatest threat, the rising Saint's Order and their dragon-killing magic.

Zoe learned the hard way that magic always comes with a price. The potion that once made her performances legendary also nearly destroyed her life, costing her both her music career and her self-respect. Now clean and determined to stay that way, she's rebuilt her life from the ashes of addiction.

But when Seb tracks her down with a ring that could hold the key to defeating the Saint's Order, Zoe faces an impossible choice. The only way to unravel the ring's secrets is to dive back into the same dangerous magic that once nearly claimed her soul.

Seb's first instinct is to force her compliance, until his dragon recognizes her as his fated mate. With time running out, Seb must choose between protecting his people and protecting the woman his heart claims as his own. But for Zoe, the choice is even more devastating: save dragonkind and risk losing herself, or refuse and watch her mate's world burn.

Get your copy of DRAGON CHAINED today.

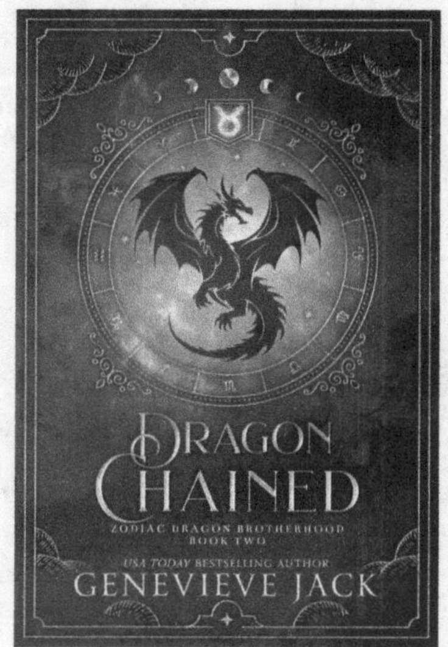

USA Today bestselling and multi-award winning author Genevieve Jack writes wild, witty, and wicked-hot paranormal romance and romantic fantasy. She believes there's magic in every breath we take and probably something supernatural living in most dark basements. You can summon her with coffee, wine, and books, but she sticks around for dogs and chocolate. Her novels feature badass heroines, fiercely loyal heroes, and fantasy elements that will fill you with wonder. Learn more at GenevieveJack.com.

Do you know Jack? Keep in touch to stay in the know about new releases, sales, and giveaways.

facebook.com/AuthorGenevieveJack

instagram.com/authorgenevievejack

bookbub.com/authors/genevieve-jack

tiktok.com/@Genevievejackbooks

More From Genevieve Jack!

The Zodiac Dragon Brotherhood

Legacy of Fire

Dragon Ascending

Dragon Chained

The Treasure of Paragon

The Dragon of New Orleans, Book 1

Windy City Dragon, Book 2,

Manhattan Dragon, Book 3

The Dragon of Sedona, Book 4

The Dragon of Cecil Court, Book 5

Highland Dragon, Book 6

Hidden Dragon, Book 7

The Dragons of Paragon, Book 8

The Last Dragon, Book 9

The Angel of Paragon, Book 10

The Three Sisters Trilogy

The Tanglewood Witches

Tanglewood Magic

Tanglewood Legacy

A Shadow's Bargain Series

A Bargain With The Shadow Prince

Battle for the Shadow Prince

Bartered by the Shadow Prince

Bride of the Shadow King

His Dark Charms Duet

Lucky Me

Lucky Us

Knight Games

The Ghost and The Graveyard, Book 1

Kick the Candle, Book 2

Queen of the Hill, Book 3

Mother May I, Book 4

Logan (companion novel)

The Wolves of Fireborn Pack Trilogy

Fated Bonds

Feral Instincts

Forever Mated